Turning the Paige

Also by Laura Jensen Walker

Dreaming in Black and White

Dreaming in Technicolor

Reconstructing Natalie

(Women of Faith Novel of the Year, 2006)

Miss Invisible

Daring Chloe

A GETAWAY GIRLS NOVEL

Turning the Paige

Book Two

Laura Jensen Walker

ZONDERVAN.com/
AUTHORTRACKER
follow your favorite authors

ZONDERVAN

Turning the Paige

Requests for information should be addressed to:

Zondervan, *Grand Rapids, Michigan 49530*

Library of Congress Cataloging-in-Publication Data

Walker, Laura Jensen.
Turning the Paige : a Getaway Girls novel: book two / Laura Jensen Walker.
p. cm.
ISBN 978-0-310-27698-2 (softcover)
1. Divorced women—Fiction. 2. Book clubs (Discussion groups)—Fiction. 3. Mothers and daughters—Fiction I. Title.
PS3623.A3595T87 2009
813'.6—dc22

2008033277

Published in association with the literary agency of Alive Communications, Inc., 7680 Goddard Street, Suite 200, Colorado Springs, CO 80920. www.alivecommunications.com.

Interior design by Christine Orejuela-Winkelman
Interior illustration by Ruth Pettis

Printed in the United States of America

09 10 11 12 13 14 15 • 22 21 20 19 18 17 16 15 14 13 12 11 10 9 8 7 6 5 4 3 2 1

For Anne "Defender of the English Language" Peterson

Beloved friend, encouraging first reader, and amazing woman of God with a generous spirit, brilliant mind, and fabulous wit. You left us way too soon.

(George Clooney didn't know what he was missing.)

You have been my friend. That in itself is a tremendous thing.
I wove my webs for you because I liked you.
After all, what's a life, anyway? We're born, we live a little
while, we die. A spider's life can't help being
something of a mess, with all this trapping and eating flies.
By helping you, perhaps I was trying to lift up my life a trifle.
Heaven knows anyone's life can stand a little of that.

Charlotte's Web

Thanks, Anne, for lifting up my life.

Fiction reveals truths that reality obscures.

Jessamyn West

The Beast was after me.

No matter where I went, there he was. Big. Furry. Silent, staring. And wearing his ever-present blue coat.

Guess the yellow dress and brown hair must have confused him. He thought I was his Belle. An understandable mistake — we both love to read. Although I've never been a princess.

And this place was crawling with them.

Finally the Beast moved on in search of the real Belle and Eric shifted beside me.

"Not much longer, honey," I said. "Look — we're nearly at the halfway point."

"Great."

"I know it's a little cheesy, but this was one of my favorite attractions when I was a kid. I never miss it when I come to Disneyland."

"Even on your honeymoon?" My gorgeous brand-new husband looked at me over his sunglasses. "Standing in line with hundreds of people to get into 'It's a Small World' isn't exactly my idea of romance. Give me a white sandy beach in the Cayman Islands any day."

"I know. But we've got our whole lives to do that. I couldn't disappoint my mom. Not after she and Dad scrimped and saved to surprise us with this honeymoon. They're not rich, you know, so this was a really big deal to them. Can't we just enjoy it?"

"I'd enjoy it a lot more if I were sipping a Mai Tai with you on an isolated beach."

"We can have Mai Tais at the hotel tonight."

Eric stared at me and his face softened. "Now *that* I'm looking forward to." He gently rubbed his thumb across my chin — the chin he always called adorable — then pulled me to him and gave me a long, slow kiss.

The line stared and I blushed. Eric held up my left hand. "We're on our honeymoon. Isn't my bride beautiful?"

I blushed again as the crowd cheered.

Eric whispered in my ear. "I love you, but you owe me a honeymoon. And," he paused, "the Indiana Jones ride is next."

1

"You never really understand a person until you consider things from his point of view ... until you climb in his skin and walk around in it."

To Kill a Mockingbird

My mother killed my marriage. Stomped all over it with her Pepto-Bismol pink pumps and ground it to divorce dust.

Okay, maybe that's not entirely fair. Mom wasn't solely responsible for the destruction of my marriage. Like many couples, Eric and I had some problems. But the biggest one was my mother. I turned the page in my wedding album on what would have been our five-year anniversary to a close-up of the two of us—happy, bright, shining, and in love. So in love. But that was then and this is now.

My fingers moved up the glossy page to the cleft in Eric's jaw. I loved that Kirk Douglas cleft and had spent many happy hours kissing it. And the delicious lips above it. Now someone else was kissing them.

I slapped the album shut. And as I shoved it back into

the closet, the phone rang. I walked over to the nightstand to check the caller ID. Probably a telemarketer.

As the phone continued to ring, I squinted at the name. Now where'd I put my reading glasses? By the time I finally found them, the answering machine had clicked on.

"Paige?" My mother's querulous voice filled the air. "Are you there? Or are you out again? Seems like you're never home anymore." She released a loud sigh. "I was hoping you could come over for just a minute and pull down my other quilt from the top of the linen closet. This one's getting too hot and heavy." She lobbed one of her famous guilt grenades. "Oh well, guess I'll just have to make do. Talk to you soon."

My turn to expel a loud sigh.

Mom's "for just a minute" was never that. Every time I went over to her house—several times a week since Dad died—she found "one other little thing" for me to do. "Since you're here, would you mind bringing the new bag of cat litter in from the garage? It's too heavy for me."

Translation: Clean out the dirty litter box and refill it.

"Could you look up the number to Animal Control? I think I've got raccoons or possums under the house."

Translation: Call the County and take care of it.

"Would you run up to the store and pick up some chicken? Breasts are on sale. Oh, and could you pick up a couple other things for me too?"

Translation: Do all my grocery shopping.

Since Dad died nearly three years ago, I'd become the go-to girl for anything and everything my mother needed. Mom was of the old school, accustomed to having my father handle everything, from balancing the checkbook to pumping gas, and had never really learned to do things on her own, or establish any kind of independence. And at her age, I didn't see that changing.

She also had the mind-set that family should do everything for one another, and considered it an imposition to ask for help from people who didn't share her same blood. Which meant everything fell on me.

My brother Patrick and sister Isabel had seen the writing on the wall and gotten out of our Sacramento hometown years ago. Patrick, the youngest, was a free spirit, going his own way and dabbling in different things. Last we'd heard, he was living on an ashram somewhere in India. Staying in touch wasn't exactly his thing.

As for Isabel, after getting her MBA from Berkeley, she'd moved to Chicago to join an investment firm. There she'd steadily risen up the ranks to the executive level where she was now a corporate muckety-muck in a high-rise office overlooking Michigan Avenue. Isabel, who's two years older than me, is married to David, another executive who shares her same career drive and Dom Perignon tastes. They work hard and play hard, flying all over the world to exotic vacation spots—beginning with their elopement to Barbados two years ago.

Mom still hasn't forgiven her for that. "How could your sister go and get married without any of her family there?" she'd asked me. "A wedding is a celebration for the whole family—not just the two of them." She released one of her signature sighs. "But then your sister's always been selfish. I'm glad I have at least one daughter who puts others before herself. I can always count on you, honey."

No pressure there.

Don't get me wrong. I love my mom. And I always try to honor her as the Bible says. But what about that Scripture that says "do not exasperate your children"?

A siren split the air. Mom's ringtone.

I knew if I answered my cell, she'd wheedle me into stopping by and I'd be late to book club. I'm thirty-five years old and I haven't learned how to say no to my mother. Grabbing my phone, I set it to vibrate and tossed it in my purse. Then I headed out the door, eager to meet the girls on our latest adventure.

Last year, at the start of our book club season, Becca, the founder of the club, had suggested that rather than just sitting around discussing the books we read, we start to live out some of the adventures in the books instead. And boy had we ever. We'd gone sailing, camping, hiking, blind dating, even rafting down the river—courtesy of Huck Finn—but our biggest adventure came when we traveled to Paris to take cooking lessons after reading *French Women Don't Get Fat.*

Ah, Paris. *J'adore.* We'd all fallen head over heels for the beautiful, cosmopolitan city, but Chloe, my karaoke-singing pal who used to not have a daring bone in her body, had taken a sabbatical from work to return to the City of Light for an extended stay. She was there even now, painting and living out her French adventure.

Not that I'm jealous or anything. *C'est la vie.*

Last month for our April book club adventure, in honor of *Kidnapped,* where young David Balfour goes on the run through the Scottish Highlands, I took the girls to the annual Scottish Games and Gathering in a nearby town. I'd have preferred Scotland—especially since I'm part Scottish—but two trips to Europe in one year wasn't in anyone's budget.

We settled for Woodland.

There we had a blast watching the Highland dancers and pipers, tasting Scottish delicacies, and watching different athletic competitions including the hammer throw and haggis hurling. But our favorite event was checking out all the men in kilts.

Shades of Mel Gibson. Talk about freedom.

Today we were enjoying the freedom of a hike in the foothills north of Sacramento.

"This hill's too high," Kailyn whined.

"You think that's high—just wait'll we get to Yosemite," Becca said. "This is great practice for our *Into Thin Air* climb in a couple weeks."

Annette, who'd been steadily puffing alongside me for the past hour, sat down abruptly. "I need to rest, y'all. Isn't it about time for our picnic, anyway?"

"Works for me. Hey guys," I called to the rest of the group as I sank to the ground beside Annette, "time to eat." Kailyn hotfooted it over to us but stopped short. She looked at her new white shorts and then down at the ground with a dubious expression.

Annette removed the denim overshirt she'd tied around her waist and spread it out on the grass beside her à la Sir Walter Raleigh. "There you go, Queen Elizabeth. Now your royal designer shorts won't get ruined."

"Thanks, Mom. You rock."

"That I do," Annette said. "Madonna has nothin' on me. Well, except money, rock-hard abs, and an estate in England. Although ... I used to live in England too."

"On an estate?"

"Nah. In an Air Force dorm when I was stationed there in the seventies. My roommates and I formed a girl band and played at weddings and bar mitzvahs. We really rocked those receptions." She hummed a little "Bohemian Rhapsody" as she began removing food items from her backpack and setting them on a small tablecloth.

"Bunch of wusses," Becca grumbled as she and Jenna joined us. "I don't know how you ever expect to scale a mountain when you can't even make it up a little foothill."

"I don't expect to scale any mountains," Annette said. "I'll just watch you."

"Ditto." I smiled up at Becca.

"Aw c'mon, that's not fair. The point of these adventures is for all of us to do them together."

"Then you need to pick adventures that all of us are physically capable of doing."

"You tell her, Mom." Kailyn stuck out her tongue at her risk-taking roommate.

"If we all trained together, we could get in shape to climb," Jenna said. "We could work out together every morning. I could probably even get us a group rate at the gym."

"No thanks," Annette said. "I already do a morning workout every day with my husband."

"*Every* day?" Becca's eyes gleamed beneath her dark spiky bangs. "Who says the sex drive wanes as you get older?"

"Eww!" Kailyn gave Becca a playful shove. "That's my parents you're talking about."

"And this parent was talking about walking, not nookie."

I faced Becca. "Can't we compromise on the mountain climbing? You've got a mixed group of women here and not all of us are in as great shape as you and Jenna."

"I know!" Kailyn's blonde ponytail bobbed as she jumped up. "We could go to one of those indoor rock-climbing walls instead, with those rubber thingies where you put your feet. That doesn't look too hard, plus we'd be protected from the elements."

"I'm sure that's just what Sir Edmund Hillary said when he was climbing Everest. 'Gee, let's stay inside so we're protected from the elements,'" Becca said.

"Shut up, nature girl."

I clapped my hands the way I used to when my siblings fought. "Time out. Hey, Jenna, aren't there less extreme mountains at Yosemite we could climb instead? Say with some pretty waterfalls or something?"

"Well, there's Vernal Falls. Technically, it's at the top of a mountain."

"Yeah, with *steps*," Becca said dismissively.

"Narrow *steep* steps cut into the cliff."

"Annette, didn't you, Tess, and Chloe go up a bunch of narrow steps to look at the gargoyles in Notre Dame?"

She nodded.

"Well, you can certainly do these steps then," I said. "And so can I. Tess will too. Where is Tess today, anyway?"

"She had a date with James. They were going to an exhibit at the DeYoung."

"Nice. Blowing us off for a guy and art," cynical Becca said.

Works for me.

"Not just any guy," Annette said with a small, secret smile. "This is love."

"Twoo wuv."

"Mawwiage is what bwings us togevver today." *The Princess Bride* is one of my favorite romantic movies.

"Does anyone else think it's ironic that Tess's last name is the same as his first name?"

"No. I think it's a God-thing," Kailyn said.

"Yeah, right." Becca snorted. "It's just a coincidence."

"A God-incidence," Annette corrected her.

Becca rolled her eyes. "Here we go with the God-stuff again."

Jenna and Becca were the two non-churchgoers in our group. Jenna never seemed bothered by our occasional God-mentions, but Becca was. I think it was something to do with her upbringing, but she'd erected a clear No Trespassing sign on that part of her life.

"Well, I don't know about y'all," Annette said, changing the subject, "but I'm really looking forward to when we read Maeve Binchy."

"Me too. I love all her books. Especially *Circle of Friends.*"

"Ooh, I loved that movie. The guy who played Benny's boyfriend was hot."

"I didn't like the way it changed the ending from the book though."

"Movies never get it right. Hemingway hated the Hollywood adaptations of his novels."

"I don't blame him," I said. "Did you ever see *A Farewell to Arms* with Rock Hudson? Talk about overwrought."

"Rabbit trail, guys." Becca executed an exaggerated bucktoothed, rapid-chewing motion with her teeth and then fixed Annette with a stare. "What kind of adventure can we look forward to from a Maeve Binchy home-and-hearth saga?"

"You'll have to wait to find out. Patience is a virtue, you know."

"Virtue isn't all it's cracked up to be."

A well-muscled pair of calves jogged into view and my heart did flip-flops. Those calves looked very familiar. What was Eric doing here?

Only it wasn't Eric. My heart began beating normally again as my eyes lifted to the blond surfer-dude body atop the muscular calves. *Twice* in a week would have been a bad sitcom.

Thursday when I was shopping at Whole Foods, I looked up from the mushrooms into Eric's startled face. Could the cleft in his chin have gotten any deeper? A trickle of sweat escaped from my left armpit.

"Paige ..."

Then my right armpit betrayed me. I pressed both arms

tightly against my sides before an entire sweat symphony broke out.

"Babe, did you get the portobellos?" A very pregnant, yet tiny brunette waddled our way. Even her waddling was radiant.

Brat. Only that wasn't the *B* word that flashed through my mind.

I stood there flushed and sweating like a pig in my Scottish Games T-shirt and old cut-offs while Eric's model-perfect, gorgeous, and *young* second wife gave off a luminous pregnant-woman glow in her crisp white cotton sundress.

"Hi Heather," I said in a bright, shiny voice as she drew near. "How's it going?"

"Paige." Her fingers—a little bloated I was happy to see—took possession of Eric's arm. "Good. And you?"

"Great. Just doing a little shopping for my mom."

"Oh. Good. That's good. We don't usually shop here, but I had a serious craving for portobello mushrooms and our grocery store was out."

Eric shifted from one foot to the other. "So, uh, how is your mom these days?"

"Okay."

Like you care. You couldn't stand my mother. I thought of all the fights we'd had over her. Including the last one—a real doozy a few months after Dad died where Eric had shouted, "It's me or your mom!"

He wasn't being fair. How could I turn my back on my mother? She was getting old and didn't have anyone else to look after her, especially since Dad had died. It was my daughterly duty. Eric and I had our whole lives ahead of us. Who knew how long Mom had?

Longer than us.

Eric walked out three weeks later. And less than a year

later he was married to Heather. The beautiful, twenty-six-year-old wife about to give birth to his baby. The baby that I had wanted. I couldn't take my eyes off Heather's basketball stomach.

She tugged at his arm. "Honey, we really need to get going."

"Oh, sure." Eric bagged his portobellos at the speed of light. "Take it easy, Paige." He gave me an uncomfortable smile.

"You too." They walked away, Eric's arm around Heather's expectant waist.

The telltale monthly cramp brought me back to the present and reminded me that yet another one of my aging eggs was down the tube. Forever gone. One less chance for a baby. What's a baby-wanting, good single Christian girl to do?

I must have spoken the words aloud.

"You could go to a sperm bank," Becca suggested.

"Huh?" My mind shifted back to the picnic.

"A sperm bank. You know—the place where anonymous guys go and make deposits and then you get to go and make a withdrawal? I hear they have these portfolios and stuff so you can pick your kid's genes. Like whether you want him or her to have some brilliant scientist with a PhD for a father, or a creative-artist type, or whatever. You get to choose. How cool is that?"

"I'd pick a professor—as long as he wasn't too nerdy looking," Jenna said. "That way my kid would be both smart *and* athletic."

"I'd probably go for a Bill Gates entrepreneur type so my kid would be rich and taken care of for life," Kailyn said.

"And his dear old mother too?" Annette teased her daughter.

"Of course. Paige, if you do decide to go the sperm bank

route, you'd better hurry up. I read an article in the doctor's office that said a woman's fertility starts decreasing in her early thirties and takes a big drop after age thirty-five."

"I read that same article," Jenna said. "It said a thirty-year-old woman has about a 20 percent chance each month of getting pregnant and by age 40, that chance is only about 5 percent."

"That sucks."

"But what about all those celebrities having babies in their forties?"

"They probably used donor eggs and spent big bucks on in-vitro." Becca snorted. "They can afford it."

My heart sank.

"Way to cheer Paige up." Annette put her arm around my shoulders. "Honey, just remember that God is greater than any statistics. Don't forget Sarah."

"Yeah," Kailyn said. "Wasn't she over a hundred or something when she got pregnant?"

"Only ninety."

"*Only?*" Becca grunted. "That's some fairy tale."

"Gives new meaning to 'mature moms.'" Jenna shuddered. "And not something I'd want to experience at that age. Ouch."

"You could always adopt. There are lots of orphans all over the world needing to be loved. And you don't have to be married to adopt either," Annette said.

Kailyn agreed. "Yeah. Look at Angelina Jolie. She adopted a whole brood as a single mom. Why can't you?"

"Does that mean I'll get a Brad Pitt in the process too?"

"You never know."

"I'd prefer Jimmy Stewart."

"Who?"

"From *It's a Wonderful Life*?" I said.

"Isn't he dead?" Becca asked.

"For some time now," Annette said.

"Details, details."

"What is it with you and all these old dead guys?" Becca asked. "In Paris, you were hoping to meet a Cary Grant or Fred Astaire."

"So sue me. I like older, romantic leading men with charm and class."

"What about George Clooney? He's definitely charming and classy."

"Yeah, but he lacks the requisite settling-down gene."

And I'm all about settling down.

I punched in the familiar number as I slid into my car. "Hi. Are you in bed?"

"Almost. It's after 8:30."

"I know. I'm sorry to call so late, but I just finished with book club and thought I'd run by and get that summer quilt down for you."

"Well ... if you're sure it won't be too much trouble. I know how busy you are."

Translation: Too busy to come see your poor, lonely old mother.

Fifteen minutes later, I bundled her winter quilt into an oversized plastic bag and stuck it on the top shelf of her closet. I changed her pillow shams and fluffed the lighter pink floral quilt on her bed. As I did so, I noticed crumbs on the rose-colored carpet.

"What's this?"

She peered at my outstretched hand through her glasses. "I can't see what you've got there."

"Cookie crumbs."

"Oh. Those are from my sugar-free chocolate chip cookies

that you got last time you went shopping. I like to have one cookie before I go to sleep, but I didn't realize I'd spilled crumbs on the floor. My goodness, I don't want to get ants."

Way ahead of you.

I pulled her Kirby from the closet and did a quick vacuum of the entire room, making sure I didn't bump her nightstand which held the brass urn with my father's ashes. Mom liked keeping Dad close by.

"Thanks, honey. You're such a big help. What would I ever do without you? I was going to ask Frieda to get the quilt down so I didn't have to bother you, but she's got so much on her plate right now, I hate to disturb her. Poor thing. Did I tell you her daughter's back in rehab again?"

"Yep. Yesterday when we talked." And the day before when I brought over dinner. I stuffed the vacuum back into the closet.

"I'm so glad you kids never got into those awful drugs—they just ruin a person's life. And their whole family's too. My goodness! That's why Frieda's son is back in jail again you know."

"I know. You've told me." At least fifty times. By phone, email, and in person. Neither rain nor snow nor sleet nor storm will stop my mother from gossiping about her neighbor and her less-fortunate offspring who can't hold a candle to Mom's anointed three.

"Well, all I can say is it's a good thing this isn't his third offense. Otherwise, he'd be under that Three Strikes law and spending the rest of his life in prison. And that would break Frieda's heart." She sighed. "Poor Frieda. Such a tragedy—especially since she raised her children in the church. But then, she really spoiled those kids. I tried to tell her after their daddy ran off to make sure she used a firm hand with them, but she wouldn't listen. And now look." Mom released a ponderous sigh. "You reap what you sow."

Does that apply to everyone? Better watch out.

"It's just past nine. I'd better get going. I don't want to keep you up."

"That's okay. Why don't you stay and visit a little longer?"

Because I still have a million things to do tonight before I can go to bed.

"I really can't. I've got to get home and iron my work clothes for tomorrow."

She shifted her large frame in her easy chair and frowned. "Has your boss given you a raise yet? He doesn't treat you right. You should get a different job where they really appreciate you and don't work you so hard. Don't let them take advantage of you."

Is that the pot calling the kettle black?

"I won't." I leaned over and kissed her chubby cheek. "I'll talk to you tomorrow. Sleep well, and don't forget to take your meds."

"Okay, honey. But before you go, can you let Mr. Spitz in? Otherwise he'll be tomcatting around the neighborhood 'til all hours." Mr. Spitz had an eye for the ladies.

In that respect, he was like my ex. Maybe that's why the furry feline and I had never gotten along. I went to the kitchen door and opened it to the fenced-in backyard that still held the old metal swing set that I'd spent many happy childhood hours on with my brother and sister. "Here, Mr. Spitz. Time for beddy-bye."

Nothing.

I made the embarrassing kissing noises Mom always makes when she cajoles him inside. And when that didn't work,

I rustled the bag of salmon-flavored cat treats she keeps on the counter.

A flash of gray streaked across the back stoop and between my legs, meowing loudly. "Aha. I thought that would do it." I pulled out one of the treats and tossed it to him. No way was I going to hand it to the mini cougar. I had too many battle scratches from past encounters.

Mr. Spitz batted at the snack with his paws and then began to chow down.

Mom shuffled into the kitchen in her fuzzy robe and slippers. "Aw, is Mommy's baby having a num-num?" she cooed. "That's a good boy. Does him want another one?" She reached for the bag of treats and started making kissy noises.

"I'll leave you to it then," I said, giving her another kiss on the cheek. "'Night."

"Good night honey. Drive safe now."

I was halfway down the driveway when I realized I'd left my cell on the kitchen counter. I rapped on the door as I opened it with my key. "It's just me. I forgot—are those *Oreos* in your sugar-free ice cream?" Her guilty look was all the answer I needed.

"Remember what the doctor said? Are you *trying* to go into a diabetic coma?" I shined my Food Police badge and opened her pink freezer door—yes, my mother has a pink refrigerator, my father's fortieth-anniversary present to her—to find a carton of cookies-and-cream ice cream smiling at me.

Why was I not surprised?

When I got home from Mom's, I turned on my laptop and googled sperm banks.

Wow. You really could determine the make and model of your child—hair, eyes, skin, and more. Kind of like picking out a new car. Or breeding a horse.

But the more I read, the more uncomfortable I became. Donors are identified by number and have profiles that generally include their height, weight, hair and eye color, age, ethnic origin, and sometimes, education and profession. It all seemed so calculated and cold and brave-new-worldish. As I continued to surf, I wondered what the motivation was for men to become sperm donors.

I soon found out. For some, it was altruistic—wanting to help childless women like me conceive. But for others, it was ego—wanting to spread their seed as far as they could.

Or money. Guess that's why they call it a sperm *bank.*

The latter motivations creeped me out a little and raised a few red flags. What if a child I gave birth to, created with sperm from a specific donor, grew up, fell in love, and wanted to marry someone who just happened to be the offspring of a sperm donor as well? The same fruitful sperm donor.

Scary. Heartbreaking. And devastating.

There was also the small matter of how all this reconciled with my faith. Was it even biblical?

I shut my laptop and scrubbed my hands at the kitchen sink.

2

> A single woman, with a very narrow income, must be a ridiculous, disagreeable, old maid! The proper sport of boys and girls; but a single woman, of good fortune, is always respectable, and may be as sensible and pleasant as anybody else.
>
> *Emma*

I've always had sensible, respectable jobs but never a great income. Like my current temp job in a call center. Before this, I'd worked at an insurance company for more than a decade—starting in the mail room after getting my associate's degree and working my way up to administrative assistant to the marketing manager.

That's where I met Eric.

I'd just returned from lunch and was sitting at my desk fretting over my new haircut in my compact mirror. The chin-length bob was long in front and shorter in back. Way shorter than my usual mid-length style. But I'd been bored and feeling reckless, so I'd given my stylist carte blanche to try something new.

George loved the movie *Chicago*, so he modeled my cut on Catherine Zeta-Jones' bob, which fit her perfectly, but was a little too much for me. At least I thought so.

"Whoa. Great haircut!" Bill, my boss, said.

"I'll second that," an unfamiliar male voice agreed.

I looked over the top of my compact to meet the greenest pair of eyes I'd ever seen—like the Scottish countryside I'd seen in pictures. This guy had to be wearing colored contacts.

He wasn't, I found out later.

"Paige, this is Eric Turner. Eric, this is Paige, my all-around Girl Friday."

"Very nice to meet you." Eric's intense green eyes sent a 7.9 earthquake through my entire body.

Four months later I was Paige Turner.

Yeah, yeah, I know. Spare me the jokes. I've heard them all.

I was thirty and Eric was thirty-five when we got married, with both our biological clocks ticking louder than Big Ben. Not wanting to waste any time starting a family, we began trying on our honeymoon to get pregnant.

We tried for two years straight. And nothing.

And all the while, my mother would say helpful things like:

"I'd like to be a grandma before I'm eighty."

"You're not getting any younger, and neither are your eggs."

"All the women in our family are fertile-Myrtles. It can't be your fault. Eric's sperm count is probably low. He should get that checked."

He did get it checked and it was fine. And if I'd had any doubts, his tiny new wife's pregnancy confirmed his sperm count was more than adequate.

I tugged my shirt down to cover my muffin top—wishing

my slight bulge was due to pregnancy rather than too many muffins—and answered the phone. "Landon Wireless. This is Paige. How can I help you?"

"You can take this bleepedy-bleep phone and stick it where the sun doesn't shine!"

Would that be Alaska?

"What seems to be the problem, sir?"

Blankety-blank, stream of invective. "What doesn't seem to be the problem? My phone keeps cutting in and out all the time."

"Is this when you're driving? Perhaps you're out of the service area?"

"It happens all the blankety-blank time! I want a new phone, or you can cancel my contract!"

"If you hold just a moment, sir, I'll see what I can do for you."

Thankfully, the next call was easier.

"Landon Wireless. This is Paige. How can I help you?"

"Can you please make my phone work?" an elderly woman's voice quavered.

"I'll do my best, ma'am. Can you tell me what the problem is?"

"Well, I keep trying to call my granddaughter in Michigan, but nothing happens."

"Are you pushing the green Send button after you finish dialing?"

"I don't see any Send button. Where is it?"

"You'll find it in the upper left-hand corner of your phone, ma'am."

"Oh, goodness. You're right. There it is. Thank you, dear."

"You're welcome. And please call back if you have any more problems."

She didn't let out even one sigh. If it had been Mom, she'd have been sighing and complaining all over the place.

"Landon Wireless. This is Paige. How can I help you?"

"You can help me by removing these crazy charges from my bill!"

"What charges are those, ma'am?"

"These ones to 'Dial-a-Hot-Chick.' I never called there."

"I'm sure you didn't, ma'am, but I see you have multiple lines on your account. Someone else in your household could have dialed that number."

"I don't *think* so! My husband certainly wouldn't and my son knows he's not allowed to call places like that."

"How old is your son, ma'am?"

"Fourteen."

Well of course he wouldn't call "Dial-a-Hot-Chick." His teenage hormones are totally under control.

"I can go ahead and research that for you, but it will probably take me about ten minutes or so. Would you like me to put you on hold or call you back?"

Working in a call center isn't exactly my dream career—it started out as a temp job two years ago—but it pays the bills and keeps me busy. Besides, I haven't quite figured out what my dream career is yet.

I was shoving my chair back to go to the cafeteria when my email pinged with a message from my sister. My successful sister who'd known what her dream career was ever since high school. I double-clicked the message. Group email of course. More efficient. And yet it fulfilled Isabel's family duty of keeping in touch.

> Hey everyone, check out the pix from our Bermuda getaway. We had a blast! If you ever get the chance, you have to go.
>
> Love, Isabel and David

Yeah. In what universe?

I scrolled through the photos of my tanned, fit, size-six sister and her equally tanned and fit husband, snorkeling, strolling on the beach hand-in-hand, and sipping drinks with those little umbrellas while gazing adoringly at one another.

Then I hit Delete.

My email pinged again almost immediately.

> Did you see those pictures of your sister? Why is it that she and her husband can go to all those exotic places but never make it back home to visit us? I'll bet David visits *his* family.

I'll bet he does too. But that's because David's parents are laid-back, low-maintenance Florida retirees who don't lob a steady barrage of familial duty guilt grenades at their offspring, and let them live their own lives. Isabel once told me that she really likes her in-laws and has fun with them—especially her mother-in-law.

What a novel concept. Eric certainly never had fun with his mother-in-law.

"Honey, do we really need to go to Pancake Carnival with your folks for breakfast after church this week?" Eric asked.

"We always go to Pancake Carnival."

"I know. So why not go somewhere different this week? Like La Bou, maybe? Their croissants are great."

"Mom can't have croissants with her diabetes. Way too many carbs. That's why she always orders the scrambled egg platter at the pancake house. They don't have scrambled eggs at La Bou."

"I know. I thought it would be nice to have breakfast just the two of us for a change."

"But we have breakfast just the two of us all the time during the week. And Mom would really be hurt. She looks forward all week to seeing you on Sundays."

"She can see me in church."

"That's not the same. There's no time to actually talk in church. That's why we always go out to breakfast afterwards. She likes to find out how your week went and to catch up on everything."

"You mean grill us about why you're not pregnant yet? And offer up her latest words of wisdom?"

"She's just trying to help. She really wants to be a grandma."

"And I really want to be a father. But I'm tired of talking to your family about it. Especially your mother. It's none of her business."

Well it is. Kinda, sorta. It will be her grandchild after all. Wisely, I didn't say that out loud though. "I'll call and tell her the subject is off-limits. Okay?"

"Which means we're going to Pancake Carnival on Sunday."

"What do you have against Pancake Carnival?"

"It's not the stupid Pancake Carnival!" Eric grabbed his jacket. "I need some air. I'll be back later."

The door slammed behind him.

I kept Mom's email as new, not up to sending my normal placating reply just yet. Then I grabbed our latest book club selection and headed to the cafeteria, stomach growling.

"Whatcha reading?"

Mouth full of croutons, I looked over the top of my book at Brooke, the nineteen-year-old new hire who'd just started in the call center last week. Pointing to my full mouth, I finished chewing as Brooke dropped into the chair opposite me and continued texting away on her cell.

After swallowing, I took a swig from my water bottle and answered, "*Into Thin Air*."

"What's it about?"

"An ill-fated expedition to Mount Everest."

"Is that the mountain in Washington?"

"No. That's Mount Rainier. Everest is in Tibet. It actually borders Tibet and Nepal. It's the highest mountain in the world."

Brooke chomped her gum as her fingers flew over her phone sending text messages. "So did people die and stuff?"

"Several. It's very sad."

"I don't like sad books. I'm all about happy endings."

"If you'd like to see something happy, take a look at this." Arthur, my sixty-something coworker who'd recently been downsized from his high-tech company and started temping with us, slid into the seat next to Brooke and displayed the latest pictures of his granddaughter.

"Ooh. Too cute. She's adorable. Isn't she, Paige?" Brooke said.

"I've always thought so." My eyes drank in the dimpled three-year-old with laughing cobalt-blue eyes who could give Suri Cruise a run for her cuteness. I flipped to the next picture where a clearly delighted granddaughter was blowing a spit bubble at her grandpa. I could almost hear her joyful giggle.

My ovaries clenched.

I sighed and passed the pictures back to Arthur. "Don't forget; if Samantha ever needs a babysitter, I'm ready, willing, and able."

"Well, Grandma and I get first dibs," he said, "but next time we're watching her, you should come on over. And maybe you could bring along some of that pear tart you learned to make in Paris."

"Deal."

With a few minutes still left on my lunch break, I decided to reply to my mother's email before she called me at work—which she did all the time, even though I'd asked her not to. Mom wouldn't know a boundary if it came up and bit her in the butt.

> Hi Mom, Need to keep this brief—lunch hour's almost over. Yes, I saw Isabel's email and I'm glad they were able to have a romantic getaway. Couples need that.

My fingers stilled at the keyboard. Maybe if Eric and I had been able to have more romantic getaways, we'd still be together. I puffed out a sigh and resumed typing.

> Don't forget, you have that appointment with Dr. Pond at 4:30. I'll pick you up a few minutes before 4. C-ya then. Love, me.

I was getting off at 3:30 today, instead of 5:30, using another two hours of sick leave to take my mother to her doctor's appointment. Not even halfway through the calendar year so far and already I'd used up almost all of my sick leave on her behalf.

Good thing I never got sick.

But Mom had had a couple fender benders lately, so I wasn't comfortable with her driving. Problem was, I couldn't afford to hire Morgan Freeman to drive her around like Miss Daisy, and she refused to *bother* her neighbors by asking them for a ride, or to take the bus—"Do you know what kinds of people ride the bus? The dregs of society. I don't want some mugger or rapist stealing my purse or something worse."

And so, it was left to me. "Blood is thicker than water," she always said.

Yeah, but how much blood am I going to have left before you suck me dry?

As I started to put my headset back on, I noticed a new email from Chloe.

In Paris.

Forgetting the headset, I clicked it open. Instantly the screen was filled with Van Gogh's *Starry Night Over the Rhone.* The cobalt sky and golden stars had been one of my favorite paintings at the Musee d'Orsay when we'd visited a few months ago. I scrolled down to read her message.

> *Bonjour mon amie!*
>
> Ryan's here visiting, so I took him to the Orsay today, and just as I'd expected, he fell in love with my Impressionists too. We had crepes for lunch at that great little place near the Eiffel Tower, and tonight we're going to Jacqueline's for dinner. She's making Coquilles St. Jacques and made me promise to send you, her favorite American student, the recipe. ☺
>
> How are all the Getaway Girls? Especially Aunt Tess? Has the distinguished James popped the question yet? *Mon dieu!* I must dash or we'll be late to Jacqueline's.
>
> *Au Revoir!* C.

I smiled to myself. I knew Chloe and Ryan would wind up together. We all did. Except Chloe. She couldn't see what was right in front of her eyes.

As for Tess, it was obvious she and James were head over heels and it was just a matter of time before the more mature couple got married. It seemed almost all the girls were getting together with someone, except me. And Becca, the serial dater.

At least she had dates. The only regular date in my life was my mom.

Not exactly the couple I'd been dreaming of.

3

Straddling the top of the world, one foot in China and the other in Nepal, I cleared the ice from my oxygen mask, hunched a shoulder against the wind, and stared absently down at the vastness of Tibet.

Into Thin Air

After lunch, I stared absently at the printer that always seemed to jam or break whenever I touched it.

"Uh-oh. Broke again? Maybe it's time to put up a 'Paige-free-zone' sign," Joe, one of the IT guys, said.

I blushed as I looked up into his seriously cute face which was grinning down at me. "Probably a good idea. I think I'm hazardous to its health."

"I hope you don't have this same effect on your boyfriend."

"That would require actually having a boyfriend."

His baby blues gleamed. "So you mean there's hope for me after all?"

Push those butterflies down, I told myself. It's just part of his flirting repertoire. He probably says that to everyone. Play it cool. Don't let him know you have a crush on him.

"You never know." I smiled, hoping he wouldn't notice the sweat I could feel beading above my lips. "The question is, is there hope for the printer?"

"Leave it to me. I have the magic touch." He popped open the side door, squatted down, and fiddled around in the bowels of the machine for a minute, then straightened and stood up, holding out a couple pieces of crumpled paper in his hands. "There's the culprit. Good as new now."

"Thanks. Maybe we should put up that 'Paige-free-zone' sign now."

"Only for the printer."

Three minutes later I had a date for Friday night—my first in over a year.

Yes! I spent the remainder of my work day in a fog

As I approached Mom's neighborhood, I stared at the detour signs blocking the street in front of me, my usual route. Good thing I left a little early as I get lost easily. I have no sense of direction, a familial malady I inherited from my mother. For years, I thought that north—since it's at the top of the compass—was always just in front of me, no matter which way I was traveling.

But Annette steered me straight. And bought me a compass which I kept in the glove compartment. One of these days, though, when I've saved up enough money, I'm going to buy a GPS unit. Meanwhile, I've learned to compensate. I always make sure I travel the same route to work, church, the grocery store, or any other frequent destination, including my mother's house. That way I know exactly where I'm going.

Not today though.

I turned right and followed the detour signs through her neighborhood. And as I drove through the streets less traveled,

I noticed a new flower shop on the corner in place of what had formerly been a thrift store.

The happy yellow sign with the unique name bade me stop.

I pushed open the front door and was greeted by chimes and Peter, Paul & Mary singing "Where Have All the Flowers Gone?" Except they weren't the only ones singing. A loud, seriously off-key voice was emanating from the back.

"Hello?" I said.

The off-key singing stopped and Peter, Paul & Mary were turned down. "Be right there."

I looked around the sunny, eclectic shop. Cheery yellow walls were offset by shelves and pedestals holding a variety of whimsical vases and flower books while tin watering cans and buckets bursting with blooms dotted the green stamped-concrete floor.

In one corner, an antique claw-foot tub overflowed with a bed of daisies, while in another, an old Radio Flyer red wagon was filled with mini roses and topiaries in different-sized terra-cotta pots. Above the wagon hung a framed print of Wordsworth's daffodils poem.

I closed my eyes and murmured the words of my favorite poem from college English. "I wandered lonely as a cloud, that danced on high o'er vales and hills, when all at once I saw a crowd, a host of golden daffodils."

"Ah, another Wordsworth fan," said a male voice behind me.

My eyes flew open and I jumped at the same time.

"Sorry. Didn't mean to startle you."

Hand over my still-rapid-beating heart, I turned around to face a guy not much taller than me with a neatly trimmed beard and dark brown hair who was giving me a pleasant smile.

And wearing clogs. Green.

"That's okay. I just didn't hear you."

He gestured to his rubber-soled feet. "Yeah, these puppies are pretty quiet. If I ever get tired of being a florist, I could become a cat burglar and really clean up." He grinned and stuck out his hand. "Hi. I'm Marc. Welcome to A Host of Golden Daffodils. How can I help you?"

I shook his hand and was surprised to discover he had quite a strong grip. "Paige. Nice to meet you. I'm looking for something a little cheerful for my mother. Maybe a bouquet of daisies or something?"

"Is your mom in the hospital?"

"No, but she has a lot of health issues. In fact," I looked at my watch, "I'm on my way to pick her up and take her to a doctor's appointment, so I don't have a lot of time."

"No prob. I know just the thing. Give me two minutes." He disappeared into the back again. A second later, he popped his head around the corner. "What's your mom's favorite color?"

"Pink." I thought of her bright refrigerator and closet full of pink floral caftans and polyester print tops. "Definitely pink."

True to his word, two minutes later he returned with a gorgeous, predominantly pink bouquet with touches of green and yellow.

"That's beautiful. She'll love it." I peered at the floral mix. "I recognize the yellow daisies, but what's the rest? I'm afraid the only flowers I know by name are daisies, roses, daffodils, and tulips."

"These large pink ones are Gerbera daisies," he said as he began to wrap the bouquet in cellophane. "And these smaller lily-looking ones are alstromeria—which last a long time. I also included one of my special favorites, Bells of Ireland." He pointed to a tall lime green stalk with bells up and down it and a tiny white flower in the center of each bell. "They've always been considered a symbol of good luck."

"I thought that was the four-leaf clover."

He winked. "Aye. But sure and begorrah, the Irish have lots of good luck symbols, don't ye know?"

"You're Irish?"

"Half."

"What's the other half?"

"Italian."

"Quite a combination."

"Best of both worlds. Great beer and dancing—and great food and music." He whistled a familiar snatch of music from what I think was something from *La Bohème* as he handed me the bouquet.

I definitely had to see that opera one of these days. Then I noticed the clock behind him. Oops. What I definitely had to do was get a move on. "Thanks again." I paid for the flowers and hurried to the door. "I'll be back."

"Good. I hope the doctor's visit goes well. And next time you come, be sure to allow more time for your next flower lesson."

"I'll do that."

As I headed out the door I heard music begin again. Only this time it was "You Don't Bring Me Flowers" with Neil Diamond and Barbra Streisand.

How come all the nice, sensitive guys always had to be married or gay?

Thankfully, I had my date with Joe. He's definitely not gay. Or married. Divorced, like me, I'd heard through the grapevine.

One thing's for sure—no way was I going to tell Mom about my date. She'd want to know everything. For now I'd just keep it to myself. Besides, it could turn out to be a total disaster.

Mom loved the flowers—even moreso when she found out they came from A Host of Golden Daffodils. "I hear the owner's really sweet. And cute. Frieda's trying to set him up with her daughter."

"Yeah, good luck with that," I said under my breath as I helped her out the door.

There was nothing wrong with Mom's hearing. "Why do you say that? Frieda says he's very nice."

"He is."

"But?"

"But what?"

"I can tell when there's a but coming, young lady. Whenever I talk to you about some nice man, you always find something wrong with him. So what's wrong with Marc the florist?"

"Isn't it obvious?" I hooked our seatbelts and backed out of the driveway.

"Isn't what obvious?"

"Never mind." Far be it from me to shatter her romantic illusions. "Did you bring your list of meds and write down any questions you have for Dr. Pond?"

"Of course. What do you think I am? Senile? I'm only sixty-eight, you know."

"I know. It's just that last time I took you to see him, there were things you wanted to ask, but you didn't remember until we got home. Then you had to call in to the office the next day and go through that long phone menu just to leave a message for his nurse. And then it took her a couple days to get back to you—which you weren't very happy about."

"I know." She waved a piece of paper at me. "That's why I wrote my questions down this time, Miss Smarty Pants."

"Okay, good." Not wanting to get into an argument, I changed the subject. "So, how was your day? Did you go for a walk?"

"You know I can't walk well with my bad legs."

"But exercise will help that. Remember? That's what Dr. Pond said."

"Yeah, well he's a slim Jim. He should try living in this body. It's not so easy to get around."

It would be if you lost a little weight and quit eating junk food all the time.

But I didn't say that out loud. If I did, Mom would just get mad and take it out on me. That's why I'd finally learned to let her doctor ask those questions.

Let her take it out on him instead.

"Catherine, good to see you." Dr. Pond rested his hand on Mom's shoulder. "What brings you in today?"

"My legs. They're really aching. Isn't there some pill or ointment or something you can give me to ease the pain?"

"We've been over this before. Your legs ache because you're not moving around enough. You need to increase your circulation, and the best way to do that is to move."

"You try moving when you're my size."

"Another good reason to lose some weight. It's really not healthy for you to carry around those extra pounds. Have you been following that diabetic diet plan I gave you last time?"

"Yes-s-s."

Dr. Pond and I lifted our eyebrows in unison.

"Well, I'm trying to, but it's not easy changing the way I've eaten my whole life. My daughter's a big help, though. She's one of those gourmet cooks and always making me something healthy that tastes good." She sent him a disappointed glance. "Too bad you're already married. She'd make a good wife."

My face burned. Not so sure Eric would agree with you there, Mom.

"I'm sure she would—I can already see she's a good daughter."

That's me. Trusty and loyal. Like a dog. I even fetch and carry too.

"Yes she is. Don't know what I'd ever do without her. By the way, what are we having for dinner tonight, Paige?"

"Rosemary chicken, brown rice with mushrooms and onions, and steamed green beans."

"Brown rice?" Mom made a face. "I like white rice."

"Brown rice is much better for you." Dr. Pond shone a penlight in her eyes and frowned. "How's your vision these days, Catherine?"

"Not so good." She sighed. "I think I need stronger glasses."

"Did you ever go to the ophthalmologist I referred you to?"

"Not yet."

"Not yet?" He stared at her and then began to flip through her records. "I referred you months ago."

"But Paige wasn't here to take me—she was in Paris."

"Mom, you never told me Dr. Pond referred you to an ophthalmologist."

"I forgot."

"I guess this brown rice isn't so bad after all," Mom said that night after she shoveled in a second forkful. "Actually, it's pretty good."

"Seasoning makes all the difference. I cooked the rice in chicken broth instead of water and added sautéed onions and mushrooms."

She gave me a wide grin. "Sautéed? With butter?"

"Uh-uh. Olive oil. It's healthier."

Mom made a face. "You and Dr. Pond are in cahoots."

"You got that right. Since you won't take care of yourself, we will."

Dr. Pond had given my mother a stern talking-to that afternoon about not following up with the ophthalmologist. "Catherine, you can't mess around with your eyes—especially with diabetes." Then he'd walked us out to the referral desk where he'd instructed them to get her an appointment with the eye doctor as soon as possible.

"Can I at least have some dessert?"

"Sure. We've got sugar-free chocolate pudding with whipped cream."

"Fat-free and sugar-free whipped cream, I suppose."

"You can't even taste the difference."

"Oh yes you can." She closed her eyes and a look of pure bliss stole over her face. "Real cream is rich and thick and doesn't have that artificial aftertaste. Same with butter. I *can* believe it's not butter." She licked her lips. "Buttercream frosting too. Not that pretend stuff they're trying to pass off as real in the grocery store bakeries today."

If I didn't distract my mother from her food fantasies, she'd work herself up into a feeding frenzy and sneak all sorts of bad stuff once I left. Or worse, send poor Frieda to the store to buy cans of frosting and whipped cream. "So, what movie do you want to watch tonight?"

Her eyes flew open. "What'd you bring?"

I reached for my tote bag and began pulling out DVDs: *The Quiet Man*, *McClintock*, and *Rio Bravo.* John Wayne was Mom's leading man of choice. Then I grabbed *Oklahoma*, *Brigadoon*, and *Seven Brides for Seven Brothers.* Musicals were also a special favorite of hers. Both of ours, actually. With that in mind, I'd once brought *Moulin Rouge* over for her viewing pleasure. Although Mom thought Nicole Kidman was talented—albeit "too skinny"—the frenetic camera cutting and MTV-feel of the musical gave her a headache. So now I stuck to the classics she preferred.

"I just can't decide between *McClintock*, *Seven Brides*, or *Brigadoon*," she said. "What do you think?"

Not *McClintock*. Can you say sexist? That whole spanking thing to show who's boss? I don't think so. But I know better than to raise that objection with Mom. She'd just go into her anti-feminist diatribe and tell me that kind of attitude was why I didn't have a husband.

Conveniently forgetting the fact that she drove my husband away.

"Okay, Mom. I'll see you in a little bit." I had hung up the phone and sighed.

Eric shot me a look of annoyance. A look that was becoming all too familiar of late. "What is it this time?"

"She can't find her copy of *Rio Bravo*."

"So tell her to watch another John Wayne instead. She's got the whole library, doesn't she?"

"Actually, I think it's just an excuse for me to come over for a little while. She's lonely."

"Why doesn't she invite Frieda over?"

"A neighbor isn't the same as family. I feel bad for her now that she's all alone. It just breaks my heart. Isabel never comes home to visit and who knows where Patrick is these days?"

"Timbuktu, if he's smart," Eric said under his breath.

"What'd you say?"

My husband crossed the room and rested his hands gently on my shoulders. "Do you ever wonder why your brother and sister left town when they did?"

"Because they're selfish and everything is all about them."

"Is it selfish to want to live their own lives?"

"No. But they didn't have to abandon Mom in the process."

He gave me a gentle look. "Didn't they?"

I pulled away. "What are you saying?"

"I'm saying that your mother can be very demanding and possessive. And probably the only way Isabel and Patrick felt they could break free of her was to leave." He paused. "I'm beginning to wonder if maybe we need to do the same thing."

"What? You mean move?"

"Maybe."

I stared at him. "We can't move. All your clients are here, and your friends, my friends, our church, my mother ..."

"I'm just raising the possibility—trying to think of what's best for our marriage. The company has an office in San Francisco I could always transfer to."

"Oh, I see. You want to move closer to *your* family."

"Partly. But if we lived in the Bay Area we'd still be close enough to your mom so you could see her, just not quite as often—say maybe one weekend a month instead of several times a week."

"You just don't understand the mother-daughter bond."

"Sure I do. My sister's close to my mom and they get together regularly. But Beth doesn't call or email her three or four times a day. She lives her own life and so does my mother. And Mom wouldn't have it any other way."

"But your mother still has her husband. With my siblings scattered to the winds I'm all Mom has now that Dad's gone."

"And what about me?"

"Why don't we watch *Brigadoon*, Mom? That way we get both Scotland and Gene Kelly."

She released a blissful sigh. "I love Gene Kelly. Although ... that Howard Keel's pretty easy on the eyes too. What a voice.

Plus, he's got those six strapping brothers in *Seven Brides.* I love their dance at the barn raising."

Oh yeah. That's one of my favorite scenes. But talk about a sexist movie—kidnapping a bunch of women, caveman-style, for a little feminine companionship?

As I cleared the table, I began humming the love song "Come to Me, Bend to Me" from *Brigadoon.*

"Honey?"

"Yes, Mom?"

"Let's watch *Brigadoon.*"

4

> Ria's mother had always been very fond of film stars. It was a matter of sadness to her that Clark Gable had died on the day Ria was born.
>
> *Tara Road*

My sister Isabel has it easy. She has no sense of family duty and hasn't been close to Mom since she was a kid. Isabel started pulling away in junior high, and when she entered high school, she became even more independent, filling her days and nights with activities—singing in choir, becoming student body president, and in time, captain of the girls' softball team. My folks basked in the compliments from her teachers and coaches: "Isabel sings like an angel. Your daughter's a natural-born leader. All the other girls on the team really look up to her."

Isabel was their golden child. A golden child who was never home.

Mom and Dad were always suggesting she invite friends over, but our shabby ranch circa the 1950s, replete with chalky pink toilet and tub in the lone bathroom, embarrassed her. Our mother embarrassed her too with her constant whining and guilt manipulation.

And her size.

Mom has always been big, although Dad always called her his *curvy* girl. As the years passed, however, and Dad's work responsibilities increased, keeping him away from home and his family more and more, she grew heavier and heavier. By the time I was a sophomore, she tipped the scales at over 250 pounds, which was anathema to my size six sister. Mom tried to lose weight—going on every diet known to woman. And for a while, they'd work. But not for long. She usually gave up in defeat and drowned her sorrows in the Colonel's Original Recipe.

I'd tried to make up for my absent father and sister and increasingly trouble-prone brother—dusting, vacuuming, and even taking over the cooking when Mom resorted to Kentucky Fried three times a week. Nothing seemed to make a difference, though. Dad still worked long hours, my sister was still a no-show, and my brother continued his stint as a headbanger.

When Isabel moved out after winning a full scholarship to Berkeley, Mom begged me not to leave and go away to school when I graduated. "I don't want to lose both my daughters," she wailed, clutching at my arm. So although I wasn't the golden child, I stayed in town and attended the local junior college instead where I got my associate's degree. My grades were okay, but nowhere near the level of my sister's. Which was fine by me. Unlike Isabel, I never had dreams of blazing a brilliant academic trail, getting a bunch of letters after my name, and soaring to the top of the corporate ladder.

The only ladder I wanted to climb was the white picket fence one, with an adoring husband, a bunch of laughing kids hanging onto my legs, and a lovable mutt barking at the bottom.

My siblings and I couldn't be more different.

Including Patrick. We never knew where Patrick was, or when or if we'd hear from him. He didn't make it to my wedding because he was backpacking through Europe at the time. And a year after Dad died, he showed up on Isabel's doorstep to see her on his way to India, where he said he planned to live on an ashram and study with some guru or another. Since then we'd had a couple postcards, but that was all. On the fridge is the most recent picture I have of him—long-haired, flashing me the peace sign from a commune in Colorado ... from four years ago.

My brother definitely marched to the beat of his own drummer. Isabel too. And me?

I was too beat to march.

Thursday night when I got home from work, there was a message from Isabel on my answering machine.

"Don't faint, but this is your big sister calling. How's everything? Still working at the call center? Anytime you want something a little more exciting, just let me know. I'd be happy to pull some strings for my baby sister. That is, if you're finally ready to cut the umbilical cord."

Easy for you to say.

I opened the fridge and pulled out the bag of baby carrots and my bottle of low-fat Ranch dressing.

I kneaded the back of my neck. Those call center complaints really took their toll. Usually by the end of the week, all I wanted to do was stay home and veg out—which I rarely got to do, since weekends, or at least one day out of them, were Mother time.

But this weekend—tomorrow night!—I had a date. With Joe, of all people. I'd been crushing on him for months. Most of the girls at work had. And yet he'd picked *me.* What were the odds? Finally I could join the rest of the Getaway Girls who were dating.

About time.

All our twentysomething members—Becca, Jenna, and Kailyn—never seemed to lack for dates, or at least the possibility of dates. (Kailyn can be pretty picky.) And Chloe, who was so devastated when that creep Chris dumped her just before their wedding last year, now has Ryan, even if she doesn't realize it yet. Annette and Tess are both in great relationships, and they're over fifty.

At thirty-five, I've been the in-between one. Kind of applies to all areas of my life.

I'm in between careers—still not sure what I want to be when I grow up.

In between residences—renting my duplex, but thinking of becoming a grown-up and buying a house.

And definitely in between men. Although no way am I going to say that to Joe. I don't want him to think I'm a loser. But truth is, I've only had a few dates in the two and a half years since my divorce—heavy emphasis on the few, and I don't want to blow this one.

The one thing different I bring to our book club table is that I'm the only divorcee in the group. Not a label I ever wanted to wear.

Snap out of it!

I could hear Cher's *Moonstruck* voice in my head as I bit into a baby carrot. Great movie. Sooo romantic. One of these days I really needed to get tickets to *La Bohème*, even without a Nicolas Cage in my life.

Hmm. I wonder if Joe likes opera?

Thinking of Joe, I'd better figure out what I'm wearing tomorrow night...

An hour later I glance at all the discarded clothes piled on my bed and strewn around the room. Apparently I'm wearing nothing. There's not a single outfit in my entire closet that will work. Which means I have to go shopping.

And I hate shopping. Unlike Kailyn who pants and starts to hyperventilate at the mere thought of her favorite activity, or Annette who can shop for six hours straight to find the best bargain.

Eric dubbed me Diana the huntress for my shopping proclivities. I'd go in a store, knowing exactly what I wanted, head straight to the specific rack, remove what I was hunting for—jeans, skirt, black T-shirt, whatever—proceed to the cash register without passing go, pay, and leave.

I grabbed my purse and drove to Macy's down the street. Thirty minutes later I returned home with a pair of black jeans and a crisp white button-down with wide cuffs and a shirttail to be worn out. Classic, understated, and not trying too hard.

Later, I dug out my old pedicure and manicure set and spent nearly all of *Ugly Betty* and *Grey's Anatomy* making my nails pretty while glancing up at McDreamy. I haven't cared about my toes and nails since we were in Paris.

At work the next day, Joe gives me that smile and reminds me that tonight's our date—as if he needs to remind me—and reconfirms that we'll meet at a casual seafood place he wants to take me to.

"The best crab in Sacramento," he says.

I arrive at the restaurant at 6:52 and wait in my car for twelve minutes so that I won't be early (How desperate would that appear?) and not on time either (shows a woman who is overanxious and not carefree and fun like I want Joe to think I might be). A few minutes late is always perfect.

Joe must have thought so too since he isn't anywhere to be seen.

The hostess asks, "Dining for one, or are you waiting for others?"

"I have a date," I say with more force and enunciation than necessary.

"Do you want to wait here or in the bar?"

The few chairs in the entry area are taken, so I go to the bar. Although I'm not much of a drinker, a small glass of wine would be nice about now. Take the nervous edge off and settle those butterflies that are dive-bombing against the sides of my stomach.

"Got stood up too?" says a voice beside me. A guy in his forties leans on the bar, cradling his super-sized beer.

I glance both ways to make sure he's talking to me. "No, I'm waiting for someone."

"Yeah, I was too."

My petite glass of wine arrives and before I take a sip, a wave of beer scent washes over me as my new buddy on the next stool leans in.

"My girlfriend and I broke up last year. Tonight was my first big date since then. But then she sent me a text when I got here saying she couldn't make it."

"That's … unfortunate," I said, turning away from Beer Breath.

My phone beeps.

"Oh, it's happening to you too. Maybe our dates are really with each other." At this he laughs heartily yet with a tinge of hysteria.

I access my voicemail and listen to Joe's message. "Paige? I was hoping to catch you before you left. I'm so sorry, but my baseball game went into overtime. Raincheck? I promise to make it up to you. I'll call you this weekend. Gotta go. I'm up to bat."

How did I miss his call? Stupid phone. I had it on vibrate and didn't hear it.

"My girlfriend cheated on me too," Beer guy is saying as I drop some cash on the bar and leave. When I get back to my car, I see the time. My first date in forever lasted all of sixteen minutes.

The next day I'm tempted to call Joe on the pretense of asking how his game went. But talk about a flimsy excuse. And overeager. Desperate.

I set the phone down. He said he'd call, so I'll just wait to hear from him.

But I refuse to sit by the phone. Too pathetic. Instead, I decide to go to the nearby farmer's market and pick up some fresh fruits and veggies. I scoop up my wallet, keys, and cell, this time making sure it's not set on vibrate.

When the Getaway Girls were in Paris, we'd learned from our French chef and mentor Jacqueline that French cooking is all about fresh ingredients, locally produced. And although I couldn't go to the outdoor market every day like Jacqueline did, I usually tried to go at least once a week to one of the many open air farmer's markets around town.

Wandering through the food stalls, I pick up onions, carrots, zucchini, early apricots, and strawberries. Plump, sweet strawberries. I wipe away the juice that trickles down my chin. The other thing I love about the farmer's market is that they let you try the merchandise before buying. I buy an extra basket of strawberries for Mom.

When I finish up at the market, I drop by my neighborhood grocery store to pick up bread and milk and some sugar-free angel food cake to go with Mom's strawberries. As I turn down the bread aisle, I bump into another shopper's cart. A very pregnant shopper.

They're everywhere.

"I'm sorry. I didn't see you."

She giggled. "You just made my day. I'll have to tell my husband that."

Sure. Rub it in. You've got the hubby and a baby on board. I give her a weak smile as she waddles away.

After I finish grocery shopping, I stop by the cleaners and pick up my dry cleaning. And all the while, my cell stays silent. Not even one vibration. When I return home in the early afternoon and set my packages down on the counter, I notice that my answering machine is blinking.

About time. He'd better grovel.

I hit Play and a tinny, computerized voice comes over the machine. "Paige Kelley, you only have two days left to claim your valuable vacation package to Lake Tahoe. Blah, blah, blah ..." I slap the Delete button.

There's only one thing left to do.

I put away the groceries and begin yanking pans out of the cupboard. Then I begin assembling all the ingredients I'll need: onions, garlic, fresh basil, parsley, spinach, tomatoes, mushrooms, tomato paste, noodles, ground turkey, and cheese. I spend the next hour and a half chopping, shredding, dicing, sautéing, simmering, sprinkling, and assembling. At last I slide the pan of lasagna into the oven to bake.

And while it's baking, I lose myself in my latest paperback, deliberately refusing to think about Joe the jerk who didn't call.

Later, while the lasagna's cooling and I'm chopping onions for salad, it's not as easy to dismiss Joe from my mind. Why hasn't he called? And why, if he wasn't going to call, did he even ask me out in the first place?

I'll never have another date.

I'm never going to get married again.

I'm going to wind up alone and childless and dependent upon the kindness of strangers in my old age.

I think back to the giggling pregnant woman from the grocery store today. And then she's replaced with the neon billboard image of Heather's very pregnant belly.

It's not fair. My eyes begin to water. That should be *my* baby, not hers. Eyes streaming, I chop harder.

The phone rings.

Maybe I won't wind up alone after all.

"Hello?" I mumble into the receiver, trying to hide a slight sniffle.

"Are you cryin', honey?" Annette says.

I was right. Completely alone.

"No. Chopping onions. What's up?"

"Well-l-l," she drawls, her voice turning all mysterious, "remember last weekend how I said Tess and James were in love?"

"Yes, and I said it was 'twoo wuv.' "

"And then what did you say?"

I wiped at my eyes with a towel, trying to remember. Then it came back to me. "Mawwiage is what bwings—oh my gosh! They're getting *married*?"

"Yes ma'am," Annette said in her Texas twang. "He proposed over a romantic lunch at the Cliff House." Her voice crackled with excitement. "Isn't that the best news?"

"Wonderful! So spill. I want details. How'd he ask her? When's the date? Where are they getting married? Has she told Chloe yet?"

"Slow down. I don't know any more than that. Tess really couldn't talk, but she promised to call tomorrow with all the details. I was thinking though that maybe we could take her out to lunch after church instead and get the straight scoop in person. What do you think?"

"I think that's a good idea, but," I pulled open the fridge to check the contents, "I've got an even better one. Why don't we have brunch here instead? I'll make some quiche and fruit salad, and we can check and see if any of the other girls are available and turn it into a surprise celebration of her engagement."

"Great idea. Love it! What can I bring?"

"How about some nice fresh croissants from La Bou?"

"M'mm, love their croissants. I'll get a mixture of plain, almond, and chocolate."

"Sounds good." I scribbled down the menu and drummed my fingers on the counter. "Now, is there anything else I'm forgetting?"

"Oops, I almost forgot. Tess said she doesn't want us emailing Chloe because she's calling her in Paris late tonight. She wanted to do it right away, but it was the middle of the night over there."

"You'd better make sure you tell the others too. Otherwise I could see Becca or Kailyn spilling the beans."

"My baby girl's good at that. But don't you fret. I'll call them next. And thanks for the brunch offer. That's so sweet. I'm sure Tess will really appreciate it."

"Well, she's the first one in our group to get engaged. That calls for a celebration."

"You're tellin' me. Now if I could just find nice guys for the rest of you ..."

"From your lips to God's ears."

I hung up the phone and stifled a sigh. Tess was fifteen years older than me and she was getting married again. Not that I begrudged her her happiness. She deserved it, especially after having lost her husband when her boys were so young and having to raise them alone all these years. But where was my nice guy? When would it be *my* turn?

You had your turn with Eric and you blew it.

No I didn't. He's the one who left, not me.

And why did he leave again?

Because of my mother.

Only your mother?

And because I couldn't get pregnant.

You sure about that? Are you being fair?

Well, look at his life now. He's got what he always wanted. And what do I have? Nothing. At least Tess had her boys to keep her company after her husband died.

All I have is my mother. And a silent phone.

I removed a couple portions of the still-warm lasagna, wrapped them in foil, and stuck them in a plastic container to drop by Mom's later, along with some of the salad. Although ... my eyes slid to the wall clock: 5:10. If I took it over now, I could pop into Golden Daffodils before they closed and pick up some pretty flowers for Tess's brunch tomorrow. Covering the remaining lasagna with foil, I stuck it in the fridge along with the rest of the salad, grabbed my keys and Mom-offerings, and slammed the door shut.

As I exited the freeway and pulled up to the red light at the intersection, I noticed an old homeless guy on the side of the road with a skinny yellow Lab at his feet who looked like he hadn't had a good meal in weeks. The man was holding up a sign that said, "Will work for dog food. God bless."

Grabbing a twenty from my purse, I rolled down my window partway and extended it to him. He doffed his grimy baseball cap and I could see his rheumy eyes glistening. "Thank you, ma'am. God bless you."

"And you." The light turned green and he stepped back, nodding at me. I glanced in my rearview mirror as I drove through the intersection and saw him squat down and hug his dog.

Now my eyes were glistening.

Five minutes later, I pushed through the florist's front door.

Marc looked up from the cash register, a smile of recognition lighting up his friendly bearded face. "Hey, Paige. Good to see you again."

"Hi. Hope I'm not coming too late to pick up some flowers."

"Not at all. For your mom again?"

"No, a friend who just got engaged. I'm having a brunch for her tomorrow and wanted to have some kind of pretty centerpiece I could give her to take home."

"Do you know what kind of flowers you want?"

"Not really. Um, something with roses, maybe, for romance?"

He gave me a mock menacing frown and nodded to the wall clock. "You were supposed to come back when you had more time for your flower education."

"Sorry. This was kind of a last-minute thing."

"Okay, you're forgiven. Come on back and let's see what we can find. Watch your step though. I haven't had time to clean up yet and there's stuff all over the floor."

I followed his rubber-clogged feet to a cluttered back room full of buckets of greenery, knives and scissors, rainbow colors of ribbons, scads of paperwork, and a carnival of colored glass lining the walls.

"So, how long have you been a florist?"

"Three years. I apprenticed with a larger florist called the Flower Cart until a few months ago, and then decided to open my own shop."

"And how do you like it?"

"Love it. What's not to love about being my own boss and being surrounded by beauty all day?" He opened the walk-in and gestured to a bucket full of deep red roses just inside the door. "Aren't those glorious?"

Glorious?

Marc was definitely cut from a different cloth than most of the men I knew. "What about some of these for tomorrow?"

"Not unless you're marrying your friend. Red roses are a sign of love and passion."

"Really?" I could feel my face warm. "What about yellow ones? Do they mean something too?"

"Certainly. Friendship and joy." He inclined his head to a bucket of pristine white roses next to the red. "White, of course, signifies purity and innocence."

"What about orange?"

"Desire and enthusiasm."

"Lavender?"

"Enchantment and love at first sight."

He stopped before a trio of rose buckets bearing varying shades of pink blooms. "Pink roses also express friendship; dark pink signifies gratitude and appreciation while light pink signifies grace, admiration, and joy."

"I had no idea roses had so many different meanings."

"Not just roses. Most flowers have specific meanings associated with them."

"Serious?"

Marc grinned. "Looks like I need to enroll you in Flowers 101." Then he looked at his watch. "Unfortunately, we'll have to continue our lesson another day."

My eyes dropped to my own watch: 5:40. How'd that happen? "I'm sorry, I didn't mean to keep you past closing."

"That's okay; I enjoyed the company. I just have a final delivery to make before 6:00—I let my delivery driver off early today." He gestured to the light pink roses. "Some of these, for joy?"

"Perfect."

He lifted six stems from the bucket and plucked three pretty pink tulips from another bucket. Finally, he reached overhead into a smaller bucket and gently removed a delicate white flower.

I sucked in my breath. "Oh, that's beautiful. What is it?"

"A cymbidium orchid, for love and beauty."

"I'm not sure I can afford an orchid—aren't they terribly expensive?"

"Not this one. It's my gift to the bride-to-be." He lifted his shoulders and smiled. "What can I say? I'm a sucker for romance. Besides," he winked, "she'll need a florist for her wedding. If she likes this, maybe she'll give me a shot."

"I'm sure she will. I'll definitely recommend you." I followed him out of the walk-in, his rubber-soled clogs making a squeaking noise on the linoleum, and watched as he worked his floral magic at the back table, snipping the stems and tightly arranging the flowers into a low, square, clear glass container with the orchid in the center.

"Gorgeous. She'll love it! Thanks so much." We returned to the front and I pulled out my wallet. "How much do I owe you?"

"Twenty." He marked my Frequent Buyer Club card that he'd had me fill out on my first visit.

"Twenty bucks? That can't even cover the cost of the roses—never mind the tulips and your labor. Seriously, what do I owe you?"

His teeth flashed above his dark beard. "Call it my wedding promo price. Just make sure your friend comes and checks me out. Deal?" He held out his hand.

I placed a twenty in his hand and shook it. "Deal. Thanks. And now I'll let you go so you can make your delivery. Thanks for the flower introduction too."

"No problem. Give me a call so we can schedule the next class in your floral education."

"Will do."

As I slid into my car, my eyes lit upon the thermal bag on the passenger seat.

A minute later I was knocking at the driver's side of Marc's yellow delivery van. He rolled down the window. "Did I forget something?"

"Yep." I handed him a foil-wrapped square. "My home-made and very healthy lasagna. Consider it payment for my first class."

5

> You can't stay in your corner of the forest waiting for others to come to you. You have to go to them sometimes.
>
> *A. A. Milne*

Mom unpacked the thermal bag and looked up at me in surprise through her thick glasses. "I thought you were going to bring me two pieces of lasagna so I could have one for lunch tomorrow."

"I was, but I wound up giving the other piece away."

"You gave *my* lasagna away? To who? Some homeless person, I'll bet." Her eyes narrowed behind her glasses. "What have I told you about that? You need to be more careful. Those panhandlers can be dangerous. I heard on one of those undercover investigation shows that some of them make more than $50,000 a year from the handouts suckers give them."

"It wasn't a homeless person. But what if it had been? What would be so wrong with that? Jesus told us to feed the hungry."

"That's why they have soup kitchens and the canned food closet at church." She removed the tinfoil, set her square of lasagna onto a plate, covered it with a paper towel, and stuck it in the microwave. "So which hungry did you feed?"

"Marc, the florist down the street."

"Well why didn't you say so in the first place?" she beamed. "Wait'll I tell Frieda. She was so sure that *her* daughter was the right match for him. Hah. Shows how much she knows."

Shows how much you know. I doubt either daughter is a match for him.

Mom frowned. "Why didn't you just invite him over here for dinner?"

"Because he had a delivery to make, and besides, it was just a spur-of-the-moment decision, it didn't mean anything. He did me a favor, and I was simply thanking him."

"What kind of favor?" Her eyes gleamed.

I wasn't about to tell her about our Flower 101 class; she'd read all sorts of things into it that weren't there. "He gave me a discount on a floral arrangement for Tess—oh no, I left the flowers in the car! I hope they're okay." I raced out the back door.

She peered closely at the flowers when I returned and set them down on the kitchen counter. "Well, he certainly does good work, doesn't he? Look at all those pretty pink roses. What'd Tess do to merit a dozen roses?"

Mom's vision was getting worse by the day, but I knew she was sensitive about it, so I tread carefully. "It's a mixture of roses and pink tulips, but the tulips haven't opened yet, so they look like rosebuds."

"You still didn't answer my question."

"What question is that?"

She expelled a loud sigh. "I asked what Tess did to merit so many roses—roses and tulips."

"Got engaged. Isn't that wonderful? We're going to have a little Getaway Girls celebration for her tomorrow after church."

"Tess *James* got engaged? Isn't she over fifty?"

"Just. She turns fifty-one later this year."

"Well, you better get a move on, missy. You don't want her to leave you in the dust now, do you? You're going to have to do more than give that florist a little piece of lasagna in tinfoil—you need to make him one of your fancy gourmet dinners if you want to fan his interest. You know what they say: the way to a man's heart is through his stomach."

Or through his baseball team. I was tempted to tell her about Joe to shut her up, but what was there to say besides the fact that he stood me up? Like I really wanted anyone knowing that. Especially my mother.

I picked up the flower arrangement and slid off the bar stool. "I have to go, Mom. I've got a million things to do before tomorrow. I'm helping out in Sunday school and I need to prep the quiches tonight for the brunch. Plus my house is a mess. Good night." I kissed her on the forehead. "Enjoy the lasagna. I'll talk to you tomorrow. And don't forget to eat the salad I brought too. Dr. Pond said you need to eat more greens."

"Okay, honey. Good night. I'll talk to you tomorrow."

Locking the back door, I pulled it shut behind me. Whew. Made it past the Mom-quisition.

As I drove away, I smiled to myself. She'd never know that I'd substituted wheat noodles for white in her favorite lasagna. Sometimes I had to be sneaky to get her to eat properly. Her diminishing eyesight, even with her glasses, concerned me though. Mom had developed cataracts a few years ago and had surgery to correct them, but there was always the possibility she could get them again, especially with her being diabetic. Thankfully we were meeting with the ophthalmologist soon.

I stopped at the grocery store on the way home to pick up some more eggs, kiwis for the fruit salad, and Red Vines, my favorite snack of choice. When I got home there were two messages on my answering machine.

At last. I hit Play and waited, trying to be cool. Breathe in, breathe out.

"Woo-hoo!" Kailyn screeched, hurting my ears. "Mom just called and told me about Tess. Isn't that great? Chloe's going to be so stoked!" Her voice lowered to a reasonable decibel level. "Not to worry; Becca and I promise not to say a word to Chloe. Oh, and we'll both be there tomorrow for brunch. I'm bringing champagne for mimosas and some sparkling cider so Mom can have a virgin one."

"And I'm bringing black armbands," Becca's voice chimed in the background. "Another good woman goes down for the domestic count."

"You're so cynical," I heard Kailyn say to her roommate as the message beeped to an end.

I pressed Delete and waited for the second message. Please be Joe. Please be Joe.

"Hi Paige," a familiar male voice said.

Not Joe.

Did you really think he'd call? C'mon, don't you know a brush-off when you hear it? I returned my attention to the message that was babbling away.

" ... got your number from your Frequent Buyer Club card. Anyway, I just had to call and tell you how amazing that lasagna was." Marc's blissful sigh punctured the air. "I haven't had lasagna that good since my mom passed. And that's high praise since her recipe came from my great-great Sicilian grandmother. Anytime you want to send more my way, feel free. Oh, and one word for you: phalaenopsis."

"Fail-a-what?" I powered up my laptop and did a search

on Google, guessing at the spelling. A raft of unusual foreign-language items popped up. Doubtful. I scrolled to the bottom where it asked, "Did you mean to search for *phalaenopsis*"?

I don't know. Maybe. I clicked on the link.

Ah ... orchids. Beautiful orchids. I clicked open one of the myriad entries. Familiar-looking flowers I'd seen around, but had never known what they were. I continued to read and learned that phalaenopsis is also known as the moth orchid because the arrangement of flowers on the stem looks like moths or butterflies in flight.

I looked closer at the picture. It did sort of look like moths flying. I learned that phalaenopsis has also become America's favorite orchid, partly because it's well-suited to growing at home.

Wonder if Marc grows any? The man definitely likes his flowers.

Surfing through another entry, I found a gorgeous gallery of photos. Vivid colors of fuchsia, deep coral, and yellow, as well as spotted varieties in different colors and a unique gold orchid with purple lines arching through each of the five petals.

But it was the simple and elegant white one with the touch of yellow and splash of deep pink at the center that I liked the most. It looked almost ethereal.

My eyes flickered to the white flower in the center of Tess's arrangement. The moth orchid—too hard to remember phala-whatchamacallit—might even be more beautiful than hers. What had Marc called it again? Simba-something? I did another Google search.

Cymbidium. I stared at it. It was pretty gorgeous too. And as I gazed at the pictures of the lush orchid, I realized I'd seen it before—on corsages women wore to church on Mother's Day.

Church. Tomorrow. Helping with the toddlers in Sunday

school. Which meant no time to clean or prep for the brunch before leaving in the morning.

I closed my laptop, washed my hands, and began assembling the ingredients for the two quiches. After I finished preparing them, I covered both pie tins and carefully placed them in the fridge, oven-ready for baking in the morning. Then I cleaned off the counters, swept the floor, loaded the dishwasher, and went to clean the rest of my duplex.

Two hours later I was finally finished. And exhausted.

What I needed was a nice hot bath filled with my favorite bath salts. As I soaked in the eucalyptus-scented tub, I pushed all thoughts of Joe the jerk out of my mind and realized that right now, Tess was probably sharing her good news with Chloe. In Paris.

Paris. What an amazing trip that was. The most wonderful trip of my life—other than my honeymoon. I shifted in the water. The last thing I needed to think about now was my honeymoon.

I closed my eyes and thought of Europe.

Paris had whet my appetite to see more of that old-world continent. Who knew? Maybe next year the Getaway Girls could manage to work in a trip to England or Ireland—perhaps even Scotland, the land of my ancestors, in homage to all the Jane Austen, Maeve Binchy, and Rosamunde Pilcher we were reading.

I thought of the Mark Twain saying Becca was always quoting: "Twenty years from now you will be more disappointed by the things that you didn't do than by the ones you did do. So throw off the bowlines. Sail away from the safe harbor. Catch the trade winds in your sails. Explore. Dream. Discover."

It would be fun to explore and discover Great Britain. I'd have to suggest that to the girls tomorrow at brunch. But before brunch, I was looking forward to helping out with the adorable toddlers in Sunday school, which helped to fulfill—at least a little—one of my longings.

"You a booty-head!"

"I not a booty-head. I'm Emily and I'm fwee." The chubby-cheeked toddler held up three fingers.

I knelt down between the battling tots. "Very good, Emily. You're a big girl, aren't you?" She nodded and stuck her thumb in her mouth, her fine blonde hair falling forward and brushing her arm as I turned to my other young charge.

"Tyler, it's not nice to call people names. You need to tell Emily you're sorry."

"No!" He thrust out his lower lip.

"Okay then, we're going to time-out." I took his little hand in mine.

"Sowwy, sowwy, sowwy." The apology tumbled out all in a rush as I led him to the designated discipline corner of the Sunday school room and squatted down in front of him. "You need to learn that you can't call people names and you can't talk back to grown-ups either. So we're going to stay here for a bit while you think about that, okay?"

He nodded, his big Bambi eyes bright with unshed tears. Then a lone tear escaped and trickled down his cheek.

My heart clenched, and I longed to scoop him up in my arms, give him a giant hug, and kiss away his tears, but I knew that I had to stand firm or he wouldn't learn. Instead, I sat down on one of the hard plastic kiddie chairs and ignored him, affecting an absorbed interest in my fingernails.

A couple interminable minutes passed, and I could hear the other children laughing and giggling behind us as they enjoyed their snack.

"Miss Paige?"

"Yes Tyler?"

He sniffed. "I weady to 'pologize now."

"Go ahead."

His lower lip trembled and he ducked his head. "I sowwy fo talking back."

"Thank you, Tyler. I forgive you. Now can I have a hug?"

He nodded and thrust himself into my arms.

Is there anything better in the whole world than holding a child in your arms? Nothing else even comes close. I patted Tyler's little back and gave him a tickle, which elicited a delighted giggle.

Okay, so making a child laugh comes a close second.

I stood up and held my hand out to him. "Shall we go apologize to Emily now too?" He nodded and we walked over to the snack table where all the kids were slurping their juice boxes and eating goldfish crackers.

"Emily?" I said.

She turned to face us, her silky white-blonde hair fanning her sweet, cherubic face.

"I sowwy for cawing you a booty-head," Tyler said. "You not a booty-head."

"'S okay." Emily slid out of her seat and hugged him in a death grip. "You not a booty-head eever." She pulled back and patted his face. "Wan' some juice?"

Tyler nodded eagerly and she thrust her juice box at him. "I share wiv you."

I knew there was a reason I volunteered to help out with the toddlers instead of the teenagers.

Not that I have anything against teens. I just can't relate to most of them. Their clothes, their obsession with electronic gadgets, and their music. I know that makes me sound like a dinosaur, but I've always been old for my age. Maybe it's because I hang around Mom so much.

Becca and Kailyn are forever trying to introduce me to what's new and hot on the contemporary music scene, but my inner gray-bunned English teacher revolts at the bad grammar and cacophony of sound without a melody. "You're hopeless," Becca said when I clapped my hands over my ears as she blasted her latest preferred rap offering.

At least I was in good company. Tess and Annette's hands flew to their ears as well. Of course, they're both fifty.

"Ooh, everything looks beautiful. You've really outdone yourself." Annette's crow's feet crinkled as she took in the sight of my dining room table set for brunch with my best linens, china, and crystal stemware.

"Do you think it's too much?"

"Maybe for Becca, but not for Tess. She'll love it."

"Hey," Becca said. "I can appreciate the finer things in life now and then." Her worn Birkenstock sandals slapped against the hardwood floor as she followed us into the kitchen. "Especially when it smells as good as this. Whaddya got cookin', Paige?"

"Quiche. Two kinds: quiche Lorraine and spinach and mushroom."

"Thanks for making a meatless one," Jenna said.

"No worries. I've got your vegetarian back." I glanced beyond her back. "Where's Kailyn?"

Annette shrugged her round, middle-aged shoulders as she layered her La Bou croissants on a platter. "Don't know. Now that she's not living at home, I don't keep tabs on her."

Kailyn had recently moved away from home and in with Becca. We all turned to our fearless book club leader, who flopped her palms out. "Don't look at me. I thought she'd be here by now. Said she had to stop and pick up something on the way."

The front door slammed and Kailyn's perky voice chirped, "Where is everyone?"

How is it possible for even a voice to be blonde?

We trooped back to the dining room to find not just Kailyn, but also Tess, waiting. Kailyn held up a bottle. "I had to stop by the store to get the champagne."

"Never mind that." Annette barreled past her daughter towards Tess. "I need to see that ring!"

The rest of us followed close behind. And then the phone rang.

"Hello?"

"Paige, I'm so, so sorry about Friday night," Joe said. "How can I make it up to you?"

Now he calls? He couldn't pick up the phone all day yesterday? Did he break his dialing finger at baseball or something? I could hear the girls oohing and aahing over Tess's ring. "I'm sorry," I said. "I can't talk right now. I have company." And then I hung up.

"Pesky telemarketer, huh?" Jenna said.

"Something like that."

The phone rang again and I snatched it up on the first ring. "I *said* I can't talk—

"Why are you being so mean?" Mom's injured voice sounded in my ear.

"Sorry. I thought you were someone else."

"That's still no way to answer the phone. I raised you better than that."

"Yes you did." I mouthed *sorry* to Tess and the girls. "What do you need, Mom?"

"Don't I even rate a hello, how are you?"

The timer dinged and I hurried into the kitchen, cradling the phone to my ear as I grabbed the hot pads and opened the oven. "Sorry. Hello. It's just that the girls are all here for

Tess's brunch and I'm pulling the quiche out of the oven as we speak."

"Well why didn't you say so?"

You didn't give me a chance.

"I forgot they were all coming over or I'd never have called and bothered you."

"That's okay. I've got a quick sec, what do you need?" Annette appeared beside me, grabbed another hot pad, and removed the second quiche, setting it on the wooden cutting board next to the stove.

Thanks, I mouthed.

"I'll make it quick," Mom said. "When you came over last night, I forgot to tell you I'm all out of my sugar-free ice cream. I was hoping you could pick some up for me today, but you're busy, so I'll see if Frieda can get it for me instead." There was a pause, and then a faint shuffling noise. "Frieda's car's not there." She sighed. "She's probably at the jail again, visiting her lawbreaking son."

Before Mom could launch into another one of her "poor-Frieda-look-how-her-kids-have-turned-out" litanies, I jumped in. "I'll bring you your ice cream over later, Mom, okay? Right now I need to get back to the brunch."

"Of course. I didn't mean to keep you. Have a good time. I'll see you later. Bye, honey."

"Bye, Mom." I hung up the phone and puffed out a blast of air.

"Don't they hurt, Paige?" Becca asked, with an innocent expression on her face.

"What?"

"Those apron strings. They're tied so tight, they're cutting off all your circulation. Must be really hard to breathe."

"Cool it, Becca," Tess said as I felt my face heat up.

"I'm just sayin' ..."

I didn't put much stock in Becca's dig. She was always making snarky comments about mothers. Besides, she was young. However, Tess and Annette were a different story. I respected both of them. And yet each had at different times over the past few months gently suggested that maybe I needed to learn to set some boundaries with my mother.

Clearly they didn't know my mother.

6

> Nora Johnson thought that men might regard travel as fast. Men preferred to marry safer, calmer women. Women who didn't go gallivanting too much. It was only sensible to have advance information about men, Nora Johnson told her daughters. That way you could go armed into the struggle.
>
> *Tara Road*

The next day at work, Kari the receptionist buzzed me. "Hey Paige," she said. "Can you come to the front desk, please?"

"What do you need? I was just getting ready to go to lunch."

"You're going to want to come up here," she said, sounding all mysterious. "Trust me on this."

As I approached her desk, I saw why. A huge bouquet of roses sat on the counter. Deep coral roses, bordering on orange. And nestled in the bouquet was a card with my name on it.

"I didn't know you had a boyfriend," Kari said.

"I don't." My cheeks warmed.

"Well who are they from?" Her eyes gleamed with curiosity.

I opened the card.

> I'm sorry. I'm really not a jerk. Let me make it up to you with dinner tonight?
>
> Hopefully, Joe

I could feel the corners of my mouth curving upward.

"So? Who are they from?"

"A date." My turn to be mysterious. If Kari knew they were from Joe, pretty soon the whole office would know and start talking and speculating. Workplace romances were great gossip fodder. And that was the last thing I wanted.

Besides, this wasn't really a romance—just a date. A first date. When I got back to my desk, I emailed Joe.

> Thanks for the roses. They're beautiful. And I'll take you up on your dinner offer. You don't have a baseball game tonight, do you?

I removed the card so none of my curious coworkers could snoop. And as I started to tuck it into my purse, I noticed that the flowers came from A Host of Golden Daffodils.

What did Marc say the color orange stood for again?

Joe and I decided to give the seafood place another try, only this time I followed his car to the restaurant after we got off work. We did the first date getting-to-know-you dance. "So, what do you like to do in your free time once you're released from call center prison?" he asked over our shared calamari appetizer.

"Read, cook, watch movies."

Spend time with my mother.

How boring was that? I needed to punch it up a little or the date would be over before it even begins.

I took a sip of my water. "A little hiking, camping, sailing ..."

Once apiece comes under the heading of little, right?

"And I went to Paris with some friends at the beginning of the year."

"Sounds like you're a Renaissance woman."

Yeah, in my dreams.

"What about you? What do you like to do—besides play baseball?"

"You're not going to let me forget that, are you?" His mouth turned up in a wry grin.

"Forget what?"

He smiled his thanks. "I enjoy a good action movie now and then, but mostly I like to be part of the action. I run, bike, work out, and in addition to my baseball team, I'm also on the coed softball team from work. Hey, you should think about joining!"

I choked on my calamari.

"You okay?"

I nodded, coughing. "Fine. Just went down the wrong way." I took a gulp of water.

Change the sports subject, and quick.

"Are you from California originally?"

"Born and bred. My folks met at Berkeley during a Vietnam protest." He delivered a sardonic smile. "They were some of the original sixties hippies."

"Unlike my parents. They got married in the late sixties, but that whole cultural revolution of the time passed them by. Of course when they said their I do's, Dad was already thirty and working in the Campbell's Soup factory, and Mom was pushing twenty-nine and a checker in a grocery store."

"How'd your folks meet?"

"He went through her check-out line one day after work. Their eyes met over the rutabagas and that was it."

"Serious?"

"That's what they always told us."

"Us. So you have brothers and sisters?"

"One each—an older sister, Isabel, and a younger brother, Patrick."

"Isabel, Patrick, and Paige," Joe said reflectively. "Nice, substantial names." He grimaced. "Unlike what my parents saddled us with."

"Joseph's pretty substantial."

"That's why I picked it. That and the fact that it was my grandfather's name."

"*You* picked it?"

He nodded. "When I was nine. I got sick of all the kids making seagull noises at me and flapping their arms whenever the teacher called my name."

"Your name was Seagull?"

Joe looked around and lowered his voice. "Livingston Seagull. As in Jonathan Livingston Seagull. But if you repeat that to anyone, I'll have to kill you."

"Don't worry. Your secret's safe with me," I whispered. "But why didn't they just call you Jonathan?"

"Too establishment. But I had it better than my sisters—Harmony and Breezy."

"Did they change their names too?"

"Breezy did. She's been Susan for years now. But Harmony kept hers, and it suits her. She's the only one who of us who followed in my folks' hippie footsteps. She and her boyfriend Ben own a lavender farm up in Oregon."

"Are your parents still here?"

"Nope. They live just down the road from Ben and Harmony."

The waiter arrived with our Alaskan King Crab legs which we tore into with gusto. I dipped a forkful of tender crab meat into the tiny crock of melted butter, raised it to my lips, and shut my eyes in rapture at that first rich bite.

Mmmm.

"It's nice to see a woman who enjoys her food and doesn't worry about her weight," Joe said. "But how do you work off the calories?"

Work off? As in work out? Me?

What we had here was a failure to communicate.

The next day I dropped by Mom's after work to do her laundry. Her increased girth and vision difficulties made me nervous about her navigating the rickety step into the garage, so I'd relieved her of that once-a-week job. Besides, I could do my laundry at the same time, which saved me a trip to the Laundromat. I was very careful not to mention anything about Joe, however—from the date that wasn't to the date that was. Knowing my mother, she'd be picking out wedding invitations before our second date.

If there was even going to be a second date.

Joe was nice enough and really cute, but I wasn't sure we really had much in common. He was such a jock. And I'm, well, not. Plus, he's really into hip-hop and when I asked what his favorite classic movie was, he said *Die Hard 2*.

Before Mom could ask what was new and I spilled the Joe beans, I told her about Tess's brunch and my getaway-to-Britain travel idea for next year.

"Why do you want to go gallivanting all over the world? You already went to Paris. I'd think that would be enough." She expelled a heavy sigh. "You're just like your sister. Your brother too. I don't know how I raised three kids who have to be going all the time, especially overseas. What's wrong with America? And what's wrong with staying home?"

Maybe you should be asking Patrick and Isabel that question.

"There's nothing wrong with America. There are lots of places I'd like to see in the U.S. too." I ticked them off on my fingers. "Alaska, Washington, the Carolinas, New York, New England … I've always wanted to visit New England in the autumn and see all the fall colors. It's supposed to be breathtaking."

"It is."

My head snapped up from the clothes I was sorting. "When did you go to New England?"

"I didn't. But I used to have a calendar from there and it was real pretty. Your dad and I talked about going there on our honeymoon, but we couldn't afford it. Instead we drove up to Placerville where we spent the weekend in a cabin and fished."

I knew about the fishing honeymoon. Not exactly on my list of romantic things to do on a honeymoon.

Like Disneyland's romantic?

Eric never did get his island honeymoon. At least not with me.

Don't go there. Focus on the here and now.

In their entire marriage, my folks never traveled outside of California—except when my father took my mother to Reno to see Tom Jones in concert for their fortieth wedding anniversary. Too expensive, they always said. Everything was too expensive with three kids and a mortgage on one blue-collar salary in the Golden State. But the house had been paid off years ago and Dad's life insurance had left my mother comfortably well off for the first time in her life. Which gave me an idea …

"Hey Mom, why don't you and I take a trip to New England this fall?"

"You must be kidding."

"Why? You can afford it now, and by then I'll have more vacation time. We could do a road trip and see a lot of the U.S. together that way."

"You must be out of your ever-lovin' mind. I couldn't sit in a car that long."

"Okay. Then we could fly into Boston, rent a car, and drive all through Massachusetts, New Hampshire, and Vermont."

"No thank you. I'm just fine sticking close to home. Besides, you know I've never been on a plane in my entire life. And I don't see any reason to get on one now. I like keeping my feet firmly planted on the ground."

Of course you do. I slid a sideways glance her way. "Would you get on a plane to go to Chicago to see Isabel and David?"

She hesitated. But only for a second. "Your sister and her husband are used to flying all over the world. They're the ones who need to get on a plane and come out here to visit *me*. Us. Do you know it's been over a year since I've seen your sister?"

Not wanting to go down that familiar long and whining road, I opted for a diversionary tactic. "Mom, if you could go anyplace in the whole world, where would you want to go?"

"Nowhere. I'm just fine here at home. People would be a lot better off if they were satisfied with where they were."

That's my mother, Catherine the Explorer. We should change her name to Dora.

"Come on, play along. Isn't there even one place in the entire world you'd like to visit if you had the chance and money was no object?"

"And I didn't have to fly?"

"And you didn't have to fly. You were magically transported to wherever you wanted to go without having to set one foot in a plane."

"Well-l-l ... if you put it that way ..." Her face took on a dreamy, far-off look. "I'd like to go to Scotland to reconnect with my Scottish roots. Your Great-Grandpa Gallie, my grandfather who died when you were little, used to tell me stories about the Highlands when I was a little girl. He'd say, 'Aye, lassie, there's no place on God's green earth more beautiful than the rugged Highlands of Scotland.' He always wanted to go back to visit but never got the chance. My dad used to dream of going there someday too and taking my mother and me, but there was never enough money."

She sighed. Not one of her usual sighs. This one was full of longing and regret.

"How come you never told me this before?"

"You never asked."

Who knew? My mother had hidden depths. Or at least, hidden dreams ...

The next day at work was a bear. The day after that too. Customers complaining left and right and demanding that I get them a new phone "or else."

I used to think I was a people person, but customer service has a way of knocking that out of you. By the end of the week, all I wanted to do was turn off my phone, stay in bed, and pull the covers up over my face.

That's just what I did on Friday night—all except the pulling the covers over my face part. Too tired to cook, I made a gourmet dinner of microwave popcorn—mixing in a little white chocolate that I'd melted—and root beer, placed it on a tray, and retreated to my bedroom where I stuck in *Rear Window,* one of my favorite Hitchcock films. I did pull the covers over my face near the end though when my beloved Jimmy

Stewart was being attacked by the killer from the apartment across the way.

Thankfully, it had a happy ending. I puffed out a blissful sigh as the credits rolled. That's how I prefer my movies. And my books.

If I could only get my life to line up like that.

As I rinsed in the shower the following morning, I realized I had nothing on my schedule for the day except grocery shopping, and that could wait until tomorrow. It wasn't often I had a free Saturday and I planned to take full advantage of it.

And *not* sitting in the stands watching a coed softball game.

Joe had invited me to his game, but as far as I'm concerned, the only thing worse than actually playing team sports is watching them. Besides, what if one of the players hurt themselves and they needed a substitute? I wouldn't put it past Joe to pluck me from the stands and make me play.

I'd much rather play in the sand.

An hour later, having packed the necessary provisions: journal, Bible, iPod, latest book club selection, and lunch, I was on my way to the ocean. Driving west on Interstate 80, I began humming "All by Myself."

Remembering my promise to the Getaway Girls to try and set some boundaries with my mom, I decided not to call and tell her I was going to the beach for the day. Past experience proved that she'd ask me to stop by for just a minute to do a quick errand, since it was "on the way." This time I decided I'd call her on my way back into town. Then if there was something she needed, I could drop by on the way home and not worry about being delayed.

Meanwhile, Point Reyes beckoned me.

Years ago, I'd discovered the miles and miles of gorgeous and secluded coastline in Marin County, where I loved to simply sit and look out to sea with the sound of the pounding surf in my ears, the sea breeze on my face, and the smell of the ocean in my nostrils.

There's nothing like the smell of the ocean in the morning.

Or afternoon. Or any time of day for that matter.

An hour and a half later, I pulled into the parking lot of Drake's Beach, where local legend has it that Sir Francis Drake stopped to repair his ship, the *Golden Hind*, before crossing the Pacific.

Grabbing my bag, I once again admired the impressive white sandstone cliffs as I made my way to the sand, and wondered if that was what the White Cliffs of Dover looked like.

Hopefully I'd get a chance to find out in person with my Getaway Girls next year.

A few clusters of people were already taking advantage of the seashore: an older couple walking hand-in-hand, a young couple smooching in the sand, a jogger getting his morning exercise, and some kids building a sandcastle as their moms looked on.

Shucking off my flip-flops, I dug my toes into the wet sand as I walked along the shore, enjoying the natural semi-pedicure and being careful to step around the slimy seaweed. And all the while I walked, I kept an eye out for sand dollars. Finally I picked up a perfect, sun-bleached one, completely intact. I brushed the sand off, admiring the intricate star pattern. Not for the first time was I grateful to live only two hours away from the ocean. It'd be great to live right on the coast, but California real estate prices made that impossible.

At last I retreated to a sunny stretch of sand away from the increasing clusters of people where I could enjoy my solitude and catch up on my reading. I pulled out *Tara Road* from my beach bag and settled in to continue reading the Irish saga of two women who switch houses, and lives, for the summer.

How cool would that be? I'd trade my life for a woman's in Dublin in a heartbeat. Or London ... Paris ... Edinburgh ... I still couldn't get over how not once in my entire life—at least that I could recall—had my mother ever mentioned wanting to visit Scotland and reconnect with her Scottish roots.

An hour later, I set *Tara Road* aside and picked up my Bible, continuing my reading in the first chapter of James. "Do not merely listen to the word, and so deceive yourselves. Do what it says. Anyone who listens to the word but does not do what it says is like a man who looks at his face in a mirror and, after looking at himself, goes away and immediately forgets what he looks like."

I gazed thoughtfully out to sea. *Is that what I do?*

I'd been going to church since I was a kid and had listened to the Word of God my whole life. But did I actually do what it said? Yes, I tithed my 10 percent, helped out in Sunday school, supported overseas missionaries, worked behind the scenes every year in the Christmas production, and always gave money to the homeless holding signs on the freeway off ramps.

But was that enough?

I continued reading and came to the final verse in the first chapter. "Religion that God our Father accepts as pure and faultless is this: to look after orphans and widows in their distress"—

A siren split the air.

Intent on the Scriptures, it took me a minute to realize the siren sound was coming from inside my purse. I dug around, finally found my cell, and flipped it open. "Hi Mom. What's up?"

"Paige?"

"Who's this?"

"Frieda. I stopped by your mother's house because I've been calling and calling and she didn't answer. So finally I used the key she gave me and let myself in."

I dropped my Bible. "Is Mom okay?"

"Well, I'm not sure, honey. She said she tripped over Mr. Spitz and fell. And now she can't get up." Frieda lowered her voice. "And I can't lift her either."

I grabbed my blanket and began stuffing everything into my beach bag. "Is she conscious? Can she talk?"

"She's a little woozy, but ..."

"Frieda, call 911." A stab of guilt pierced my breast.

"Paige, she can talk. Just a minute." Frieda's voice grew fainter. "Catherine, here's Paige."

"Honey?" Mom's voice wobbled. "Can you come over and help me up? I'm too heavy for Frieda."

So much for setting boundaries. "I'm out of town, Mom. It's going to take me awhile to get there. Are you in pain?"

"I bumped my head so I'm a little dizzy, and my hip really hurts."

My guilt was instantly replaced by fear. What if she had a broken hip? I'd heard too many stories of older people breaking their hips and then going rapidly downhill—sometimes never to recover. I grabbed my beach bag and sprinted toward the car. "You need to hang up and call 911."

"I probably just had the wind knocked out of me," she said weakly. "I don't need an ambulance. I'll just wait for you."

"Mom, I'm two hours away! And you could have a concussion or something. Now please just hang up and dial 911."

"I don't want sirens coming and all the neighbors watching. I'd be embarrassed."

Better embarrassed than dead.

"I'm on my way, but it's going to take me awhile to get

there." I unlocked my car and threw all my stuff into the back before sliding into the driver's seat and buckling my seat belt. "Don't worry, though, everything's going to be okay, Mom. Put Frieda back on the phone now, please."

There was an indistinct muffle and then Frieda's voice. "Yes, Paige?"

"Frieda, I need you to hang up right now and dial 911 please."

"Well ... I'm not sure ..." I could tell that Frieda, never the most assertive of women, was looking at Mom, who wrote the manual on assertive and was probably shaking her head no. "Your mother said she doesn't want an ambulance ..."

"I don't care what she wants. This is what she *needs.*" I hit the steering wheel in frustration. "I'm sorry. I didn't mean to take it out on you, Frieda, but I'm worried about her. She could have a serious injury. She *needs* to go to the hospital. Would you please call 911 and stay with her until they get there? Tell Mom I'll come straight to the hospital."

"Okay ... if you think that's best ..."

No, what's best is that I handle this myself.

As always.

7

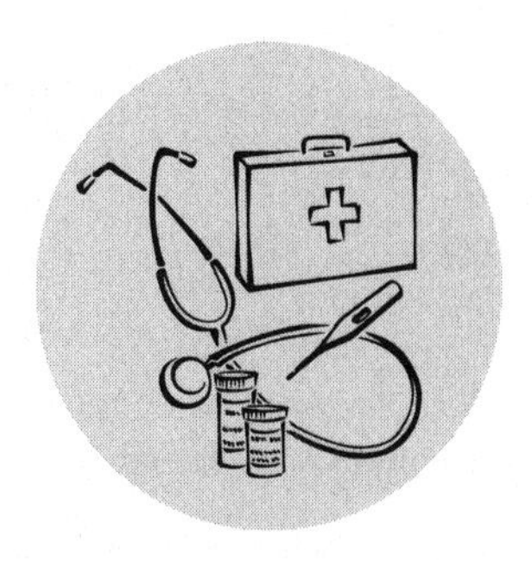

> Just living is not enough. One must have sunshine, freedom, and a little flower.
>
> *Hans Christian Andersen*

I hung up and punched in 911 from the parking lot, gave the dispatcher Mom's address and all the details I knew, then gave her my cell number so she could call back and tell me which hospital they took her to.

As I drove, I prayed. *Please Lord, don't let her have a broken hip.* I debated whether I should call Isabel or not, but decided against it until I had more information. Besides, what could she do from Chicago anyway?

Nothing. As usual.

I should never have left town.

Why not? How could you have known this was going to happen?

I couldn't. But still. I should be there.

And you will be soon.

I hate that she's all alone.

She's not alone. Trained professionals are on their way—probably already there and taking good care of her.

But they're not family. She should have family with her. And why hasn't that 911 operator called me back?

I checked my phone as I sped down the highway.

No bars showing.

Perfect. Just perfect. I threw the phone in my purse and punched the gas pedal.

I made my best guess at which hospital she'd be at and an hour and a half later, I pushed through the emergency room doors and hurried to the registration window. "I'm looking for my mother, Catherine Kelley, who should have been brought in a little while ago. She fell and hit her head."

"Kelly." The woman in scrubs behind the window tapped her keyboard and looked at her computer screen. "No ... no, sorry. We don't have anyone named Kelly here."

"Are you sure?" I asked, longing to hop over the counter and check for myself. "That's Kelley spelled with an 'ey.'"

"Oh." She tapped her keyboard again and frowned. "I'm sorry. No Kelley either. You sure she was brought here?"

"No. I just assumed she would be since it's the closest hospital to her house." The words came tumbling out all in a jumble. "I was out of town, her neighbor called me, then my cell went out and I couldn't get any more information." I could feel my eyes starting to well up.

"Don't worry, honey. We'll find her. Just let me check." She punched some more information into the computer. "Here she is." She looked up and gave me a reassuring smile. "She's down at Mercy General on J Street. Do you know where that is?"

"Yes. Thanks so much." I drove past the landmark brick hospital every time I went to Kailyn and Becca's condo. I bolted out the ER doors. Twenty minutes later I was talking to the doctor in the hallway outside my mother's room.

Not exactly McDreamy. McSteamy, either, but kind.

"Fortunately your mother has no factures, only a mild concussion. She also has several abrasions to her left hip and thigh area." The middle-aged doctor continued. "She's going to be really sore tomorrow. I've admitted her for observation. The CAT scan was unremarkable, but I'd like to run a few more diagnostic tests. A concussion, no matter how slight, is still a head injury. She's also dehydrated so we're giving her fluids—"

"Dehydrated? But Mom drinks water constantly," I mumbled. He frowned as he looked at her chart. "Has she been having vision problems long?"

"She had cataracts a few years ago and surgery to remove them. Lately she's been having sight problems again, so I took her to the ophthalmologist's. He ran some tests. We're supposed to get the results this week."

"I see." He frowned again and tapped his pen on the clipboard. "I understand your mom lives alone?"

"Yes, since my dad died a few years ago. But I'm always over there—at least two or three times a week."

"Well, for her safety she'll need someone to stay with her once she's released."

"No problem. I can do that."

He continued, gently. "Have you given any thought to assisted living? With all her health problems, she really shouldn't be alone. I'll have the social worker bring you some literature ..."

Right. No way would I ever put my mother into one of those places. As a little girl, we'd gone to visit my great aunt at one of those assisted living/nursing home facilities and I'd caught a glimpse of some large, nasty bedsores she had when the aide came to change her bed and had to move her.

Not a sight I'll ever forget.

Neither would I forget the time when our high school youth group went to sing Christmas carols at a nursing home. As we started to leave, one frail, elderly woman, her eyes brimming with tears beneath a halo of snow-white hair, clutched at my arm with her liver-spotted hands and said, "Please take me home. Please get me out of here. Please."

"That's okay." I restrained myself from slapping the clipboard out of the doctor's manicured hands.

"Can I see my mom now?"

"Yes, of course. She may be asleep. Please contact me if you have any questions or concerns."

"Thanks." I pushed open the door.

Mom's loud snoring told me she was asleep the moment I entered the room. Monitors flashed numbers. An IV bag hung from a tall pole. I approached her bed, wincing at the large goose egg on her forehead. Carefully, I leaned over and kissed her cheek. "I'm here, Mom. Don't worry, everything's going to be all right."

She looked so pale. So still. What if this happened again? What if she didn't survive the next fall? For the first time since I could remember, I longed to hear her voice.

I began to stroke her hand and kissed her cheek again. "I'm here, Mom."

Her eyes fluttered and she looked my way, as if trying to focus. "Isabel?"

Ever the attentive, though unnoticed daughter, I pushed open the door of Golden Daffodils, half an hour later, intent on getting some flowers to brighten up Mom's hospital room when I returned later that night.

Marc hurried over, concern etching his friendly features. "Paige, how's your mother?"

"Okay. Just a slight concussion and some bruises, but

they're keeping her in the hospital overnight. She's sleeping right now." Then I realized. I stared at him. "How did you know?"

"I saw the ambulance go by, and Frieda came over to get some carnations for Catherine and filled me in." He grinned. "You should know by now that the blue-haired brigade is faster than high-speed Internet."

"I just pray they never get the hang of texting." I pushed my hand through my hair.

"You look like you need a drink." Marc steered me over to a garden bistro set near the front counter where he commanded me to sit on one of the metal chairs. "Unfortunately all I can offer you is bottled water or tea."

"Tea will be fine."

"Okay, and then we'll continue with your flower education. Back in a sec." He disappeared into the back room.

While he was gone, I realized that I'd forgotten to call Isabel. Fishing out my phone, I punched in her number. Naturally it went straight to voicemail, so I left her a brief message and asked her to call me back.

"Here you go." Marc returned with a small tray holding sugar, Splenda, a creamer pitcher, and two steaming mugs of tea. He set it before me on the bistro table. "I had a feeling you might be a woman who likes milk in her tea."

"Your feeling was right. Thanks." I sprinkled in some Splenda, topped off my mug with milk, and blew on it before taking a sip. "Mmm. This is great. Thank you."

The phone rang, but Marc ignored it.

"Don't you need to get that?"

"Nah. Annie will pick it up."

"Annie?" The ringing stopped.

"My right-hand woman. She came with me when I left the Flower Cart. She's great." He swigged his tea.

A head poked around the back doorway. A cropped redhead with spiky platinum tips and a pierced eyebrow. "It's for you, boss-man. One of your regulars."

"Okay. Thanks." The head disappeared and Marc excused himself to go pick up the phone at the counter.

I sipped my Earl Grey, trying not to eavesdrop, but it was impossible with the counter right in front of me.

"Yes, Mrs. Kowalksi, white lilies would be the best choice for your granddaughter's First Communion. Some freesia too, I think. But not too much. We don't want the flowers to overpower her." Marc scribbled on a pad. "I'll take care of that for you, no problem. Thanks."

He hung up and turned to me with a smile. "Pop quiz. Why white lilies for a young girl's Communion?"

"Because they're a sign of purity?"

"Very good. And freesia?"

"You got me there. I don't even know what freesia is."

He crooked his index finger. "I'll show you. Just be careful in those flip-flops. I don't want you slipping and falling."

"Me either. I don't think the neighborhood could handle two ambulances in one day." I followed him to the back where Annie's spiky head was bent over the work table. She was working with a vivid array of unusual flowers that looked like they belonged on some tropical island.

"Annie, this is Paige; Paige, Annie."

"Nice to meet you."

She raised her head and smiled, which allowed me to see her black T-shirt that read *Nobody puts Baby in the Corner.*

"Ditto. So are you coming to work here?"

"Oh no. What I know about flowers would fill a bud vase. Marc's trying to educate me."

"He's a good teacher."

I peered closer at the arrangement she was working

on. "That's different. What's that red, waxy-looking thing called?"

"Anthurium." She gestured to a stalk with vivid orange and purple spikes right next to it. "And this is Bird of Paradise, or strelitzia, as we call it."

"Do you like those?" Marc asked, nodding to the flowers in front of Annie.

"They're really striking," I hesitated, not wanting to offend. "Honestly, though? Not really my thing. A little too stark for my taste, I'm afraid. I like softer, prettier flowers like roses. And daisies. And those, for instance," I nodded to a nearby vase of pale pink blooms.

"Hah!" Marc said to Annie, whose pierced eyebrow was puckered into a scowl. "Told you." His teeth gleamed in a wide grin above his beard. "I knew we were kindred spirits. Oh, and those are peonies by the way; Sarah Bernhardts."

The front door chimed and Annie left to greet a customer.

"I hope I didn't hurt her feelings."

"Annie? Nah. Her feelings aren't that easily hurt. We just have an ongoing debate about what constitutes beauty in flowers. Like you, I prefer the softer varieties, while Annie leans to the dramatic and unusual. But that's good because we have customers who want both."

"How long have you two worked together? She looks young."

"She is. Nineteen. Makes me feel old." He sent me a rueful grin. "Annie started at the Flower Cart her junior year in high school so we've worked together nearly three years now. Her brother Toby works here too—he's my delivery driver. Now let me show you that freesia." He led me over to a ball-shaped bouquet of multicolored roses. "This nosegay is for a wedding tonight. See these small white flowers tucked in here? That's freesia."

"Reminds me of the moth orchid." I leaned in to smell the fragrant bloom. "Is it part of the orchid family?"

"No, although they look a little alike. Freesias are a bulb plant—like tulips or daffodils."

Annie returned and plucked some tulips from a nearby bucket just in time to hear Marc say, "Freesias stand for innocence."

"Most people don't know or even care what flowers mean," she said. "They just want *pretty*. One of Marc's many eccentricities." She sent him a wicked grin. "They're legion."

"Says the girl with the pierced eyebrow and the penchant for Puccini," Marc shot back as she returned to the front.

"Puccini?"

"Opera. *Madama Butterfly? La Bohème—*

"I love *La Bohème.*"

"Me too! Did you get to see Baz Luhrmann's fabulous production when it came to San Francisco a few years ago?"

"No." I felt my cheeks grow hot with embarrassment. "Actually ... I've never seen *La Bohème*, except in the movie *Moonstruck.*" I shrugged, bracing myself for his "Well then how could you love it?" reaction.

"Great movie," he said without missing a beat. He began plucking flowers from buckets. "I can work on your mom's bouquet and continue your floral education at the same time. Did you want tulips?"

"Depends. What do they mean?"

"In general, perfect love. Although each color means something different: purple symbolizes royalty, white ones express forgiveness, and red tulips mean true love."

"What about yellow tulips? They're so happy looking."

"They are. Today, they represent sunshine and cheerful thoughts, but years ago, they represented hopeless love."

"I prefer the sunshine."

"Me too." He chuckled.

"Mom needs a little sunshine right now, so let's use yellow tulips. What else would go well with them?"

"How about these Blue Magic irises?" He selected several of the deep blue blooms and held them next to the bright yellow tulips. "Irises mean faith, hope, wisdom, and valor."

"Well, two out of four's not bad, and that color does look great with the yellow."

As he arranged the flowers, he continued talking. "So what do you do, Paige?"

"Work in the call center for Landon Wireless."

"Ah. So you're the one I should call when I have problems with my phone?"

"I'm your girl."

He looked at me over the top of the flowers and I could feel myself blushing, but he continued as if he hadn't noticed. "Are you an only child?"

"No, although it often feels like it. My older sister moved to Chicago years ago and my brother's overseas."

"So all the responsibility for your mother falls on you?"

"You got it."

"Been there, done that," he said. "My friends always teased me about being a mama's boy, but as the only child of a widowed mother, it was up to me to take care of her."

"That's what I'm sayin'. None of my friends seem to understand that. Granted, I'm not the only child, but I might as well be. That's why I feel so bad that I wasn't there when she fell today."

"You can't be there 24/7," Marc said gently. "Don't beat yourself up about it. Remember, the doctor said it wasn't serious and they're releasing her tomorrow." He offered the finished bouquet to me for inspection. "What do you think? I added a few chrysanthemums for fullness, and also because they stand for cheerfulness and rest."

"It's beautiful. She'll love it. Thanks so much. Your mother must be proud to have such a talented son."

"She is. Was." His eyes flickered. "She passed away a couple years ago."

"I'm so sorry."

Idiot. Don't you remember he already mentioned his mother was gone when he thanked you for the lasagna?

"That's okay. She's home now. No more cancer. No more pain."

"Hey boss-man," Annie skipped into the back, a triumphant grin splitting her face. "I just got us another wedding. A tropical one, no less, so you-know-who gets to design the bouquets." She pumped her fist in the air. "Yes!"

After I left the flower shop, I swung by Mom's to pick up her robe and slippers, toiletries, and a change of clothes. While I was there, Isabel returned my call. "So what's up with the mother-unit this time?" Her sigh echoed in my ear and sounded exactly like Mom's, although I didn't dare tell her that.

"She's been having some more vision problems, and apparently she didn't see her cat earlier and tripped over him and fell. The doctor says she'll be fine though and he's releasing her tomorrow. She has a mild concussion and a bruised hip. Not a broken one, thankfully."

"Is it cataracts again or do you think she's getting dementia?"

I sucked in my breath. "She does *not* have dementia—she was perfectly fine and lucid Tuesday when I went and did her laundry. As for whether it's cataracts, that's what we think, but we're not sure. We'll get the results from the ophthalmologist Monday."

Isabel only focused in on one part of my response. "You're doing her laundry?"

"Hers and mine together. It saves me a trip to the Laundromat."

"Let me see if I've got this straight." I could hear her fingernails drumming on her desk. "You're already shopping, cooking, and cleaning for her, and now you're doing her laundry too? What's next? Bathing her? We've had this conversation before. When are you going to face facts, little sister? If Mom can't do basic household tasks herself, it's high time we check out an assisted living situation."

"I'm not moving Mom out of her home and into one of those places."

Isabel released another sigh. "It's not the ghetto. And it's not like it was thirty years ago when Aunt Joan lived in one. They have really nice facilities for the elderly now with all kinds of activities—bingo, singalongs, square-dancing ..."

"And when was the last time you saw our mother square dance, pray tell? I am *not* going to put her in a home and that's that. I really have to go now." I hung up the phone trembling and sat down at the kitchen table.

Two people in one day?

I looked around the beloved, familiar kitchen I'd grown up in and where my mother had first taught me to make chocolate-chip cookies when I was little. I took a deep breath and let it out slowly.

I knew what I had to do.

8

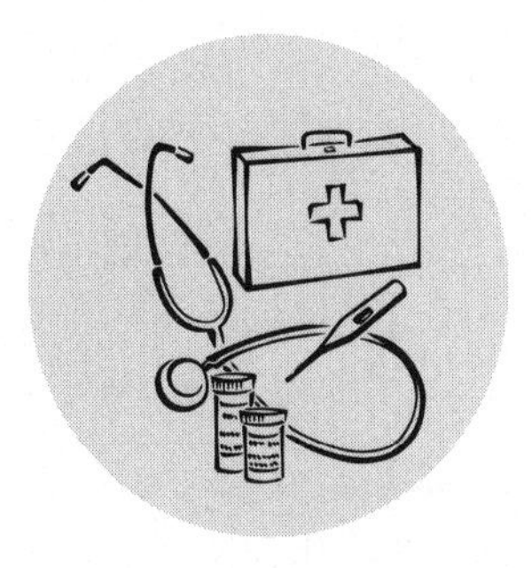

Give me a girl at an impressionable age, and she is mine for life.

The Prime of Miss Jean Brodie

"Paige, are you sure you want to do this?" Annette shot me a concerned look over her mocha at Dunkeld's later that week, where we were meeting to discuss the details of our next book club adventure. We'd pushed together two tables in the crowded café so all the Getaway Girls could fit.

"It's the right thing to do."

"For who?" Becca said. "You or your mom?"

"For both of us. Mom can't stay alone any longer—it's not safe. And I live alone so it makes sense for me to move back in with her."

"Let me ask you again," Annette said gently. "Are you sure you *want* to do this?"

"Want has nothing to do with it. Sometimes you just do what you have to do, no matter how hard it is. That's life."

Becca snorted into her hot chocolate. "That's not life, that's prison. What about *your* life? You already spend most of your time with your mom ... if you move back home she'll consume every waking minute of your existence. You're not that old." She gave me an appraising look over her blueberry scone. "You could still meet someone."

Gee, thanks. Love you too. Oh, and by the way, you have a chocolate mustache.

I pointed to her upper lip.

She swiped at it with a napkin. "But how's that going to happen if you're at her beck and call night and day? Besides, I thought you wanted to have a kid. What happened to that idea?"

"I do want to have a child ... someday." Visions of adorable, chubby-cheeked toddlers danced in my head. And my arms ached to hold a baby of my own. Resolutely, I pushed my kiddie longings aside and squared my shoulders. "Right now, however, I don't have a child, but I do have a mother. And she needs me. Simple as that."

"What about your sister and brother?" Jenna asked. "Can't they help?"

"Yeah." Kailyn's perfect features settled into a scowl. "Why do you always have to do everything?"

"Good question. I've been asking myself that for years. And if I ever get an answer, I'll let you know."

"But Paige, you can't make your entire life revolve around your mother," Annette said. "You need some kind of balance. When will it be time for you?"

"God only knows. But he does know."

I thought back to my beach reading in James. "And he also commands us to look after orphans and widows in their time of need. Well, this is my mother's time of need." I lifted my tank-topped shoulders. "Stuff happens. Life isn't always about what we want; it's also about duty and commitment and putting others first—doing what you have to do. And this is something I have to do."

"Paige is right," Tess said. "I never wanted to be a widow and raise my sons alone, but as she said, stuff happens. My husband died and I did what I had to do. Paige is doing what she has to do and it's not going to be easy for her, or her mother." She fixed the group with an unwavering stare from behind her red glasses. "We need to support our fellow Getaway Girl, not tear her down."

"Thanks, Tess. I appreciate it." Tears pricked my eyelids, but I held them at bay.

After she'd been released Sunday from her overnight hospital stay, I'd taken Mom home where I'd prepared soup and sandwiches for lunch, made sure she took her Vicodin at the right time, and while she was napping, quietly cleaned out her pink fridge and freezer.

I got rid of all the sugary and starchy no-no's she wasn't supposed to have and filled it with healthy fruits and vegetables and lean meats instead. That night I cooked a healthy dinner of lean, pecan-encrusted pork chops—no Shake 'N Bake or heavy breading for diabetics—a small helping of baby potatoes cooked in olive oil, and tons of greens. Afterwards, I popped in *The Quiet Man*, her favorite John Wayne, but before it was even halfway through, she was fast asleep in her recliner.

Monday morning I took her to the ophthalmologist's where he informed us that Mom didn't have cataracts, but diabetic retinopathy.

Essentially, she is legally blind.

The doctor spoke while I sat dazed, listening to something about "the center of her eye." The "macula," I think he called it. He said she can't see details and blah, blah, blah, but all I could focus on was the word "blind." The doctor actually uttered my mother's name in the same sentence as the word "blind." How could that be?

He continued speaking. Finally I heard the magic word, "surgery." I took a deep sigh of relief and silently thanked God. Evidently laser surgery has proven to restore some eyesight, depending on the extent of damage. The ophthalmologist said sometimes more than one laser surgery was required. But in Mom's case, he offered no guarantees that her sight would improve if she had the eye surgery.

My heart sank. Then I heard him say, "Catherine, I explained to you after your cataract surgery, that unless you made the necessary lifestyle changes, this would happen." I sat in stunned silence. Mom had never shared that piece of vital information with me. This could have been prevented?

I restrained myself from reaching out and throttling her.

What good would it do at this point anyway? The damage was done. I released a long slow breath. And as we left, a nurse handed Mom literature regarding diabetic retinopathy and laser surgery.

Once we were in the car going home, she didn't feel like talking about surgeries. She had more important things to think about. Like my moving back home.

"You can have your old room back! It will be as if you'd never left."

Now there's a happy thought. As if the past fifteen years never happened. No husband, no house, no career, no nothing.

You don't have *a husband now.* Or *a house. Kids either. And you certainly can't call working in the call center a career.*

Well all righty then. Moving on …

Mom insisted that I not pay rent, and I insisted I would. "I'm not going to live here for free. It wouldn't be right. I'm thirty-five years old and working. I'm going to pay rent—the same amount I pay for my duplex."

"That's ridiculous. You're my daughter, this house is paid off, you don't need to pay anything to live here."

"The only way I'm moving in is if I can pay rent. I'm not some out-of-work slacker who's going to live off her mother."

"What kind of mother charges her kids rent? Frieda's kids have had to move in with her at different times over the years, and I know for a fact that not one of them has ever paid rent."

That's because they're unemployed, in rehab, or just out of jail.

I recounted our rent discussion—and our stalemate—to Tess when she called the next day.

"I'm afraid I have to agree with your mother on this one," she said.

"What?"

"Think about it. The reason you're moving out of your own place and back in with your mom is to help take care of her, right?"

"Right."

"And part of that care means you'll be doing the cooking, cleaning, laundry, and ferrying her to all her errands and doctor's appointments, correct?"

"Yes-s-s-s," I said slowly.

"So if you think about it, in essence you'll be taking on a second job. Why should you have to pay for that privilege?"

"I hear what you're saying ... but I still don't like the idea of moving in and not paying any kind of rent. It's just not right."

"So if it will make you feel better, then just pay a fraction of what you paid at your duplex," Tess said. "Remember, it's all about compromise."

Mom accepted the compromise—after a little grumbling—and we were both happy.

The setting sun filtered through the bookstore blinds,

casting fingers of gold on the café floor. I drained my latte and set my mug down on the table, resolute. "It's a done deal," I told the book club. "I've already given my notice to my landlord and I'm moving to Mom's as soon as I can."

Becca and Kailyn exchanged a glance across the table. "Um, not to be all mercenary and selfish," Kailyn said, "but would you mind telling us how much you pay for rent? Our condo's coming up for lease renewal soon, and it's gotten way too expensive. We need to find another place to live, and soon."

"Yeah, think maybe you could recommend us to your landlord?" Becca cast me a hopeful look.

"Maybe. If you pay me enough."

"But we can't afford—" Kailyn broke off. "Oh, I get it. You're kidding."

"That's me. Always the kidder."

"But what are you going to do with all your stuff?" Jenna crossed her tanned, athlete's legs. "Didn't you say your mom's house is pretty small?"

"And cluttered?"

"Yes. That's going to be one of my first major projects, sifting through all the clutter and downscaling—not just my stuff, but Mom's too. We'll see which of my things fit in and whatever doesn't, I'll put in storage or sell at a yard sale."

"Or maybe sell to your friends who are hopefully moving into your duplex? That way you won't have to move it or pay for storage."

"That's our Becca, always thinking of others," Tess said.

"I do what I can." Becca gave a slight bow over the cluttered table and hit her head on the napkin dispenser. "Ouch!"

"Everyone? Please meet my roommate, Grace," Kailyn snarked.

"You're going to need a lot of grace moving in with your

mom," Annette said to me. "You do realize that you may have a hard time getting her to part with any of her stuff, don't you? Older people really have a hard time letting go and often, a tendency to hoard. We ran into that with my mama when we had to move her to a studio apartment in a seniors complex."

"Boy, did we ever," Kailyn said. "Remember all those ugly double-knit polyester pantsuits from the seventies that she insisted still had plenty of wear in them? And the stacks and stacks of *National Geographics*? And those awful crocheted toilet paper holders? Yuck."

"Don't forget the Tupperware," Annette reminded her. "We had Tupperware coming out our ears. I wound up taking a bunch of it to church to give away. Who knew one woman could use so many plastic containers?"

"I'll see your Tupperware and raise you a dozen cookie jars," Tess said with a wry grin. "My mother had tons of them in the kitchen, but then she ran out of space and my father had to build an entire wall of shelves in the family room to hold them."

I shifted in my chair and grimaced. "My mom's obsession is Precious Moments figurines. And fabric. Lots and lots of fabric. A whole roomful, in fact, just going to waste. She used to sew everything: clothes for my sister and me, costumes for the church Christmas productions, quilts, curtains ... you name it, she sewed it. But I don't think she's touched her sewing machine in a decade, and I'm certainly not going to. Yours truly has never been handy with a needle, no matter how much she needles me."

"My sister Karen, Chloe's mother, is." Tess's eyes gleamed behind her red-rectangled glasses. "I'll bet she'd love to take some of that fabric off your mother's hands."

"Hey, maybe she could make a wedding dress for her sister out of some of it?" Kailyn darted a sly look at Tess.

"Maybe not."

"Have you even set a wedding date yet?"

"Yes. July 25th."

"That's just two months away." My mouth dropped open, but then I could hear my mother's voice in my head saying, "You'll catch flies that way," so I snapped it shut.

"*Two months*?" Kailyn screeched, causing people at neighboring tables to turn and stare.

"Baby girl, you're not in the theater now, remember? You don't need to project."

"And remember, I have to work here," Becca said, "so try not to embarrass me."

Kailyn's peaches-and-cream complexion flushed tomato red. "Sorry. But Tess, why are you getting married so soon?"

"Yeah, is this a shotgun wedding?"

"Becca!" Kailyn shot a scandalized glance at her roommate.

"I'm just sayin'."

"Well, for one thing, since I'm menopausal, that would be physically impossible."

"And let me guess ... for another thing, you're waiting until the wedding night, right?" Jenna teased.

Two pink spots appeared on the normally unflappable Tess's cheeks.

"Y'all leave Tess alone now. A lady doesn't kiss and tell, or not kiss and tell—at least from our generation."

"Not just your generation," I said.

Kailyn's brow puckered in confusion. "So why are you in such a rush to get married, Tess?"

We all gave her a look from beneath raised eyebrows.

Becca added a "Duh," which Tess pretended not to hear. "Because when you're our age, you don't want to waste time."

"Then why not just run off to Tahoe this weekend instead?"

"Because Chloe would kill me if I got married while she was in Paris. After she gets home, we're going to have a small, intimate wedding in my backyard. Just family and a few friends."

"I hope that includes us."

"Of course."

"*All* of us?" Becca asked.

"Well ..."

"I'll be on my best behavior."

Tess looked at her over the top of her red glasses. "Promise?"

Becca held up three fingers in a crooked salute. "Scout's honor."

"You were never a Girl Scout," Kailyn said.

"No, but I was a Brownie for about three weeks one summer."

"That doesn't count."

"I was a Girl Scout." Jenna proudly snapped a regulation three-fingered Girl Scout salute, thumb holding the little finger, palm out, and elbow by the side. "Got every single merit badge too."

"I'll bet you did," Becca said.

"Merit badges, hah!" Annette squared her plump shoulders beneath her crisp, white oxford shirt. "Y'all ain't seen nothin' 'til you've gone through basic training." She crossed her starched jean leg. Annette must be the only woman on the planet who irons jeans. Once when she spilled some salad in her lap, a stray cherry tomato rolled down her jeans and the sharp crease split that sucker clean in half.

Jenna gave Annette a wide-eyed innocent look over her

chai tea. "Was that the basic training where you had eyebrow plucking in beauty class instead of learning to shoot M16's?"

"Yeah," Becca said. "I'm sure our country really slept well back then knowing they were being protected by perfectly groomed and manicured soldiers."

"What can I say? In the seventies we were a lean, mean *beauty* machine—not fighting."

"You tell 'em, Mom. And you guys," Kailyn sent a mock frown to Becca and Jenna, "quit giving my mom a hard time."

"Speaking of moms and hard times ..." Jenna focused on me. "Paige, you're a better woman than me. I mean, I love my mother, but I could never live with her."

"Me either. We'd have killed each other," Annette said. "That's why mama insisted on moving into a senior complex after my daddy died, rather than in with us."

My mother in a seniors complex? Leaving her lifelong home? So not going to happen.

"There are exceptions to the mother-daughter living together rule." Kailyn delivered a satisfied smile to Annette. "You and I got along pretty well under the same roof."

"Yes we did, baby girl, but that doesn't mean I want you moving back home any time soon."

"Thanks a lot."

"No offense. Your daddy and I are just enjoying a long second honeymoon." The corners of Annette's mouth curved upward.

Kailyn covered her ears and shook her head in embarrassment.

9

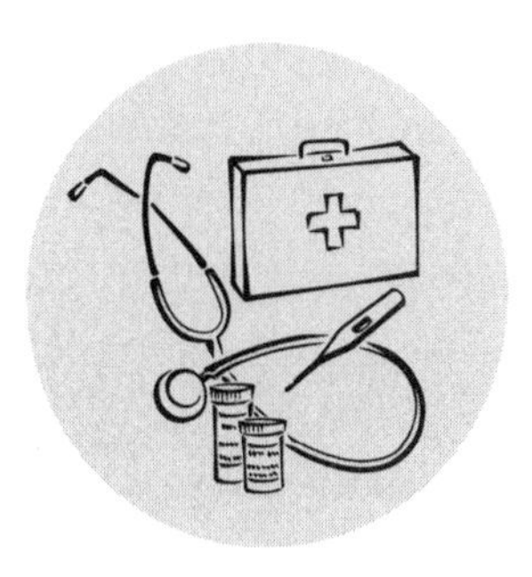

People didn't pick her out; she didn't have any kind of sparkle like other girls in the class did.

Tara Road

Over the next couple weeks, I became Paige the Purger.

No, not binge and purge—I enjoy food way too much to upchuck it on purpose—sort and purge. I sorted through all my stuff, separating it into three piles like they do on those clear-out-your-clutter shows on TV. Only my piles were the to-go-to-Mom's pile, the to-be-stored pile, and the throw-out pile.

Ruthlessly, I got rid of college textbooks, old Christmas cards, ancient cassette tapes, and my "skinny clothes" that I'd been hanging onto for years in the fantasy that someday, some year, I might be a size eight again.

I held up my black stirrup pants against my size 12 hips. Who was I kidding? I added the stretchy, long-out-of-style pants into the ever-growing throw-out pile.

Picking up a stack of photo albums, I stuck several of them

in the to-be-stored pile, but also set a couple aside to go with me to Mom's. Then I came to the final one in the stack—my white wedding album with the two silver hearts entwined on the cover.

Should I open it?

Only if you're a masochist.

Should I take it with me?

Why? Because misery loves company?

Was it time to get rid of it? I cut my eyes to the throw-out pile.

Uh, yeah. Ever hear of moving on?

But it was an important part of my life. *Was* being the operative word.

He's moved on; why can't you? You can't still think you're going to get back together, can you? The man's remarried. And his new wife's going to give him the baby he always wanted. Remember?

Yesssss, but I said vows. In church. Before God. And I meant them. My eyes moved uncertainly from one pile to another.

True. But Eric's married to someone else now; he's no longer married to you. That would be called bigamy. Move on.

Hesitantly, I approached the throw-out pile and set the photo album on top of my old stirrup pants. A second later though, I snatched it back and stuck it on the storage pile.

Does someone have a problem with letting go?

Oh shut up.

I stuffed the throwaway pile into two large black garbage bags and took them out to the trash. Then I packed all the stuff for storage into boxes, labeled and stacked them next to my couch, ready to be carted off to the small storage unit I'd rented. Although Mom had a garage, our family home was from the fifties when they only needed one-car garages.

And that one-car garage was already crammed full of

stuff, including the car my mother never drove anymore. I didn't want to drive it either. Maybe it could serve as extra seating since Mom wasn't into my chenille couch. Only two years old, it was much more comfortable than hers. I'd tried to talk her into getting rid of her ancient brown and orange floral fake-velvet couch and using mine instead.

"But your dad and I saved for months and months to buy this couch." She sent me an injured look from the recesses of its concave cushions. "I love this couch."

"I know you do, but it's almost thirty years old and it's really not in style anymore." I didn't add that it was also ugly as sin.

"Since when have you cared about style? I think you've been hanging around that Kailyn a little too much."

"I thought you liked my couch."

"I do. It's very pretty. But I want my own couch in my own living room."

"Okay. I guess I'll put my couch in storage then."

"If you want, you can bring your wingback chair," Mom conceded. "I know how much you love it and it is real pretty."

"Thanks." Of course the pink and blue pattern would totally clash with her shrieking orange and brown velvet, but I didn't want to argue or be ungracious. Especially since she hadn't balked at my bringing my bookcases. Mom had never been much of a reader, but she knew the importance books held in my life and was willing to make room for them.

Just not in her living room.

"Do you think we could move one of your curio cabinets into the dining room or your bedroom, so I can put one of my bookcases in the living room?" I asked one Saturday morning a couple weeks before the move.

"And split up my Precious Moments?" She looked at me as if I'd suddenly sprouted horns and a tail.

"Think of it as a trial separation. They'd only be one or two rooms away. Sometimes it's fun to mix things up a bit." Yet even as the words left my mouth I realized how ludicrous they were.

Mom hadn't rearranged furniture in years — since the day her much-loved couch was delivered. Everything was still in the same place it had been since I was a kid. The only thing different was the dining room table. Since Dad died, she didn't use it, preferring instead to eat in front of the TV or at the kitchen table. So she'd pushed it up against the wall, instead of in the center of the room where it had stood for years. There the sturdy oak table had become the repository for half-finished craft projects, her computer — a joint Christmas gift from my sister and me two years ago — and a mountain of *Sunset* magazines which she insisted she kept for the recipes.

Guess she liked reading the recipes and salivating over them or something, because she sure never made any of them. But then, my mother had never been much of a cook. Her standbys were burnt meatloaf, hot dogs and mac 'n' cheese from a box, which she doctored with Velveeta, and fried chicken, often undercooked. Soon enough, KFC supplanted even that.

We had Kentucky Fried Chicken buckets all over the house. Mom washed them out after we'd scarfed down all the drumsticks and used them to store buttons, elastic, safety pins, and whatever else struck her fancy.

My mother was the Queen of Packrats.

She never met a knick-knack, piece of junk mail, or fast-food condiment packet she didn't like. Two kitchen drawers alone were crammed to the hilt with nothing but rubber bands, junk mail, and twisty-ties.

Billions and billions of twisty-ties.

I scooped out several handfuls. "Why don't we throw out a lot of these? You don't need this many."

She jutted out her chin. "Yes I do. I use them all the time."

"For what?"

"Lots of things."

"Like what?"

"Loaves of bread, baggies of coins, my bags of bingo chips ..."

"But you don't need more than a hundred for that. How about if we just keep fifteen or twenty?"

"Well ... I think twenty-five or thirty would be better."

Of course you do. Whatever I suggest is never enough.

Painstakingly, I counted out twenty-five twisty-ties, set them to one side, and dumped the rest into the garbage. Then I pulled out fistfuls of coupons from the same drawer and started rifling through them.

"Most of these coupons aren't good any longer. Here's a couple from the drycleaner's that expired last year, one from a dentist offering tooth-whitening that you don't need with your dentures, and several pizza and fast foods." I fixed her with my unflinching Food Police Stare and tossed them in the trash. "They're expired anyway. And look: you even have a two-for-one from that Chinese restaurant that went out of business five years ago."

"I always liked their sweet-and-sour pork."

Yeah, that oil-soaked breading is really great for your diabetes. I started to sigh, then checked myself. I was *not* going to become my mother, the Queen of Sighs. I finished cleaning out the drawer and then headed to my old bedroom that I'd shared with Isabel growing up.

After I moved out, my parents had turned it into a sewing room. Dad built Mother a sewing table with drawers on each side to hold her bobbins, needles and thread, and other sewing miscellaneous. Mom was delighted not to have to lug her heavy sewing machine to the dining room table every time she wanted to sew.

She hadn't sewed in years, though. At least a decade. Yet the room was bursting at the seams with fabric and craft stuff. Boxes of yarn and craft supplies were stacked willy-nilly, my old dresser overflowed with material, and our old white bunk beds were piled high with bolts and bolts of cloth.

Mom picked up a bolt of rich emerald green velvet and ran her hands lovingly over the plush material. "This would make a beautiful Christmas skirt or dress for you," she said, "but I just can't see well enough to sew anymore. You really should learn how to sew, honey."

"Not in this lifetime."

She released a heavy sigh and set the velvet back down. "Where did I go wrong? Neither of my girls likes to sew or even crochet." She sighed again. "At least you cook, unlike your sister."

It's called self-defense.

My entire family had been relieved when I'd started cooking in the eighth grade. Dad gave me a big hug and murmured out of Mom's earshot that he could go the rest of his life without the Colonel's Original Recipe.

Not that I was the most adventurous cook in the beginning. I started slow with basic things like tacos, burritos, spaghetti, and all kinds of casseroles swimming in cream of mushroom soup. As I gained in confidence, I graduated to pastas, stews, and Sunday pot roasts. And by the end of my senior year I was whipping up exotic stir-frys, beef stroganoff, and Cornish game hens served on a bed of wild rice with a raisin-orange sauce.

I loved cooking for my family. It gave me a sense of purpose and satisfaction, plus it was nice to know there was something I could do that Isabel couldn't. And besides all that, it was fun! I loved experimenting in the kitchen and trying out new recipes. That's why our Getaway Girls trip to Paris and studying cooking under a real French chef had been such a dream come true for me. I'd loved learning inside tips from Jacqueline Marceau. And the goat cheese tart she'd taught me to make was always a big hors d'oeuvre hit here at home.

During our lessons Jacqueline had suggested that I consider becoming a chef since it came so naturally to me. But I wasn't even tempted. I cook for the love of it and if I started doing it for money, then it would be work. Bye-bye fun.

I hummed as I began preparing lunch—spinach salad with chicken, grapes, diced apples, and celery. When I finished the salad I tossed it with Mom's favorite dressing—ranch. She preferred the original, but I always used non-fat or light.

Someone had to watch out for her health.

In the mood for a picnic, but knowing Mom couldn't sprawl out on the grass with me, I decided to make it an indoor picnic instead. I pulled out a red-checked tablecloth from the middle drawer of the buffet and spread it over the kitchen table. That's when I noticed the huge blue stain in the center and pencil-sized blue dots spattered all around it. "What happened here?"

"Don't you remember? You kids were fighting and one of you, probably your brother, knocked over a container of blueberries."

"And you still have this stained tablecloth?" I pulled it off the table. "You should just throw it away."

"I was planning to cut it up and make it into napkins."

"When? That stain had to have happened more than twenty years ago." I gentled my voice. "You said it yourself—you're not sewing anymore. Why don't we just get you another red and white checked cloth, okay?"

She released a loud sigh. "Okay."

After we finished lunch, I continued with the purgeathon

while Mom kicked back at the kitchen table, munching on a pear. I opened the door to the little-used pantry that had become a junk catch-all over the years. "Wow. Look at all these flower vases you have—you could start your own florist's shop."

"Those are from all the flowers your dad sent me over the years, plus some from you and your sister."

"But there must be at least fifty vases in here."

"Sixty-three altogether."

She counted?

"Seven came from you and your sister and fifty-six were from your dad." She sent me a proud smile. "Your father sent me flowers every Valentine's Day and anniversary for the last twenty-seven years of our marriage."

"So what happened the first fourteen years?"

"Oh, we couldn't afford such extravagances then. With five hungry mouths to feed it was enough just to pay the mortgage and bills and put food on the table. But as you kids got older and your dad kept moving up at work, things got easier." She got a faraway look in her eyes. "I still remember the first time he sent me roses ... It was our fifteenth anniversary and I'd just gotten home from getting my hair done because your father was taking me out to dinner that night, when the doorbell rang. I opened the door and there was this large bouquet of the prettiest pink roses I'd ever seen. They even came in a beautiful pink glass vase."

"I remember that vase. You never let us touch it." I rummaged through the rows of glassware until I found what I was looking for. Carefully I removed the tall, pale pink vase with fluted edges and held it out to her. "Is this it?"

Mom's eyes misted as she took it and set it on the table. "That's the one. I still remember what your dad wrote on the card." She closed her eyes and recited:

> To my sweetheart who made me the happiest man in the world 15 years ago when you said "I Do." Looking forward to the next 15 years. And the next. All my love, Bob.

My eyes misted too and I leaned down and gave her a big hug. "I really miss him," she choked out.

"Me too, Mom. Me too." I patted her back as the tears trickled down my face. I plucked a couple napkins from the table, handed one to my mother, and then we both blew our noses in concert.

"Hey, why don't we keep this vase out on the middle of the table so you can see it all the time? I'll keep it stocked with fresh flowers. What do you say?"

"Well ..." she hesitated. "I wouldn't want it to get broken."

"It won't get broken. There's no kids running through the house or curious little hands to touch it."

Great. You've done it now. Brace yourself for the when-am-I-going-to-become-a-grandmother speech.

Before Mom could begin that familiar refrain, I steered the subject back to the vases. "I know math's never been my strong suit, but if Daddy sent you roses twice a year for the past twenty-seven years, that's only fifty-four vases."

"He also sent me roses on my fiftieth birthday. Don't you remember?"

How could I forget? I was a senior in high school and when I got home from school that day, the first thing that greeted me was the biggest bouquet of vivid pink roses I'd ever seen. For a minute my heart skipped a beat and I fantasized that my secret crush, Rick Bartlett, the captain of the basketball team and the coolest guy in school, had at long last come to his senses and realized that he loved me and not Brenda, the bubbly blonde co-captain of the pom-pom girls.

I snatched up the card and read the words.:

> To my sweetheart: Fifty roses for your fiftieth birthday, with all my love. When I look at you, honey, I still see the beautiful girl I married.

Awww. I counted and there were indeed fifty long-stemmed roses. Then and there I determined that I was going to marry a man as romantic as my dad. And somehow I knew it wouldn't be Rick Bartlett. My father sent my mother a dozen red roses every Valentine's Day and a full bouquet of pink ones on their anniversary—only there the numbers varied; one rose for every year they'd been married.

"Hey, wait a minute." I looked at her and frowned. "That still only brings us to fifty-five. Didn't you say you had fifty-six vases from Dad?"

Mom's face turned beet red. "Yes. The other one was something special just between your dad and me."

"Come on. 'Fess up."

She shook her head, a secret smile tugging at her lips. "No. There are some things that are just between a husband and wife."

Then why did you always want to know everything about Eric and me—including each unsuccessful effort to conceive?

I pushed those thoughts away and focused on the matter at hand.

"Mom, I know you have a lot of sentimental value attached to some of these, but nobody needs fifty-six vases. Especially since several of them look exactly alike." I pulled out a dozen dark green glass vases that are standard issue at most florist's shops and lined them up in front of her. "See? Besides, they're just hidden away in the pantry collecting dust anyway. How 'bout if we whittle them down to say ten or so—the ones that have the most significance to you, and then get rid of the rest?"

"It would be a sin to just throw them out. Such a waste."

"We won't throw them out. We'll recycle them. We can donate them to the Salvation Army. Or ..." a lightbulb flashed on, and not the swirly ice-cream cone fluorescent ones that take so long to brighten, but the old-fashioned, instantly bright one from days gone by. "We could give them to Marc at Golden Daffodils to reuse. What do you think of that?"

She beamed. "I think that's a wonderful idea. In fact, why don't you go over there right now and take them to him?"

"Uh, kind of in the middle of something here."

"But I'm a little tired, honey. Could we finish de-cluttering later? I'll just pick out a dozen or so of my favorite vases and then I'd like to take a nap."

Nothing like a little matchmaking prospect, no matter how off-the-mark, to change my mother's mind in a heartbeat.

Once again, I was glad that I'd decided to keep the Joe thing under wraps. Not that there was much to the Joe thing—we'd been trying to go out again ever since our initial seafood dinner, but couldn't get our schedules to line up. He was always so busy with all his sports stuff and I was busy with Mom and the move. We emailed though and had managed on Wednesday to have a quick lunch away from work. Really quick. We only had an hour lunch and didn't want to eat at any of the restaurants in the area and run the risk of running into any of our coworkers. Some of them were nearly as bad as my matchmaking mom. Instead, we'd driven twenty minutes each way to a little burrito place and crammed down chicken burritos in a hurry.

I had heartburn the rest of the afternoon.

Fifteen minutes later, the remaining forty-three vases—Mom had kept her top thirteen—clinked against each other in the box as I pushed opened the door to Golden Daffodils with my hip.

The familiar chimes sounded and Annie looked up from the counter where she was writing something. Her face split into a huge grin. "Hey Paige, how's it goin'?"

"Good. And you?"

"Can't complain. Just took a big order for a 50th-anniversary party. The boss-man will be stoked when he comes in."

I felt a stab of disappointment that Marc wasn't there to see my donation. As particular as he was about flowers, I figured he'd especially appreciate the vintage vases. As I approached the front counter I saw that today Annie was sporting a lavender tee with the slogan *I like my Picassos on black velvet.*

"Cool shirt." Carefully I set the box of vases on the counter. "I'm more of an Impressionist girl myself. Especially van Gogh—although technically I think he's considered a post-Impressionist. His *Starry Night Over the Rhone* is amazing. I got to see it in Paris."

"You've been to Paris? No way! I'd kill to go to Paris. When did you go? How long did you stay? Is it as fabulous as they say? Marc's been too. He loves to travel. Besides Paris, I think he's been to London, Dublin, Spain," Annie scrunched up her face in thought, "and Portugal. Oh, and Italy too. He took his mom there before she died."

"He was really close to his mother, wasn't he?"

"Oh yeah. He was her only kid so they were pretty tight. In fact," she giggled and a little snort escaped, "when I first met him I thought he was gay. I mean, come on: sweet, sensitive guy, close to his mom, works with flowers, loves opera, and wears those goofy rubber clogs?"

"So ... he's not?"

"Oh no. He's as straight as they come."

Assume much? I could feel the heat creeping up my neck.

Annie noticed my red neck and waved her hand dismissively. "Don't worry about it. Everyone thinks so at first. But Marc's quite secure in his masculinity. It doesn't bother him. Except of course when he asks a woman out and she's all surprised and stuff. He said maybe he should wear a football jersey and start tossing back six-packs and scratching and belching or something." She grinned. "But of course then he wouldn't be Marc. He's definitely not the typical guy."

Definitely not.

"Has he ever been married? Or engaged?"

"Not yet. Although he came pretty close once."

"What happened?"

She shrugged. "I'm not really sure. I think it was something about opposites attracting and then seriously repelling. Something like that. He still dates though."

"He does?"

"Oh yeah. Once women realize he's straight and available, they fall all over him."

I'll just bet they do.

The door chimes sounded and I turned around to see a stunning Asian woman with the kind of long, glossy hair you see in those expensive shampoo commercials.

She click-clacked her way to the counter in her size zero jeans, snug, V-neck black T-shirt, and black stiletto mules.

"Is Marc in?" she asked Annie in a breathless, baby-doll voice.

No wonder the women fall all over him. One strong breeze and she'd topple off her skinny stilettos.

10

> Mr. Phileas Fogg lived, in 1872, at No. 7, Saville Row, Burlington Gardens, the house in which Sheridan died in 1814. He was one of the most noticeable members of the Reform Club, though he seemed always to avoid attracting attention; an enigmatical personage, about whom little was known, except that he was a polished man of the world.
>
> *Around the World in 80 Days*

Tess had chosen the classic adventure *Around the World in 80 Days* for our current book club selection, a book she'd always wanted to read. As a kid, she told us she'd loved the movie where the intrepid Phileas Fogg bet his card-playing pals that he could travel the globe in a mere eighty days—a feat that was considered impossible in that Victorian era—by utilizing new forms of transportation including steamships and locomotives.

"I loved that movie too. Lots of great Hollywood cameos in it. And of course David Niven was perfect as the quintessential Englishman calmly racing against time," I said.

Kailyn grinned. "Jackie Chan was so funny in that."

"Um, that was the remake."

The vastly inferior remake. Although I didn't say that aloud. No need to hurt Kailyn's feelings. "The one we're talking about won Best Picture in 1956 and had cameos from Frank Sinatra, Marlene Dietrich, and dozens of other film luminaries."

"Well look at you, Miss Movie Trivia."

"Remind me not to challenge you at Trivial Pursuit," Jenna said.

"My favorite part was when they crossed the Alps by balloon."

Tess's face split into a huge grin. "Good. Because that's our next adventure."

"*What*?" Kailyn's excited theater voice kicked in.

"Crossing the Alps in a balloon?"

"No. Riding in a hot air balloon over the Napa Valley."

"Sweet!" Becca pumped her fist in the air.

"Are you kidding?"

Kailyn's eyes shone. "Ever since I saw *The Wizard of Oz* I've wanted to go up in a hot air balloon."

"Me too," Jenna said.

"Well now you're going to get your chance."

Except ... there was no hot air balloon in the novel. *Anywhere*. Trains, boats, and several other modes of transportation. Even an elephant.

Just no balloon.

"I can't believe it," Tess said after we'd finished reading the book and were discussing it at her house. "Throughout all their travels, I kept waiting for that ubiquitous balloon to show up."

"Me too! And it never did."

"What a rip."

I held up a copy of the audio book I'd gotten for Mom to listen to while I read the paperback. I'd started checking audio books out from the library for her. "Look. The cover even has a striped balloon on it."

"Talk about false advertising."

"I know. It's so strange. I mean what is the one image that instantly comes to mind when you think *Around the World in 80 Days?*"

"A hot air balloon."

"Too weird."

"Oh well, it was a good idea," Annette said.

"What was?"

"Going hot air ballooning."

"Oh, we're still going ballooning," Tess said matter-of-factly.

Annette stared at her. "But ... it's not in the book."

"I know. But we thought it was, so why waste a perfectly good adventure?"

"Now that's what I'm sayin'!" Becca said. "Tess, you rock." She jumped up from her chair and did a little happy dance.

Jenna leaned forward from her position on the couch next to me and fixed Tess with an eager look. "So when do we go?"

"And what do we wear?" Kailyn asked. As the designated fashion plate in the group, she was always stylin', from the latest hair accessories down to her designer flip-flops.

I lifted an eyebrow and sent an innocent look to Tess. "I'm guessing we should leave our miniskirts at home?"

She returned my look and raised me another eyebrow. "Correct. Long skirts too. Any kind of skirts for that matter. They recommend jeans or comfortable pants." Her eyes slid to Becca's worn and trusty Birks that she wore like a second skin. "I'm afraid you'll have to swap those out for sneakers.

Closed-toe, flat-heeled shoes are the order of the day. No flip-flops either."

"No flip-flops?" Kailyn pouted, looking down at her sparkly white ones.

"Nope."

"I don't mean to rain on your parade, but have y'all really thought this through?" Annette's eyes flicked from one Getaway Girl to another. "I mean, is it safe?" She shuddered. "I've heard of balloons hitting power lines and catching fire. And I read about one woman who died when that happened."

"There's a happy thought, Mom."

"People die in car crashes every day. Does that mean you're not going to drive?"

"Yeah." Becca cut Annette a curious look. "Besides, you were in the Air Force. I thought you liked going up into that wild blue yonder."

"In a plane, yes. With a steel skin and doors and windows."

"And what—weighs six tons or whatever? Better to be in something a little lighter."

Annette lifted her chin. "But a plane has a pilot."

"Hot air balloons have pilots too," Tess said. "The pilots are all FAA certified and so are the balloons. I researched this in-depth before I brought the idea to the group."

"And Mom," Kailyn said gently, "planes crash too, but that hasn't stopped you from flying."

I'd used a version of that same argument on my mother when she balked at the prospect of my going ballooning. Problem was, it didn't carry as much weight since she had never flown in a plane and had no intention of ever doing so. "Going up in a flimsy balloon is dangerous," Mom said two nights before our adventure when we were having dinner together. "You could get hurt."

"I'll be fine. Honest."

Then we got to the real crux of the matter.

"You're being selfish. What would happen to me if something ever happened to you?"

Who's the selfish one again?

But Mom couldn't help it. She was used to being taken care of and didn't know anything else. My father had taken care of her for forty-two years, and when he died, I picked up where he left off. When Mom finally, grudgingly, consented to the laser eye surgery, which was done on an outpatient basis, I'd taken another couple days off work to ferry her to and from the appointment and keep an eye on her once she was home recovering.

The eye surgeon had told us that sight improvement was usually immediate. But that didn't happen for Mom. The damage to her eyes was too extensive and had taken place over years. Although a second surgery *might* help, she refused to have it. "The first one didn't help, and I don't want to go through it again."

Thankfully, Annette did agree to go through with our balloon adventure. "Yay, Mom!" Kailyn hugged her. "It will be a blast. You'll see."

"Just so we don't blast into any power lines."

"If to live in this style is to be eccentric, it must be confessed that there is something good in eccentricity," Becca intoned.

"Huh?"

"It's a quote from the book."

Kailyn rolled her eyes. "Leave it to you to memorize that one."

Joe and I finally got our second nighttime date. Kind of.

Realizing that our schedules were simply too difficult to

line up to find a free evening together, I agreed to attend his Friday baseball game and go out for pizza afterwards. He told me how to get to the baseball field, but I printed out MapQuest directions just to be safe.

I arrived just a couple minutes before the game started, parking my car and making my way uncertainly across the grass to the two sets of bleachers on either side of home plate. Which side was I supposed to sit on?

Luckily, Joe saw me from where he was sitting in the dugout. He stood up in the entrance and pointed to the bleachers on the left. As he did so, a couple of Paris Hilton types in the stands turned and watched me approach, then bent their heads close, obviously talking about me.

By the time I settled in and felt less awkward, a guy had hit the ball, another struck out, and Joe was up to bat. I realized that I was trying to recall the truths of the game from gym class which wasn't tapping me into enough knowledge to understand more than bases and most of the positions. What was the person called between second and third? Short stack?

No, that's pancakes.

Joe turned and gave me a small smile and wink making this somewhat worthwhile. Somewhat.

The first ball was a strike. I knew this from what the umpire said and a couple beside me who said, "Strike? Come on ump, get some glasses!"

The next pitch, Joe swung and connected. And boy did it connect. The white ball swung up toward the lights, the spectators jumped up, Joe took off running, but then a collective groan released as the ball hit the ground and everyone slowed down. Why they slowed down, I had no idea. No one caught it in the air. It nearly hit the back wall. Looked good to me.

A few more pitches later, Joe was on first base with a walk. "Yeah, he scared you, didn't he? Scared the little pitcher," the male half of the couple next to me shouted at the field. Man, people get so excitable at these things.

At least it wasn't as boring as I'd expected. However, this thought came a bit soon. An hour and a half later my eyes glassed over and ears burning from the overzealous fans on my left, the game was over and everyone on my side of the bleachers was angry.

"Can you believe that umpire?" Joe said as his first words of greeting when he approached me after the game. "I need a beer."

And for the next hour, I sat squeezed between Joe and one of his dusty-smelling teammates at a booth table as the team, wives and girlfriends, and other extraneous people rehashed the entire game.

Really having some fun now.

I nibbled on a piece of Meat Explosion Pizza in near silence, listening to baseball memories and avoiding the steady, piercing gaze of one of the women who turned out to be Joe's ex-girlfriend.

I actually prayed that Mom would call and interrupt us, give me any excuse to leave. No such luck.

Finally I told Joe I had to leave because I had to get up early for our ballooning adventure.

When our six Getaway Girls arrived yawning at the launch site at o-dark-thirty the next morning, we got to watch the three-man crew get our hot air balloon ready. They laid the wicker basket, which we'd later be standing in—no seats—sideways on the ground, unpacked the balloon, or envelope, as they called it, and stretched out the vivid-colored nylon fabric across the ground, then connected it to the basket and propane burner.

We watched in fascination as a powerful gas-powered fan

blew cold air into the envelope for what Tess said was a "cold inflate."

"Sweet!" Jenna said.

Kailyn's eyes looked as big as mine felt.

Once the envelope was partly inflated, the propane burners were then ignited, and the air inside heated up, further inflating the balloon.

"Even sweeter," Becca said as the colorful rainbow pattern filled out before our eyes.

One of the crew members held a rope tied to the top of the balloon to prevent it from swaying too much and also from rising before it was fully inflated. A few more minutes and the woven basket was standing upright. We craned our necks. "Now that's what I call a beautiful balloon."

"Niiiiice."

Jim, our pilot, extended his hand to us. "Okay, in you go."

We climbed in, one by one, and Kailyn's eyes grew even wider. "I feel like Dorothy."

"I feel more like Toto," Annette muttered.

"Don't worry. We haven't seen any wicked witches on broomsticks flying around." Our pilot lifted a bushy eyebrow. "Yet."

Moments later, we were off. Up, up, and away watching the sunrise over the Napa Valley floating gently above the treetops.

"Wow. Check out that view."

"Gorgeous."

"Spectacular."

Below us, the rising sun shimmered on rows of grapevines stretching through lush vineyards, the morning mist hovered between the mountains, and narrow country roads snaked their way through undulating hills and valleys speckled with wildflowers where cows and horses grazed contentedly.

"You should see it in March when the mustard is in full bloom," Jim said. "Talk about fields of gold."

Even Annette, who'd been so nervous about the whole balloon riding prospect, was enchanted. "I didn't realize it would be so peaceful," she said. "You can hardly tell we're even moving."

"This is so tranquil."

"And calm."

"Yet exciting at the same time," Becca said.

"Says the woman who grumbled about getting up so early," Kailyn teased.

Travel guide Tess, who always did her research, said that flights are most often launched at dawn or sunset when the wind is usually calm, which makes for both an easier launch and landing of the balloon. Flying at those times also avoids thermals—rising currents of warm air—that make it more difficult to control the balloon, she explained.

Our balloon was well-controlled. We were floating gently, almost imperceptibly, through the sky. Like a dancer in a slow, graceful ballet.

"Magical," I breathed.

Becca murmured her favorite Mark Twain quote: "Twenty years from now you will be more disappointed by the things that you didn't do than by the ones you did do. So throw off the bowlines. Sail away from the safe harbor. Catch the trade winds in your sails. Explore. Dream. Discover."

I wondered what we would discover on this Getaway Girls adventure.

"Look!" Jenna pointed. "Over there on the right. See the deer?"

We followed her finger to see a trio of does and a fawn cantering across a meadow towards a grove of trees. "Oh, look at the little Bambi with them." Kailyn raised her digital camera and began snapping away. Becca, too. And Jenna caught it all on camcorder.

I'd decided to leave my camera home, preferring to simply soak in the adventure instead and enjoy it while it was happening, rather than worrying about catching it for posterity. Besides, I could always get copies of the photos from one of the others.

"There's another one over there." Annette pointed a little to the left. "Looks like a buck."

Jim shaded his eyes against the sun. "Yeah. He's a big one."

"Look up," Tess said. "Look up."

We swiveled our heads to the sky where a multicolored checkerboard hot air balloon was drifting above us and off to the left—the wicker gondola packed with passengers. We waved in floating solidarity and they waved back.

Although there were several hot air balloon companies to choose from, Tess had selected one of the smaller, more intimate ones that was slightly less expensive—hot air ballooning isn't cheap—and where we wouldn't be crammed into a basket with 12 or 16 other people. Six passengers was the limit in our balloon, which suited us fine.

Becca released a blissful sigh. "This is the life."

"I'll say."

"Too bad Chloe is missing this," Tess said. "I bet she'd love it. My boys, too."

"I'm not going to feel bad for Chloe. The woman is in *Paris* after all and having a great time by all accounts."

Kailyn fingered the Hermès scarf at her neck—a gift from her mom when we were in the City of Light. "Think she'll bring us back any souvenirs?"

"Hopefully some chocolate."

"Or maybe some macaroons from Ladurée. I could sure go for another one of those." Annette licked her lips.

"Stop. You're making me hungry."

Jenna asked Jim how high up we'd go.

"Maybe 2,000 feet, give or take."

Becca whistled. "Now I know what they mean by a bird's-eye view."

"I had a bird's eye view when I went up in a glider in England," Annette said. "It was fun to see all the sheep on the rolling green hills — there's lots of them — and the stone cottages that are hundreds of years old. I'll never forget it."

"Wait." Jenna stared at her. "You were scared of going up in a hot air balloon, yet you flew in a glider?"

"Yeah. What's up with that?" Becca asked.

Annette shrugged. "I was young and fearless then. Now I'm old and wise." Her lips curved up. "Wiser. The thing is, I thought the glider would be really quiet since there's no engine. But it wasn't. The rushing wind, especially without a canopy, made it pretty noisy. Unlike this. I can't get over how quiet it is."

"That's because we move *with* the wind, not against it," Pilot Jim said. "We become the wind." Jim was a great guide. He told us all about the Napa area and pointed out different vineyards, houses, and restaurants as we flew over them.

I've been to Napa dozens of times. But never like this. So beautiful. So tranquil. So serene. Can I stay up here forever?

But of course we had to come back down to earth.

We landed an hour later, descending gently into a meadow of wildflowers, aided by the two-man chase crew who'd followed our balloon on the ground, keeping in radio contact with our pilot. They packed up the balloon and drove us back to the launch site where they presented us with a complimentary bottle of champagne.

"Balloonist's tradition," Jim said.

"But we don't have any glasses."

He winked and fished a bag of plastic glasses from the crew's van and passed them around. He popped open the champagne and poured a little into each of our glasses. Then he raised his glass to us, as did the crew, and they continued with another ballooning tradition, reciting the Balloonist's Prayer:

> The Winds have welcomed you with softness.
> The Sun has blessed you with its warm hands.
> You have flown so high and so well,
> that God has joined you in your laughter.
> And He has set you gently back again
> into the loving arms of Mother Earth.

"Amen!" Becca said.

"Amen," we chorused, lifting our glasses and taking a drink.

"Thanks, guys," Tess said. "This is one adventure we'll never forget."

"You guys are the best." We raised our glasses to Pilot Jim and the crew in a toast.

"And here's to Jules Verne and Phileas Fogg for inspiring this journey," Jenna said.

Annette giggled. "And to Hollywood for adding the balloon."

"To the Getaway Girls!"

11

> "When I left Queen's my future seemed to stretch out before me like a straight road. I thought I could see along it for many a milestone. Now there is a bend in it. I don't know what lies around the bend, but I'm going to believe that the best does. It has a fascination of its own, that bend, Marilla."
>
> *Anne of Green Gables*

At last it was moving day. And all the Getaway Girls helped—except for Annette, who was off on a romantic B&B weekend with her hubby. Tess even commandeered her teenage twins Tommy and Timmy to handle the big stuff, which wasn't a lot: my bed, wingback chair, three bookcases, and an armoire that housed my TV and stereo system.

Having my own TV was a non-negotiable. I didn't want to be held hostage to Mom's soap operas and reality TV shows. She watched three soap operas in a row, and had ever since we were kids. I knew more about Erica Kane, Luke and Laura, and all the citizens of Oakdale put together than I ever wanted to. But more than her soaps, my mother was totally addicted to reality TV. From the one where a group of strangers all live together in one house with cameras recording their every move, to the one where people eat icky bugs and slugs, to the granddaddy of them all, *Survivor*.

Mom found it fascinating. Me? Not so much. All the lying, scheming, and manipulation in pursuit of the big bucks was a bit too real for me. I tried to tell Mom that most of the stuff she saw on TV was set up and scripted, but because the word "reality" was associated with the show, she insisted it was absolutely true.

What was true was that moving was a pain.

I'd be lying if I said it was easy giving up my independence and my duplex which Becca and Kailyn had arranged to move into next week. It wasn't. I was accustomed to living alone and had gotten used to my solitude and to doing things my own way, but I knew I was doing the right thing.

The past couple weeks had been a crazy, chaotic time as I packed and cleaned both my place and Mom's in preparation for the big move. I stripped off the pink ballerina wallpaper in my old/new bedroom that she'd put up when Isabel and I were toddlers and replaced it with a soothing celery green paint and crisp white trim, emptied the dresser drawers of all the fabric which Tess and her sister happily came over and relieved us of, and held a joint garage sale with my mother that netted us nearly three hundred bucks.

And now, at long last, moving day had arrived. I rented a small U-Haul and on the way to Mom's my moving caravan made up of Tess's sons and four of the Getaway Girls, stopped at my storage unit where the twins unloaded my couch and several heavy boxes, and Tess, Becca, Jenna, Kailyn, and I fit in different odds and ends.

We were a well-oiled moving machine. Until we got to Mom's, that is.

Correction: Mom's and my house. When we pulled into the driveway and clambered out of our vehicles to begin unloading, Mom appeared in the front doorway in her walker and pushed open the screen door. "Hi everyone. Glad to see you finally made it. Come on in and have some breakfast while it's still hot."

The twins looked at Tess, Tess and the other Getaway Girls looked at me, and I slid the words out the side of my mouth. "She probably just nuked some coffee cake or some of those hot oatmeal breakfast bars. Let's go grab some, and then we can get moving."

Only it wasn't coffee cake. Oatmeal breakfast bars either.

Mom had enlisted Frieda's help, and together the two of them had concocted a gooey bacon-and-egg tater-tot breakfast casserole thick with two inches of American cheese slices bubbling on top. There were also mega cinnamon rolls slathered with cream cheese icing, platters of ham and sausage links, and a pink bakery box filled to the brim with two dozen doughnuts, most of them oozing with jelly, custard, or cream.

"Moving's hard work, so I wanted to make sure you had some sustenance for the job ahead." Mom smiled and nodded to Tommy and Timmy. "Especially you growing boys. When my son was a teenager, he and his friends were always hungry. Go on now. Dig in."

The twins didn't need to be asked twice. They sat down at the kitchen table and began scarfing down the bountiful breakfast with relish.

"Mom, you shouldn't have." You really shouldn't have.

"Mrs. Kelley, this is so sweet of you," Kailyn said, "but you really shouldn't have gone to so much trouble."

"No trouble at all. Frieda prepped the breakfast casserole

last night and all we had to do was pop it in the oven this morning. I microwaved the ham and sausages and she ran to the doughnut shop for me and got all the goodies. And no, Paige," she made a face, "I didn't sneak a cinnamon roll before you got here."

She filled a heaping plate and handed it to Kailyn. "Now make sure you eat all this, honey; you could stand a little meat on your bones," she clucked. "You young girls today are way too skinny."

Tommy and Timmy's admiring glances at Kailyn in her red T-shirt and shorts said otherwise as she smiled weakly at Mom and sat down next to them.

"I've got coffee and orange juice too. Paige, why don't you get the apple juice from the fridge in case anyone wants some?"

As I opened the refrigerator door, Jenna sidled up next to me and whispered so my mother wouldn't hear, "Any chance there might be something that's not loaded with meat or fat?"

I pulled out an apple and a bunch of grapes from the crisper and handed them to her.

"Thanks." She kept her voice low. "Looks like you've got your work cut out for you."

Don't I know it.

"Hey Jenna, share the wealth," Becca said when she noticed the cluster of grapes in Jenna's hand.

Mom's eyes narrowed when she saw that Becca hadn't touched the eggy casserole, but Tess intercepted her before she could say anything or release one sigh. "Catherine, thank you so much for this wonderful breakfast, and please thank your friend for her help too. This was very thoughtful of you."

"Well, I can't do a lot these days, but the least I could do is provide food."

"And we appreciate it. Don't we?" She looked at the Getaway Girls and over at her boys, who'd just crammed cinnamon rolls into their mouths. They nodded enthusiastically. "Thanks too, Catherine, for giving all that fabric to my sister. Karen's in absolute heaven sewing cute little outfits for her granddaughter. And she's planning to use the rest of the fabric for quilts. We have a program at church where we donate quilts to newborns and kids in need. In fact, Karen thought that maybe you might like to join the ladies in her quilting group and help out."

"Oh, I haven't quilted in years."

"Well then it's high time you started again, don't you think?" Tess said.

"I'd like to, but I really can't see well enough to do fine needlework anymore. That's why I got rid of all my fabric." Mom released a heavy sigh.

"But how hard can it be to make a crib quilt? I mean, I don't know all that much about sewing—that's my sister's domain—but our Nana's been quilting forever. And stopping is not an option for her even though her eyes aren't what they used to be. So last Christmas I gave her this magnifying lamp and she said it's made all the difference. Maybe it could do the same for you?"

"Well ... maybe."

Tess continued. "Karen was thinking perhaps you could also be a mentor to some of the young women who are just starting out. Maybe tell them a little about design and patterns and your sewing techniques?"

"That's a great idea." I sent a look of gratitude to Tess. "Mom, you always said you wished Isabel or I had taken up sewing so you could teach us everything you knew. Now here's your chance."

"I don't know ..." But I could see the idea appealed to her. "How would I get there?"

How else? "I'll drive you."

"Karen said she'd be happy to pick you up," Tess said.

"Oh, I'd hate to put her to all that trouble. Paige can just take me. She's such a good daughter, she takes me everywhere." Mom sent me a suffocating smile. "I don't know what I'd do without her."

Me either.

"It's no trouble at all for Karen to swing by and pick you up. You're right on her way to church."

"Well ... if you're sure. I wouldn't want to put her out."

And yet it's perfectly okay to put me out because after all, I don't have a life.

"You wouldn't be putting her out in the least. I'll give Karen your number so she can call and you two can make your arrangements." Tess looked at her watch and stood up. "And now we'd all better get a move on unloading that truck. I'm meeting James for lunch at 12:30, and Tommy, don't you have a movie date with Clemmie this afternoon?"

"Ya got that right." He shot up from his chair and slapped Timmy on the back. "Come on bro, move your lazy butt."

The next hour-and-a-half passed in a blur as we unloaded the U-Haul in record time. The twins brought in my armoire and bed which they set up in my freshly painted bedroom, Tess and Kailyn carried my wingback and floor lamp into the living room, and Jenna, Becca, and I ferried boxes to my bedroom.

All except for the heavy ones. Those we saved for the guys.

Timmy grunted as he staggered past me with a large box. "What have you got in here? Rocks?"

"Nope. Books."

"Shoulda known. You're just like my mom."

I wish. Then I'd be all wise and together. Engaged, too.

"Thanks. Once a book geek, always a book geek."

We continued carrying boxes in and the territorial Mr. Spitz kept getting underfoot. Finally after someone stepped on his tail for the third time, Frieda came and took him over to her house for the duration. I wish Mom had gone too—Mr. Spitz wasn't the only one who got underfoot—but she insisted on staying and "helping."

Tess rode to the rescue again by asking Mom for a cup of coffee to keep her out of the way. Then she sat down at the kitchen table with my mother and told her all about her upcoming wedding. As a result, the rest of us were able to make short work of the remaining boxes and odds and ends.

As we set the final box of books down next to the empty bookcases in my now-crowded bedroom, the doorbell rang. "Stay there, Mom. I got it," I yelled. I scurried to the front door and opened it to a skinny, redheaded teenager who bore a strong resemblance to Annie. Minus the platinum spikes. He was holding a spring bouquet of gorgeous multicolored flowers in his spindly, tattooed arms.

"Ooh, pretty!" squealed Kailyn, who'd followed me to the door.

The teen's eyes flickered from her to me, then back again to the curvaceous Kailyn, taking in her well-filled-out T-shirt and shorts and tanned long legs. "Uh, delivery for Paige Kelley?"

"That's me," I said.

Reluctantly he took his eyes off Kailyn and had me sign the delivery form. Then he handed me the mixed bouquet. "Here ya go. Enjoy."

"Thank you." I bent my head and breathed in the heady mixture of roses, lilies, daisies, and carnations as he loped down the sidewalk to his idling van. A yellow flower van with a familiar logo.

Everyone clustered around me in the hallway, including

Mom in her walker, having heard Kailyn's squeal. "Ooh, gorgeous! Who are they from, who are they from?"

"I'm not sure." Although I had a pretty good idea. So much for keeping the Joe thing, such as it was, on the down low.

A huge smile creased my mother's face. "I think *I* know."

"Well open the card already and find out," the girls urged.

"Okay, but give a girl a little room, would you?" Shutting the front door, I carried the bouquet over to the cluttered dining room table, setting it down next to a stack of magazines, and plucked out the card.

Paige,

Welcome to the neighborhood! Hope this means we'll be seeing much more of you now.

Your new neighbor and flower instructor, Marc.

P.S. The white carnations stand for good luck. Oh, and since you're trying to reduce your vase collection, I hope you'll like this substitute container instead.

The substitute container was a gorgeous pink-and-green floral china teapot. What a sweetie. And what a relief the flowers weren't from Joe. Or was it?

"Who's Marc?" Becca and Kailyn chorused as they peered over my shoulder.

"Yeah, you haven't told us about him," Jenna said. "Someone's been holding out."

"He's the florist down the street. Owns this great shop called A Host of Golden Daffodils. And I have mentioned him—he's the one who did the gorgeous flowers for your brunch, Tess. Remember? I said you might want to check him out for your wedding?"

"I do remember. That's one of the many items on my to-do

list I haven't gotten to yet." She looked closer at my arrangement of pink and yellow roses, white, pink, and yellow daisies, pink Stargazer lilies, and white mini carnations. "He does beautiful work, so I'll definitely be following up."

"You'd better hurry. He gets booked pretty fast."

"So ... are you guys dating?" Kailyn gave me an eager look.

"Yeah," Jenna teased, "Is this a *budding* romance?"

Everyone groaned at the bad pun.

"No. We're friends. He's teaching me about flowers." I showed them the card. "See? He even signed it 'your flower instructor.' Don't read anything more into it. That means you too, Mom." I smiled at her to show I was teasing. Sort of.

After everyone left, Mom took a nap and I began the process of unpacking. Books first, and then clothes. I never felt truly settled in until all my books were in place.

Several hours later I added the finishing touch to my final bookcase, a framed plaque on a small easel with a quote from Erasmus that read, *When I get a little money, I buy books; and if any is left, I buy food and clothes.*

12

> There were three of them. Roberta was the eldest. Of course mothers never have favorites, but if their mother had had a favorite, it might have been Roberta. Next came Peter, who wished to be an engineer when he grew up, and the youngest was Phyllis, who meant extremely well.
>
> *The Railway Children*

Isabel decided to fly home for a family duty trip the following weekend. David would be off on a deep-sea fishing jaunt with some of his old college buddies then, so she thought it would be a good time to make one of her rare familial visits.

My sister always timed her visits for a weekend. That way she didn't have to use any vacation time—"things are so crazy at work right now, there's no way I can take time off" was her usual excuse—but more important, she could keep her visit brief. She'd usually fly in late Friday night and return home Sunday night. Then she only had to spend a day or at the most, a day and a half, with as she called her, "the mother unit."

Of course, she never stayed at Mom's.

Isabel always booked a room at the Hyatt Regency downtown. She said she needed high-speed Internet—Mom was still on dial-up—and access to an on-site gym where she could work out. Truth is, she just didn't want to be with Mom 24/7.

Plus our family home wasn't grand enough for her.

"You know I've always hated that dinky pink bathroom," she said on the phone when she called to say she was coming and I invited her to stay with Mom.

Us.

I was still getting used to that *us*.

"But it's not pink anymore. Well, not completely." One of my first missions when I moved in had been to tone down the screaming Pepto-Bismol walls in the bathroom. Mom was resistant to the idea at first until I showed her places where the paint had begun to chip. With a heavy sigh, she finally acquiesced and I quickly painted over the pink with a creamy vanilla semi-gloss before she could change her mind.

I really wanted to replace the primeval pink tub as well, but I soon learned from talking to coworkers that ripping out a tub and putting in a new one was way too hard. One guy said that when he got his new tub they had to rip off the side of the house to fit it in. Talk about disruptive. I like the open air, but not that much. It was also way too expensive. Way.

No wonder so many plumbers drive Beamers.

Instead, I was now investigating the possibility of having the tub resurfaced white, which was a far more affordable option. The next item on my bathroom fix-up agenda was going to be replacing the ancient toilet. Also pink. Naturally. It wasn't just the pinkness that was the problem however—although that alone was enough to make me want to upchuck and chuck it into oblivion—but it had a tendency to keep running, so you had to always jiggle the handle to make it stop.

The hand to handle relationship got a little old.

I'd already removed the upholstered vinyl toilet seat with pink flowers and butterflies on the lid. I'd hated the too-cute bathroom aberration ever since Dad bought it for Mom over a decade ago and tried to make sure I never had to use the facilities while visiting.

There's something just wrong with sitting on a soft-padded toilet seat in the squashy indentation of someone else's butt. Seems to me germs have a much better chance of collecting in the wrinkles and recesses of a padded seat than on the smooth hard surface of a standard-issue one that I could easily clean with Lysol.

Luckily, there was an infinitesimal tear on one side of the upholstered seat which scratched me uncomfortably whenever I sat down and which I told my mother might even in time draw blood. Or at the very least, become a fertile breeding ground for bacteria.

"I've never seen it," she said when I told her about it. "Or even felt it."

I led her into the bathroom and pointed to the jagged tear that had somehow overnight mysteriously morphed into a two-inch rip. "Right there. See?"

She bent over and peered through her glasses. "Oh my goodness. That does look dangerous. I guess we'll have to get a new toilet seat."

"Not to worry. I'll take care of it." An hour later, I'd popped that squashed puppy off its hinges, tossed it in the trash, and replaced it with a new, white solid surface seat.

I'm pretty handy with a screwdriver if I do say so myself. Unlike my brilliant, gorgeous, wildly successful, and blissfully married older sister who wouldn't know a screwdriver from a socket wrench.

Not that there's any sibling rivalry.

"Thanks for the offer to bunk with you and Mom, little

sister, but I'm really not into sleeping in my old narrow bunk bed," Isabel said to me on the phone.

"We got rid of the bunk beds when I moved in."

"About time. So then where would you propose I sleep? In your double bed?" She snorted. "Sorry. I'm a little too old for sleepovers. Besides, the only person I sleep with is my husband."

Rub it in why don't you?

"You can sleep in Patrick's old room."

"In his lumpy bed? No thanks. Probably still smells of pot. No, I think I'll just stay at the Hyatt. That way I can work out in the mornings and evenings."

And avoid Mom. I'm onto you, Iz.

Isabel said she'd also pick up a rental car at the airport, which Mom thought was a waste of money. "I don't know why your sister has to go and pay good money for a car when she could use mine. It's just sitting there in the garage and it's in great condition. It gets really good gas mileage, and these days with the price of gas, that's important."

I stopped myself from releasing a sigh. No way was I going to follow in my mother's sighing footsteps. "You know Isabel, Mom. She likes her independence and doing things her own way."

Just like you.

Mom was in her element having her firstborn, favorite daughter coming home. She'd even gone so far as to straighten her room and shove some of the clutter—which had multiplied like rabbits again since my pre-move purgeathon—into her closet.

The day before my sister's arrival I took off from work a little early and snuck into the house through the back door, knowing Mom often liked to nap at this time. Not wanting to wake her, I slipped off my heels, untucked my blouse, and snaked my hand up my back to unsnap my bra. The final words of Martin Luther King's famous "I Have a Dream" speech resounded in my brain. Free at last.

Hearing muffled voices from the living room, I grabbed a bottled water, plucked a Red Vine from my secret stash, and pushed through the kitchen door just in time to hear my mother say, "My Isabel has a master's degree and has done very well for herself. She lives in a penthouse on Michigan Avenue."

"She doesn't live in a penthouse, Mom. She lives on the twenty-seventh floor. And it's not Michigan Avenue; it's *next* to Michigan Avenue." I took a vicious bite of my Red Vine and plopped down on the sagging brown and orange couch next to her timid next-door neighbor and confidante. "Hey Frieda, how are you? How's Nikki doing?"

"Really good," Frieda twittered, fluttering her birdlike hands and giving me a grateful look. "She's out of rehab now and in AA and she hasn't done any drugs for twenty-nine days now. She also signed up to take some college classes online and she got a job at Waffle House as a hostess."

"That's great. Sounds like she's on the right track this time. You must be really proud of her."

"I am." Her drab brown eyes shone.

"Frieda, did I tell you that my Isabel's met ..." Mom paused for effect and then dropped the O-bomb, "Oprah?"

"No! Really?"

Yeah, if you can call sitting in the audience and seeing her onstage "meeting" her.

My mother had done it again. Her favorite daughter's Big O connection—never mind how tenuous—trumped Frieda's druggie daughter's fresh-out-of-rehab, getting-back-on-track tale.

Mom savored a smile of victory from her throne—my wingback chair that she'd appropriated after I moved in.

"David said to give you his love, Mom, and to tell you he's really sorry he couldn't come." Isabel unfolded her napkin with her French-manicured fingers, her wedding ring with its square-cut emerald in the center—no run-of-the-mill diamond for her—catching the light and casting Tinkerbell sparkles on the table.

Yeah right. David's never been a big fan of Mom's.

"Oh that's okay, honey. A man needs to get away every now and then with his buddies. Remember how your dad always went on his yearly fishing trip with Don from work?" She beamed at us across the breakfast table. "Besides, it's nice to have just my girls with me at home again. It's been *way* too long since we've all been together."

Isabel caught my eye and mouthed the word "pow."

My sister had indeed arrived in town too late last night to come by, so we'd agreed over the phone that she would join us for breakfast where we'd discuss our plans for the day. I stayed up late cleaning the whole house not only from top to bottom, but from side to side, clearing away as much of Mom's clutter as possible, and making sure everything was gleaming and spotless.

No way was I going to let my almost Michigan Avenue sister find something to turn her perky little nose up at.

"It's nice to see the dining room table back in the middle of the room again." Isabel sipped her orange juice, her mascaraed eyes roaming the room. "But where'd you put your computer?"

"Oh, Paige set it up for me in Patrick's old room. Now it's a combination spare room and office for me."

"Nice. Paige has always been good at organizing." She inclined her expensively bobbed and weaved head to me and took a bite of her crepe. "And cooking. This is delicious. What's in it?"

"Fresh spinach and mushrooms, skim milk, a little light cream cheese, and a shaving of goat cheese. The recipe called for blue cheese crumbles, but goat cheese is better for diabetics. Skim milk too." I lifted my shoulders in my new white T-shirt, bought on my lunch hour yesterday, knowing my sister would be designer-shod from head to toe. "I fell in love with crepes in Paris and have been experimenting with different recipes that Mom can have."

"And most of them have been really good. Except for that one wheat zucchini bread." Mom made a face.

"Yeah, that was a little dry. Next time I'll add more applesauce to make it moist."

Isabel finished her crepe and reached for the bowl of fresh blueberries and strawberries, her diamond-and-emerald tennis bracelet tinkling against the side of the cut-glass bowl. "You really should think about becoming a chef." She spooned fruit onto her plate. "It would be more rewarding than working in a call center. Not only from a career satisfaction point of view, but also monetarily. Good chefs are worth their weight in gold."

What? I have two mothers now? I don't think so.

"Thanks, Iz. You're not the first person to suggest that. But I'll tell you the same thing I tell them." I smiled to soften the sting. "I don't want to cook for money. If I do, then it becomes work and not a joy. I'm happy simply cooking at home and for my friends."

Besides, if I became a chef, I wouldn't be home evenings to keep an eye on our mother.

Mom reached for the pepper, but misjudged the distance and knocked over her still half-full glass of juice.

Isabel muttered an oath and jumped up as the orange juice spattered her expensive white pants.

"I'm sorry, honey. I've gotten so clumsy lately." Patches of red mottled Mom's cheeks and she tried ineffectually to mop up the juice with her napkin, but wound up knocking over the pepper shaker in the process.

I could see the tears of frustration pooling in her legally blind eyes. "It's okay. Don't worry about it, Mom. I've got it." I added my napkin to the mix and went to get some paper towels to blot up the rest of the spill. I righted the pepper shaker and the juice glass upon my return and glanced at my sister, who still stood there scowling. "Iz, if you go put some cold water on that right away, it should come out, no problem. And if not, we've got one of those stain pens that will definitely do the trick."

The cold water worked and there was no harm, no foul. Or at least I didn't think so at the time.

Mom and Iz visited in the living room while I cleared the table and loaded the dishwasher. I could hear my sister telling Mom something about her latest work project as I approached. My mother was making encouraging mmm sounds even though I knew she had no idea what Isabel was talking about. To her, it was all blah, blah, blah. To me, too. My investment broker sister was way over our paltry savings account heads. Investment-speak was not our native language.

I rejoined them and pasted on a bright smile. "So what's on the agenda for today?"

Isabel shot a quick look at Mom's hot pink floral housecoat that snapped down the front. "Well, I thought a little shopping would be nice. I saw some beautiful pantsuits in the Nordstrom in Chicago that I think would look wonderful on you, Mom, but I wasn't sure of your size. I thought I'd wait until I got here so you could try them on. We could go to the mall and check out a couple other stores too."

"The mall?" Mom sent me a desperate look.

"Iz, Mom kind of has a hard time moving around these

days. Even using her walker, her legs hurt and she gets really tired if she walks too far."

"Okay. Not a problem. We'll forget the other stores and only go to Nordstrom."

"Oh, but Nordstrom's so expensive, honey. Why don't we just go to K-Mart or Wal-Mart? That's where I get most of my clothes."

Isabel's glossy red lips tightened. "Those stores are fine, Mom, but I really wanted to get you something nice for church and there was this one pale pink pantsuit in particular that I thought would look really nice on you."

"Pink?"

Score one for the Izmeister.

Isabel continued. "Afterwards, I thought we could have a light lunch and then," she paused for effect, "I'm going to treat us all to an afternoon at the spa where we'll be pampered with a nice relaxing massage followed by a manicure and pedicure." She leaned back in my wingback in her crisp red sleeveless blouse, white pants, and Italian red slingbacks and smiled, obviously pleased by her largesse.

I hated to pop her bubble. Or did I?

"Iz, I'm afraid Mom can't have pedicures, not with her diabetes and circulation problems. It would be way too easy to get an infection."

Her smile faded. "Oh. I didn't know that. Well, what about a manicure?"

"If the manicurist is qualified and knows not to push back the cuticles or to cut the nails too close. But it's still a bit risky. Probably just having her nails gently filed and polished would be the safest bet."

"Or maybe we should stick to just a massage," Isabel said.

Mom cleared her throat. "Honey? Don't you have to take off your clothes for that?"

"That's the general idea."

She blanched. "I could never be naked in front of strangers."

"A certified massage therapist is a professional, Mother. They're used to seeing naked bodies all day long."

"Not this naked body. The only person who's ever seen it is your father and my doctor, and I plan to keep it that way until I die." She grinned. "Then I won't care."

"The massage therapist is just like a doctor. Think of him as a doctor of aching pains and muscles."

"*Him*? A man?" Mom pursed her lips and sent a scandalized look to her firstborn. "You don't let a *man* give you a massage, do you?"

"Sure. Why not?"

"Because you don't have any clothes on!" She harrumphed. "What does your husband think about that?"

I settled back to enjoy the show. This was really getting fun.

"He thinks Peter's great. David sees him too. Once a month for a deep-tissue massage. It really helps his back and is a great stress reducer."

"Well I never."

"It's not a big deal, Mom. Everyone goes to massage therapists these days."

Yeah, right. Everyone who can afford it.

"Besides, you're covered with sheets. You're not lying there fully exposed for the whole world to see. You're in a private room with the door shut and the therapist adjusts the sheets as he, or *she*, works on different parts of your body," Isabel continued. "What do you say? It would really make you feel good and would probably even help your legs feel better too." She smiled. "And we can make sure you get a woman too. Okay?"

"Well," Mom said uncertainly. "I guess ..."

“Good. That’s settled then.” Isabel turned to me with a crooked grin. “I suppose you want a female massage therapist too?”

“Actually, Iz, thanks a lot for the offer. That’s very generous of you, but I’m going to have to pass.”

“What? Why?” She rolled her eyes. “And please don’t say you have some religious objection to the whole thing.”

“No. Not at all. In fact, some of my best friends get massages and they still take Communion.”

“Funny. So what’s the problem then?”

“No problem. I just think that you and Mom should have a mother-daughter day together since you’re going back home tomorrow. The two of you don’t get to see each other very often and Mom and I see each other all the time.”

I gave my sister a level look.

Mom’s face lit up like one of those spotlights announcing a grand opening at a strip mall. “Really? I don’t remember the last time you and I spent time together just the two of us, Isabel.”

I do.

The eighth-grade mother-daughter banquet where Mom sewed matching pink crepe dresses with sweetheart necklines and puffed sleeves for the two of them to wear. Afterwards, Isabel came home, threw herself on her lower bunk, and said Mom looked like a big pink elephant and all the girls in her class would probably start calling her a baby pink elephant now.

I could see by her eyes that Isabel remembered too.

It was right after that banquet when my sister began throwing herself into her studying and a plethora of after-school activities that kept her away from home most of the time.

“What a good idea, Paige,” Isabel said in her clipped, professional, I’m-going-to-kill-you-later voice. “But what about you? What will you be doing while we're off getting pampered and beautiful? I hate to think of you stuck here alone like Cinderella while we go to the ball." She smiled to show she was teasing, but the smile didn't quite reach her eyes.

"Oh, don't worry about me. I've got plenty to do. I might wash my car or go see one of my friends, or even catch up on some of my reading."

Mom sent a conspiratorial smile to her firstborn. "You remember what a big reader your sister's always been. She's even in a book club now, and she and her friends do all these wild and crazy things together. Why, did you know that she went up for a ride in a *hot air balloon*?"

"No I didn't." She gave me a thoughtful look and for a second I saw something else in her eyes.

What was it? A flicker of admiration?

Couldn't be. Isabel had never admired me for anything.

Ten minutes later I stood in the driveway and waved as they backed into the street in my sister's rental car. A Lexus, of course. "Bye. Have a good time. See you later."

Alone at last.

Living with Mom, I never got the chance to be alone anymore. She was always there. Occasionally Frieda drove her to the store or to the pharmacist's to pick up a prescription, but that was always during the day when I was at work. When I got home every night, there she was. Every day. Always. Like pop-up ads on the Internet.

Reveling in the unexpected solitude, I decided to use it to catch up on my reading. Since it was a warm, sunny day, I took my paperback out to the back patio and settled into the white wicker rocker for a nice, long, leisurely read.

Except the new romantic comedy that the back cover blurbs called "hilarious" didn't hold my interest. And wasn't even funny. The writer was trying way too hard.

I shut the book and decided to take a walk around the neighborhood instead. Maybe I'd even drop by Golden Daffodils to say hi and see if Marc had time to give me the next class in my flower education.

13

> We are all travelers in the wilderness of this world, and the best we can find in our travels is an honest friend.
>
> *Robert Louis Stevenson*

I pushed open the door of the flower shop and entered chaos.

Overhead, a twangy country voice was belting out the seventies' chestnut, "I Never Promised You a Rose Garden" while from the back, Marc's voice thundered over the music. "Did you find someone?"

"Not yet," Annie yelled, her head turned toward the back room and a phone clutched against her yellow T-shirt that read *Watch out or I'll use my opera voice.* "Still trying. And could you please lose the country twang-fest so they can hear me?"

The music softened by several decibels.

"Thank you!" Annie's head snapped back to the front and she punched in a phone number. When she finished dialing, she looked up. Seeing me, she gave me a quick smile and held up her index finger in a just-a-minute gesture while she spoke into the phone. "Suze? Hey, it's Annie. What's goin' on?" Her face fell. "Oh. Sounds fun. Don't suppose you'd like to blow it off and earn fifty bucks instead? Toby's sick and we're desperate." She listened to the voice on the other end. "No, that's okay, I understand. Don't worry about it. I'll find someone else. Have fun." She hung up the phone and blew out a large puff of air.

"Sounds like you guys are having a bad day."

"You can say that again. My brother, our delivery driver, is sicker than a dog and we're absolutely slammed. We've got four funerals and a wedding, a couple birthdays, and some assorted congratulations all to deliver before the end of the day."

"Don't you have a back-up driver?"

"That would be my mom." She shoved her hand through her platinum spikes. "And she's at the ER with Toby. She thinks it might be pneumonia or something."

"I'm sorry." I touched her arm. "Do you need to go to the hospital?"

Annie shook her head. "You know how ER's are. I was there for nearly three hours this morning just hangin' out in the waiting room. Couldn't do anything there, so I decided to come to work and keep busy. Mom'll call me once they see the doctor." She scrolled through her contacts on her cell. "Now I'm just trying to find someone to—"

"Any luck?" Marc called from the back.

"Nope. Still trying."

He hurried out front. "We might have to clos—Paige, hi. Sorry, I didn't know you were here."

"That's okay. I know you guys are busy and stressed."

Should I?

What? Offer to help? You're directionally impaired. Remember? And you don't even have a GPS system. You'd get totally lost.

I know. But they're really in a jam. The least I can do is offer.

You sure you want to do this? You might really screw it up. Take the wrong flowers to the wrong house or whatever.

Oh, put a sock in it.

I took a deep breath. "Can I help?"

"Really?" Marc's face lit up. Annie's, too. "Can you drive a stick?"

"I learned to drive in a VW bug."

Marc lifted his eyes heavenward. "Thank you, God!" Then he threw his arms around me and clasped me in a bear hug. "And thank *you*. You're a lifesaver."

His arms were strong, his chest solid, and his beard soft. It tickled my cheek. I wonder what would it be like to kiss a man with a beard?

Stop it.

I pushed that thought and myself away from Marc's strong, friendly-like-a-brother arms and released a nervous titter that sounded more like a snort. "I'm not sure how much of a lifesaver you'll think I am when I tell you that I'm really lousy with directions and have a tendency to get lost."

"No problem," he said. "We've got a Thomas Guide of the entire city and surrounding areas in the van. No way can you get lost with that."

Wanna bet?

"Seriously. My powers of disorientation are pretty astounding."

Annie threw me a reassuring smile. "If you have any problems, just call and we'll talk you through it. We've done that in the past. No prob."

Marc glanced at his watch. "I hate to rush you, but our first funeral begins in a little over an hour and we have to be there with the flowers an hour in advance. Come on back. We need to get you loaded up and start moving."

I followed him to the familiar back room that today was

bursting with more flower arrangements than I'd ever seen, with another one in progress on his work table. He led me over to a small wreath of white roses with a pale peach ribbon diagonally affixed to it that read "Sweet Sister," a large spray of peach and white roses with baby's breath and white carnations bearing a larger ribbon that read "Our Angel," and a white wicker basket exploding with white lilies and roses and a single peach rose in the center. That ribbon read "Beloved Granddaughter."

My eyes filled and I whispered. "Are these for a little girl?"

He nodded somberly. "Christina Jacobs. Six years old. Ran out in the street and got hit by a car. Killed instantly."

A tear slipped out. "How heartbreaking. Her poor family. They must be shattered."

Marc nodded again. Then he murmured something and I realized he was praying. " ... please be with little Christina's family as they mourn the loss of their beloved daughter ... sister ... granddaughter. Give them the comfort only you can provide."

I wiped my face and saw that Marc was wiping his as well.

"We'd better get moving." He carefully lifted the large funeral spray and had me follow him to the van with the basket and the small wreath of roses. "Could you open the door for me, please?" he asked, nodding to the back of the van. "It's unlocked."

When I swung open the door I saw that the inside of the van was lined with thick, rectangular pieces of foam rubber with cut-outs. Marc explained that they kept vases and baskets from sliding or falling over while the van was moving. He carefully laid the spray of peach and white flowers that would be draped over little Christina's casket on the top of one side of the foam rubber. Then he relieved me of the basket of flowers and stuck it securely into one of the foam cut-outs on the other side. Finally, he laid the small wreath of roses next to the basket. Then he pulled out the Thomas Guide from the driver's side pocket and started describing the best way to get to the funeral home.

My absolute cluelessness and total fear must have shown on my face.

"Let's go inside and I'll highlight the route for you real quick," he said. "Don't worry. It's a piece of cake."

Yeah, right.

While Marc was highlighting the streets in yellow, Annie came back and walked over to examine the wide shelf of flowers waiting to be delivered. She picked up a cobalt blue vase bursting with yellow roses and carried it over to Marc's work station. "Did you forget something, boss-man?"

He looked up, distracted. "No."

"I think you did." She read aloud the address on the card. "This birthday bouquet for Sarah Ireland is less than five blocks from the funeral home. What? You were going to make Paige come all the way back here to get it?"

"See, Paige?" Marc grinned. "Told you Annie's my right-hand. She keeps me in check."

"Somebody has to." Annie turned to me. "If you give me your cell, I'll program our number in. That way if you have any problems—not that you will," she sent me a wink over Marc's once-again bent head, "you can just call and the cavalry will come running."

"Thanks." I handed her my phone. "And prepare yourself for a few calls."

"All set." Marc handed me the highlighted map and went over the directions. "When you get to the funeral home, pull in the first driveway which will take you around back where you can unload. The flower room is the first one inside. All you have to do is set the flowers on the table, sign the clipboard hanging by the door, and they'll go ahead and arrange them for the service. Got it?"

"Got it." I hope.

Annie returned my cell and Marc glanced at my new white, lace-edged T-shirt and frowned. "I'd hate to see that pretty shirt get ruined. Some of this greenery can really stain and the pods inside the lilies are notorious for stains that don't come out." He removed a pale yellow short-sleeved oxford-style shirt from a hook on the wall with a Golden Daffodils logo over the pocket and handed it to me. "Why don't you put this on?"

"Thanks. Now I'm official."

Marc handed me the delivery sheets for each order and the keys to the van. "No, now you're official. Go get 'em, tiger!"

"And call right away if you have any problems," Annie said. "Any at all."

You bet I will. Just keep those phone lines open.

I hurried to the van, clutching my map. As I buckled my seat belt and turned the ignition, I threw up a quick prayer. *Please help me not to get lost and not to be late. Especially to little Christina's funeral.*

I should have been praying every time I got into my car.

I made it all the way to the funeral home without a hiccup. Well, one tiny one. Three blocks from the mortuary, I couldn't make a left turn where Marc had indicated on the map because the street was closed for construction. So I just went down another block and turned left there.

And I did it without calling Annie. Yes!

After the funeral home, I zipped the yellow roses over to the nearby birthday girl's house. I rapped on the raspberry red front door of a cute blue cottage. Moments later the door was opened by a pretty teen with long, curly auburn hair, gorgeous eyes the color of blueberries, and a smattering of freckles across her upturned nose.

"I have a delivery for Sarah Ireland?"

Her hand flew to her mouth. "That's me."

"Happy Birthday." I extended the vase of roses to her.

"Oh my gosh. Oh my gosh." Her hands shook as she took the cobalt blue vase so I kept mine on it so she wouldn't drop it. "I've never gotten flowers before. And roses ... yellow ... my favorite. Wow." Her eyes grew wet and her mouth split into a dazzling grin. "Mom!"

A tall, robust woman with short curly hair the same color as her daughter's hurried to the door. "What is it?" Then she saw the flowers and her mouth split into a similar grin of delight. "Who are they from?"

"I don't know."

"Want me to hold the flowers so you can open the card?" I asked.

"Would you?"

"Sure. It's all part of the service." I didn't know whether it was or not, but I was dying to know myself and I figured another minute couldn't hurt.

Sarah read the card aloud. *To my little girl on her sweet sixteenth. I'm so proud of you. You're growing up into a beautiful young woman. Just remember, though, you'll always be my little girl. Love, Daddy.*

Three sets of feminine eyes leaked salt on that one.

This delivering flowers stuff was fun. You rang the doorbell and when people answered, you got to give them a bouquet of beauty and see their eyes light up. Or spill out happy tears. How cool was that?

I delivered the next three funerals—two were at the same mortuary, which helped—and another birthday and only had to call in for help once. Then Marc said it was time for the wedding, a few miles away at a small, nondenominational church.

He helped me load the back of the van with the bouquets, boutonnieres, corsages, and two trailing flower arrangements which he said would flank the altar in stands provided by the church. The final thing Marc nestled carefully in the foam was the bride's bouquet—a nosegay packed tightly with a profusion of rich red roses with something sparkling in the center of each bloom.

"Wow. That's absolutely beautiful. What's the sparkle?"

"A rhinestone pin."

"It's so elegant. It really makes the flowers pop."

"Thanks. I think so too." He smiled and shut the back door of the van. "Okay, we ready to roll?"

"We?"

"Not that I don't have confidence in your delivery abilities. You've done a great job today, which I really appreciate, but have you ever set up flowers at a wedding before, or pinned on corsages and boutonnieres?"

Uh, no.

Way to go, Sherlock.

We climbed into the van, buckled up, and I started the engine. "But it can't be all that hard." I made my eyes all wide and innocent. "The corsages go on the guys and those boutonniere thingies go on the mothers of the bride and groom, right?"

"Close." He gave me an impish grin which made his eyes crinkle. Not that I noticed. "The main thing you want to remember is not to draw blood when you pin on the flowers. Some of those mothers-in-law can get pretty testy."

"I'm sure the mothers aren't a day in the park either." My hands clenched on the steering wheel as I thought back to my own wedding and how my mom ran roughshod over the whole thing and wound up reducing the wedding coordinator and one of my bridesmaids to tears.

"Have you ever been married, Paige?"

Here it comes. Now I'm going to have to break out in the Tammy Wynette D-I-V-O-R-C-E song which automatically makes me suspect in most Christian circles. Especially when they find out there were no *biblical* grounds for the divorce—no one committed adultery. I'd been down this road before as well-meaning church members clucked in sympathy over my divorced status. "I'm so sorry, sweetie. Was it another woman?"

No. The only other woman in my marriage had been my mother.

And she destroyed it more effectively than any affair ever could have.

"Paige?"

"Sorry."

"No, I'm sorry. I didn't mean to pry. Obviously it's a sensitive subject. Forget I said anything."

"What makes you think it's a sensitive subject?"

He pointed to my hands still clenching the steering wheel in a death grip.

"Oh." I relaxed my grip but there was no time to say more since I'd just pulled into the church parking lot and Marc was directing me where to park.

As we started to unload the flowers, he said, "You don't have to come in if it's too hard for you."

"If what's too hard for me?"

"Weddings."

"Oh, I don't have a problem with weddings. It's divorces I'm not crazy about."

On our drive back to the shop after Marc had finished

pinning on each boutonniere and corsage, he didn't bring up the *D* word again. Instead we talked about mothers.

"I loved my mother dearly," Marc said, "but she sometimes drove me crazy. At one point I thought of starting a group called Mom-Anon. *Hello. My name is Marc and I'm a Momaholic.*"

"Ooh. Where do I go to sign up?"

He chuckled. "My mom always wanted to know every aspect of my life. And she was the quintessential matchmaking Italian mother always trying to set me up with someone. Finally I had to draw some boundaries. But it was a good thing. By the time she passed, we had a really great, healthy relationship."

"Got any pencils left in that boundary drawing box?"

When we returned to Golden Daffodils Annie shared the good news that her brother was home from the hospital with a bad case of the flu. "Mom gave him some Tylenol and chicken noodle soup and then he crashed. Doc said he should be better in a few days." She grinned at Marc. "And Toby said to tell you not to give away his job while he's down for the count."

"Well ... I don't know. Paige here is doing a pretty good job and she looks way better in that work shirt than he ever did." Marc winked at me.

That wink told me he was teasing Annie, not flirting with me.

"Yeah. I'm not sure I'll be able to give this shirt up. I've gotten pretty attached to it."

"I wouldn't get too attached. My brother has some serious dandruff issues."

I looked askance at my shoulders.

"Gotcha." She smirked. "Don't worry. The shirt's been washed since he last wore it." She consulted a sheet of paper. "Only three more deliveries and then you're done: another birthday and two congratulations. Just be sure and remember to have them sign the delivery form. Otherwise, they can say they never got the flowers. And then we're out both flowers and money."

"Okay. Sorry." I'd forgotten on the first couple deliveries.

"Don't worry about it." She flicked her hand in a dismissive gesture. "When Toby first started, it took him several deliveries to get it right. Right, boss-man?"

"Right." Marc grimaced. "And a couple hundred bucks."

I tucked the clipboard under my arm and picked up a vase of mixed daisies and carnations in one hand and another, larger vase of Stargazer lilies, in the other, holding them against my front for balance.

"Here, let me help you." Marc hurried over and relieved me of the heavy lily vase. But as he did so, his hand got caught in my open work shirt. As he tried to untangle himself, his hand accidentally grazed my chest.

The exposed flesh above his beard immediately matched the color of the lilies. "Sorry." He yanked his hand away and in his haste, one of the lilies brushed against my white T-shirt leaving a dusty yellow streak in its wake.

Marc apologized again as we walked to the van. "Try some Simple Green on that in the laundry, and if it doesn't come out, let me know and I'll buy you a new shirt."

"It's not a big deal. Don't worry about it. I only paid ten bucks for it. No biggie."

We loaded the two vases into the back of the van and returned for the final arrangement. I stared at the massive, happy bouquet of yellow.

"Daffodils? I thought they were spring flowers."

"Very good. Pat yourself on the back," Marc said. "You get an A in Flowers 101."

"But how did you get daffodils in June?"

"Love can open a lot of doors."

"Yeah," Annie said. "Especially when that love is backed up with big bucks."

"Explain, please."

"A new customer contacted me several months ago when he saw the name of my shop in the Yellow Pages," Marc said. "Told me his wife's favorite flowers were daffodils and that she'd be celebrating a major milestone in early June and he wanted to send her *a host of golden daffodils* to mark the occasion—even though he knew daffodil season would be over. Said he was willing to pay whatever it took to make it happen."

"Now that's what I call love." I looked again at the huge vase brimming with sunny daffs. "So how'd you do it?"

"It's a very complicated process that includes a secret alliance with an underground grower in Holland, a startling time change where the sun only nourishes the plant for two hours every other day—except for Sundays—and a cruel plot for world domination. Bwahahahaha."

I punched his arm. "You're not going to tell me, are you?"

"Well, part of that is true. But it is quite a complicated process and if I told you all of it, I'd have to kill you." He winked. "A master craftsman never gives away his secrets."

Annie rolled her eyes.

I delivered the smaller bouquets first and saved the mass of golden daffs for my final delivery to one of Sacramento's most prestigious neighborhoods known as the "Fab Forties." There, stately, older, million-dollar-plus custom homes on large lots filled canopied tree-lined streets named after numbers in the forties. I didn't need the Thomas Brothers to get me around the Fab Forties. When I was little, my parents used to take us on occasional Sunday drives through the upscale neighborhood with a European flair where Ronald and Nancy Reagan lived when he was governor. There we'd pick out the spacious, elegant, one-of-a-kind houses we'd like to live in if we ever struck it rich. Dad would drive slowly up and down the wide streets where two-story Colonials mingled with Spanish stucco, and Dutch farmhouses nestled among English Tudors and large Craftsman bungalows, pretending we belonged.

Christmas was a special treat when all the houses were lit up in their sparkling holiday finery. I still drove through the neighborhood every Christmas season to enjoy the lights and the beautiful homes.

Homes I knew I could never afford. But it was still fun to pretend.

I checked the address on my clipboard and pulled up in front of a red brick, two-story English-style "cottage" with rosebushes out front and gaily colored flowers edging the curved walkway.

Grunting under the weight of the massive bouquet, I lifted it out of the van and carefully made my way up the flagstone walk to the arched wooden Hobbit-style door.

I rang the doorbell and moments later I heard it open, followed by a gasp. I couldn't see anything except a pair of bare feet with pink polished toes and a silver toe ring.

"Phoebe Spencer?"

"In the flesh. The very large flesh at the moment. I can't believe he did this! Where in the world did he find daffodils this time of year?"

"It's a trade secret." I shifted the heavy vase in my arms. "Okay if I give you these now?"

"Oh, I'm sorry. Actually, I'm not supposed to lift anything heavy. Do you mind bringing them in and setting them on the hall table?"

"No problem." I shifted the vase again. "If you can just guide me in, though. I can't see too well."

"Of course. Duh. Here, I'll hold onto the front of the vase," she said. "Just come straight in. There's no step or anything."

I glimpsed gleaming hardwood floor beneath the pink-polished toes and slowly inched across it.

"Good. Just a couple more steps and you're there." The polished legs of a small cherry wood table appeared in my limited vision.

"Okay, stop," she said. "Just hang on a sec while I get something to put under the vase." I heard a drawer open, some rustling, and then close again. "All right, you can set it down now. Thanks."

Slowly I lowered the vase onto a lace doily atop a small round table.

"Thank you *so* much. I really appreciate it."

At last I saw that the bare feet with the toe ring and polished toes were attached to a very pregnant woman in denim shorts and a T-shirt whose dark hair was pulled back into a ponytail. She stuck out her hand and smiled. "I'm Phoebe."

"Paige. Nice to meet you."

"Thanks for making my day, Paige." She swiveled her head to the voluminous display of daffs. "I still can't believe he did this!" She snatched up the card and tore it open, murmuring the words aloud: *Congratulations on the birth of your first baby. I'm so proud of you and know it was a difficult labor. I pray your second delivery goes much smoother. Here's lookin' at you, kid. All my love always, Alex.*

"You just had a baby?" I looked down at her enormous stomach stretching her tee tight that looked like it was about to pop at any second.

"Of a sort. My first book was just published."

"Congratulations! How exciting. What's it called?"

"As Time Goes By: How Casablanca *Got Me the Love of My Life and Other Stories."*

"I love *Casablanca*. I'm a big old movie buff."

"Me too." She grinned. "So's my husband. In fact, I need to call that sweet man right now and thank him for these amazing flowers. Thanks again for bringing them inside for me."

"No problem. And congratulations again." I glanced at her medicine ball stomach and smiled. "On *both* babies."

As I drove away I found myself humming "As Time Goes By."

14

> Mary flew into a fine passion. She could fly into a passion without making a noise. She just grew sour and obstinate and did not care what happened.
>
> *The Secret Garden*

"Where have you been?" Mom glared at me as I walked through the back door. "And where's dinner?"

"Dinner?"

"Yes. You know I like to eat early on the weekends. Here it's already after 5 and there's nothing in the oven."

"I just walked in the door, Mom. I've been working all day."

"Working? You never said you had to work today."

I cut a glance at my sister. "I told Isabel when she called earlier that I was helping out a friend and I didn't know exactly when I'd be home. We were working so hard, I lost track of time. I'm sorry. I guess I just assumed the two of you would grab a bite."

"Sorry, Paige." Isabel looked like she really meant it. "I

asked Mom if she'd like to get something to eat, but she said you'd be making dinner."

"You always make dinner." Mom fixed me with a baleful stare. "And with your only sister out here all the way from Chicago I was sure you had something really special planned for tonight."

No. That was this morning when I made the crepes. I thought that was special. Guess not.

Isabel looked at me expectantly. I knew what she was waiting for. She wanted to see if I'd explode under the impact of Mom's guilt grenade. But I've never been an exploder. That's my sister's territory. I'm more of a stuffer. And Isabel knew that.

"Mom, what's your favorite restaurant?" she asked all of a sudden.

"What?"

"What's your favorite place to eat?" Isabel glanced at her watch. "It's only 5:13 on a Saturday night. Most restaurants don't really start to get busy until after 6. I know you're hungry, so if it's not too far away and we hurry, we could get in soon and beat the dinner crowd. What do you say?"

"Well ..." Mom looked uncertainly from my sister to me, and then back again to Isabel. "I really like Outback. They have steak *and* seafood. And I might have a coupon for them too." She closed her eyes and licked her lips. "I love their crab legs."

Like mother, like daughter.

But I could tell from my sister's expression that a chain restaurant wasn't exactly what she'd had in mind. She and her high-rise husband probably never deigned to set foot in them. And it was a good bet they sure didn't use coupons. Yet through a supreme force of will, she didn't wrinkle her nose in disdain. Just swallowed. I saw.

"Okay. Outback it is." Isabel aimed a look at me. "Is there one nearby?"

"Yep. Less than a mile away."

Her clear gray eyes skimmed over me, taking in my stained T-shirt and shorts spattered with water and flecked with green. "How soon can you be ready?"

"Give me ten minutes and I'm yours."

Nine minutes later I rejoined my mother and sister clad in fresh khaki capris and a dressy black T-shirt, the ends of my hair still slightly damp from the shower.

Isabel sent me an appraising gaze. "I'm impressed. David would be too. He's always telling me I take too long to get ready." Her eyes flicked to my face. "But then again, you've never been much for makeup, have you?"

"Oh, your sister hardly ever bothers with makeup unless it's a special occasion." Mom released a long-suffering sigh. "I try and tell her that if she put on even just a little each day, she'd probably get a lot *more* special occasions. A man always appreciates a woman who makes a little effort." She patted her face and I noticed her cotton-candy-pink nails.

"Paige, you didn't say one word about *my* makeup. What do you think?" She twisted her head my direction, preening. "Isabel took me to the cosmetics counter where this nice girl introduced me to this new foundation and lipstick. She said pink was definitely my color. Your father always said that too."

"You look very nice, Mom. Very pretty. Dad would love that pink lipstick."

She giggled. "Your father always liked the look of my lipstick, but he sure didn't like the taste."

Isabel grimaced, but Mom didn't see. "We'd better get a move on if we want to beat the dinner rush."

"But I haven't even shown your sister my beautiful new outfits yet."

"You can show them to her after dinner." Isabel steered Mom to her walker. "You want to be sure the restaurant doesn't run out of crab, don't you?"

Mom moved faster than she had in years.

When we arrived at Outback, she announced to the hostess in a jolly voice, "Now make sure you give us a table, honey. No way can I squeeze this big old body into one of those tight booths."

Isabel's lips tightened. And they tightened even more when two anorexic teens sent Mom a disgusted glance as she lumbered past in her walker. I wanted to slap them silly and tell them to bulk up on some potatoes, but I settled for giving them a dirty look.

Mom got her crab and a small steak, but I suggested she skip the potato in favor of steamed vegetables. When her meal arrived, she couldn't see well enough to remove the shell from her crab legs so I had to do it for her. I also had to cut her steak. But I didn't mind.

Actually, I preferred helping. They didn't provide metal crackers for customers to use because they'd already sliced a thin crack down the center of each crab leg in the kitchen. It was up to the customer to break the shell and pull it apart, which can get tricky. Those shells are sharp and slippery and I've nicked my fingers on them in the past, drawing blood. No way was I going to let that happen to my diabetic mother.

As Isabel watched me cut up Mom's food, she attacked her chopped salad with vigor. The conversation became strained as my sister and I attempted to make small talk.

"Paige?"

I looked up to see Marc standing by our table, a pretty brunette at his side.

Very pretty. And a different girl than the one who had come looking for him at the flower shop.

"Hi," I said.

"Is this your mom and sister?"

I nodded. "Mom, Isabel, this is my friend Marc. Marc, this is my mother, Catherine, and my sister, Isabel."

He gave them a winning smile. "Nice to meet you." Then he lightly touched Mom's hand. "It's great to meet you in person at last, Catherine. Thank you again for those lovely vintage vases you donated to the shop. That was so thoughtful."

Mom beamed up at him. "You're welcome. I'm glad they found a good home."

"Me too. And thanks for loaning us Paige today too—she was a real lifesaver. We'd never have made it without her help."

"Oh, is this the fill-in delivery driver you were telling me about?" the brunette asked, moving closer to him, her gold bangles jingling on her tanned, sculpted arms.

"I'm sorry." A flicker of embarrassment crossed Marc's face. "Vanessa, this is my friend Paige and her family. Paige, this is Vanessa."

"Hi," I said.

"Hello. Marc was telling me on the way over here how frantic he was this morning without his regular driver and how you saved the day."

"I just happened to be at the right place at the right time."

"And I'm really glad you were," Marc said. He smiled at Mom again. "Your daughter was a huge help."

She beamed up at him. "Paige has always been really helpful."

Vanessa tugged at Marc's arm and said, "I'm thirsty."

They said their good-byes and moved on to their table.

"Well someone certainly felt threatened," Isabel said.

My mother patted my hand. "Don't you worry, honey.

She may be prettier than you, but you're much nicer and that's more important."

I bit back the sharp retort that rose to my lips. "Marc's just a friend, Mom." Yet I did hope my friend would find someone less witchy and possessive.

By the time we got home from the restaurant, Mom was seriously drooping and ready for bed. Yet she insisted on showing me her new clothes first.

I uttered the appropriate oohs and aahs at the pale pink pantsuit, ivory blouse, and silk fuchsia caftan. Isabel had even sprung for a pair of gold and pearl clip-on earrings that Mom loved. "I've never had real pearl earrings before," she said. "I'll have to save these for a special occasion."

Mr. Spitz was enamored with the gleaming earrings too. He nosed his gray head beneath Mom's arm and swatted at the box with his paw.

"No, no baby," she said. "That's not for you. Be a good boy now."

I lifted Mr. Spitz from her lap and carried him to his water bowl in the kitchen. Then I made sure Mom took her meds, helped her into her favorite nightgown—she had trouble with the buttons—and got her into bed. I kissed her on the forehead. "Night, Mom. Sleep well."

"Night, honey," she mumbled, nearly asleep already. "Thanks again for taking me shopping."

Isabel was waiting for me in the kitchen, drinking a cup of decaf coffee at the table, her feet slipped out of her shoes. "What a day," she said. "I don't know how you do it. Is she asleep?"

"Out like a light. This was a long day for her. She doesn't usually do that much. She'll probably want to go to the later service tomorrow." I poured some coffee and looked at my sister over the rim of my cup. "Thanks for spending the day with her, Iz. It really meant a lot to her."

And to me. I had to admit it was nice to have a break.

Isabel frowned. "I had no idea Mom had gotten this bad."

"What do you mean? She's not that bad."

My sister raised incredulous eyes over her cup. "As compared to what? Her vision has really deteriorated. I had to hold things right in front of her eyes in the store for her to even see them. And she moves so slowly! It took forever for her to walk from one place to another." Her nails drummed a staccato beat on the table. "I don't know how you stand it. She gets confused too. She called me Paige several times."

"She did?"

Maybe I'm not the unnoticed daughter after all.

"Yes. And she kept wanting to stop for sweets and when I wouldn't, she got mad and walked even slower. She's like a petulant child." Isabel began rummaging through her purse. "I really think it's time for assisted living or maybe a nursing home." She pulled out some slick tri-fold brochures and passed them to me. "David and I investigated some options and I thought maybe you and I could visit a couple tomorrow before I leave. Two of them have open houses—one at 11, the other at 1. That would give me enough time to do a quick walk through both before I need to head to the airport."

I stared at her. "Are you nuts? Or just completely clueless? Why do you think I moved back in here in the first place? The whole point was so she wouldn't have to go to one of those places. By living here I can keep an eye on her."

"But what about when you're at work? Or in Paris? Or off in a hot air balloon somewhere?" She fixed me with a level gaze. "I'm not saying you shouldn't do these things. In fact, I'm thrilled that you're finally getting out there and having these kinds of experiences. It's called living life and broadening your horizons. And how can you do that if you're tied to Mom all the time? It's not fair to you."

Fair to me? Since when did you care about what's fair to me?

"And what about what's fair to Mom? Is it fair to make her leave her home? Fair to go behind her back and scope out nursing homes on her behalf? Fair to decide without even asking her that it's time to ship her off to the old folks home?" My voice trembled, but I got myself under control. "Mom's perfectly capable of making those decisions herself, Iz. She's in full control of her mental faculties."

Isabel lifted an eyebrow.

"Yes, she gets confused now and then, but nothing serious. That's just a part of aging. It's not like she has Alzheimer's or anything."

"How do you know? Have you had her tested? You're not a nurse, Paige, or even a medical professional." She gestured to the brochures. "And these places have nurses and trained caregivers 24/7 who know how to take care of older people who have problems like Mom. Besides, it would give you a break."

"I have a break. Once a week Mom goes out quilting with the mother of one of my book club friends."

Actually, that wasn't exactly true. Mom had gone quilting with Karen exactly twice. She said it was just too hard for her to do the six-inch blocks, even with the magnifying glass. "It's too awkward to use," she said. "Plus I feel like I'm slowing everyone else down when they have to stop and help me. No, my sewing days are definitely behind me. It's best if I just stay home."

The fact that her favorite reality show was on the same night as quilting had nothing to do with her decision.

Who did Isabel think she was anyway to come in and start saying what Mom's going to do and how she's going to live?

She's not the boss of us. We're doing perfectly fine without her interference. Besides, she forfeited her daughterly interest years ago.

But I wasn't going to say that. Instead, I'd just turn the other cheek.

"I couldn't go with you tomorrow, anyway, Iz. It's my week to help out with the toddlers in Sunday school. And don't forget, you said you'd come to church with us. As tired as Mom is, she'll probably want to go to the eleven o'clock service."

Isabel called in the morning and cancelled on church. Said she had too much to do before she had to catch her plane. Big surprise. Isabel always cancelled. She said she'd try and swing by the house to say good-bye on her way to the airport, but just in case, she'd say good-bye now on the phone.

I knew she wouldn't be back. A full day and night with our mother was way more mom-unit than my sister could handle.

Mom was crushed, but she tried not to show it. She'd already had her breakfast and was dressed and waiting for Isabel in her pretty new pink pantsuit, pearl earrings, and pink lipstick.

"You're really stylin', Mom. Just wait until Frieda and the ladies at church see your new outfit."

But she'd already removed her clip earrings and set them on the kitchen table. "Yesterday was such a long day, it really wore me out. I'm not used to that. I think I'd just better go back to bed."

"Are you sure? But you're already dressed and you look so pretty."

"No, honey. I just need to sleep."

"I can stay home with you if you like."

She gave me a tired smile. "No you can't. You're helping out with the toddlers this morning. I know how much you enjoy them. Don't worry about me. I'll be fine. I'm just going to take a nice nap."

Every once in a while Mom surprised me and showed her generous side. Like now. She gets that I need my kid-fix. Mom used to attend church regularly, but she'd fallen off since Dad died. Ever since I'd moved in though, she'd started coming at least two Sundays a month. But I knew when to push and when not to.

"Okay, thanks. You get some rest now." I kissed her on the forehead. "And tonight I'll make something special for dinner and then we can watch your show together."

Little Emily was on the warpath. "Want anuvver cookie," she said during snack time.

"You've already had two cookies, Emily. That's all you get this morning. You don't want to ruin your appetite for lunch."

She stuck out her lower lip and pouted. "Don' care 'bout aptite. Want anuvver cookie." She thrust her hand out to grab a chocolate-chip one from the plate in the center of the table, but I pushed it out of her reach.

"Emily, I said no. You've had enough."

She began to wail.

I had to refrain from taking her in my arms and soothing away her tears. Even though that's what I really wanted to do. Hug her little body close to mine and make comforting "There, there, it's going to be all right" noises.

Instead, I did the appropriate grown-up thing. "Somebody needs to go to time out." I stood up and held out my hand. "Come on."

She wailed even louder.

Michelle, the Sunday school teacher, caught my eye and gave me a sympathetic, but encouraging nod as I led Emily to the time-out corner.

"I think someone's tired."

"I not tiyud," Emily hiccupped between angry sobs.

"Well I am. I think I'll just sit over here and rest and be quiet for a moment. That always makes me feel better."

Her sobs slowly subsided. "I west too." A few minutes later, she snuggled up into my lap and sniffled. "Will you tell me a stowy?"

"Can you be a good girl now?"

She nodded her silky blonde head.

"Once upon a time in a land called Sacramento there lived a beautiful little girl named Emily who—"

Tyler came running up holding his nose and pointing to Rachel, one of the other little girls in the class. "Miss Paige, Miss Paige! She just pooped in her pants."

On my way out of the classroom, I ran into John and Linda Judson. John was the lay marriage-and-family counselor that Eric and I had gone to see when our marriage was falling apart and Linda was his nice, but slightly ditzy wife.

Eric had gone to exactly one counseling session—under direction from our pastor who said divorce wasn't what Jesus would want—but that was it. He'd already made his mind up that our marriage was over and nothing was going to stop him from moving on. And what can you do when someone stops loving you?

Not much. Other than pray.

I prayed constantly for God to change Eric's heart, to make him see that what he was doing was wrong and to preserve our marriage. But it didn't work. One day I was married, and the next, I wasn't. For Eric, it was as if our union had never happened. He moved on with his life, married Heather, and now they were going to have a baby together.

John gave me a big hug and Linda followed his lead. "Paige, we haven't seen you in ages," she said. "How are you?"

"Good. Everything's good."

She glanced at the toddlers' sign on the door I'd just come through and gave me an approving smile. "I'm so happy to see you're not letting Eric's new daddy status prevent you from still loving and working with the little ones."

I gripped my purse strap tightly. "They had the baby?"

Linda's hands flew to her mouth. "I'm sorry. I thought you knew."

John sent his wife a reproving glance, then squeezed my arm. "I'm sorry, Paige."

"Don't be. The birth of a baby isn't an occasion for sorrow, it's one of joy. Was it a boy or a girl?"

Linda sent her husband a helpless look, but kept mum this time.

"John?" I asked.

"A boy."

"Good. That's good. Now he's got his Eric Jr. It's what he always wanted." I tried to give an approximation of a bright I'm-happy-for-him smile, but I could tell I didn't pull it off by the sympathetic looks in John and Linda's eyes.

15

> Every man's life is a fairy tale written by God's fingers.
>
> *Hans Christian Andersen*

If my life were a fairy tale, I'd sure hate to see reality.

I logged in at work thirteen minutes late—after making sure Mom got up and had some breakfast. On my way to work I'd called Frieda and asked if she could pop by and spend a little time with Mom this morning since I knew she was still down in the dumps over the end of Isabel's visit.

By the time I took my mid-morning break, I'd already fielded thirty-seven calls—two were from Mom, so didn't count—and was feeling confident that I'd make my stats for the day.

For the first time in ages.

"How'd the weekend with the sister go?" Arthur asked as he poured a cup of coffee in the break room.

"Okay. Fine." I shook a packet of sweetener into my coffee.

"Well, not so fine. My sister isn't the most compassionate person."

"Why? What'd she do?"

"Which time? The time she freaked out because Mom accidentally spilled some juice and got her fancy designer pants wet? Or the time she reneged—yet again—on her promise to go to church with us and hurt my mother's feelings?" I ripped open a packet of fake cream. "Or the time she tried to talk me into putting Mom into a nursing home?" Upending the cream into my mug, I stirred furiously, causing hot coffee to splash onto my hand. "Ouch!"

"Here, let's put cold water on that," Arthur said, leading me over to the sink. "That'll take the sting out." He turned on the tap and stuck my hand under the cool stream. Then he fixed me with his kind, grandfatherly eyes. "Would a nursing home or assisted living be such a bad idea?"

I yanked my hand away. "Not you too. I'm not putting my mother into one of those places."

"They're not so bad. In fact, some of them are actually pretty nice."

"Yeah, and prison's not so bad either. I hear the inmates get to wear the latest designer orange jumpsuits."

"Good thing I'm not going to prison then. Orange isn't my best color." Arthur gave me a wry smile. "Actually, contrary to what you may have heard or read, there are some excellent places out there for seniors who need a little assistance. I've checked them out myself."

My heart skipped. "Why? Arthur, you're okay, aren't you?"

"I'm fine. Addie's fine. We just want to be prepared for the future," he said. "That's why years ago we took out a long-term care insurance policy. That way if the day ever comes when we can't take care of ourselves, we'll go into a nice assisted living facility instead—probably one with a nursing home option as well. We didn't want to leave our kids in the position of having to take care of us someday. That's a big burden."

"I don't see it as a burden. Families are supposed to take care of each other."

And besides, Jesus said to take care of the widows and orphans.

"But it sounds like you've been taking care of your mother for a long time," he said gently. "Didn't you say you started cooking in high school because your mom didn't?"

"Cooking's not one of her gifts."

"Was it one of your sister's?"

I snorted. "Yeah, right. Isabel's idea of making dinner is to dial for takeout."

"And what about your brother?"

"What about him?"

"Have you heard from him lately?"

"No. Not for a couple years now. He's dropped off the face of the earth."

"So basically, all the responsibility for your mom falls on your shoulders." Arthur patted my shoulder. "I know they're pretty strong shoulders, but even the strongest ones can crack under the strain. You need to take care of yourself too, remember. There are senior agencies that can help out. Or people from your church. You don't have to be the Lone Ranger, you know." His eyes twinkled. "Even the Lone Ranger had Tonto."

Hi ho, Silver, away! I'd love to get away somewhere. Anywhere.

I know. I can tell Isabel I've booked a non-refundable around-the-world cruise and she and David will have to come get Mom and have her stay with them for a month. Wouldn't that be rich?

So not gonna happen.

"Enough about me and my problems, Arthur. How was *your* weekend?"

"Great." His eyes lit up. "We had Samantha for the whole weekend while her parents went to Carmel for their wedding anniversary. That little girl gets more beautiful every day. Smart as a whip too. She told me yesterday that I was the best Grampy in the whole world."

"She *is* smart." Then I told him about Emily's acting up in Sunday school and how much I enjoyed telling her a story after time-out. Arthur gave me a thoughtful look. "You know, Paige, you'd make a really great mother ... Have you ever thought about adopting?"

"Right now I'm too busy being a mother to my mom to bring a child into the picture."

But back at my desk, Arthur's words made me think. I'd jettisoned the whole sperm bank idea, but I still wanted kids. Could I possibly adopt someday?

Adoption costs a lot of money. You're not rich like Angelina Jolie or Madonna.

No, and I don't have their puffy lips or rock hard abs either, but my puny lips and abs do the job they're supposed to.

I looked at the clock on my computer and realized I still had a couple minutes of break time left. I googled "adoption and single women." My screen filled. As I began reading, I was surprised to discover that adoptions by single parents had really jumped in the past two decades. And that single women tended to adopt internationally because the process was much faster and they could get younger children—American birth mothers usually chose to place their babies with couples rather than singles.

What really surprised me, however, was that more and more single women in their forties and fifties were adopting. And adoption agencies were welcoming these older moms with open arms because they were more settled and financially independent.

Not exactly your life.

Oh well. It was a pipe dream anyway. Besides, there's Mom to consider.

You mean the woman who's been saying for, I don't know, forever, *that she wants grandchildren?*

Grandchildren from her own flesh and blood. I'm not sure she's all that big on adoption.

So ask, already. What can it hurt?

The voice in my head sometimes sounded strangely like Barbra Streisand kvetching in one of my favorite old musicals, *Funny Girl.*

We'll see. Eventually. The timing's not right just now.

I coughed to dislodge a sudden tickle at the back of my throat and took a swig of water from the bottle I always kept at my desk. Those thirty-seven calls earlier must have really dried out my throat. Noticing the time, I put my headset back on and prepared for the next round of incoming.

Wonder if I should grill some nice fish for Mom tonight? We haven't had salmon in a while and next to crab, that's her favorite seafood ...

My phone rang. "Salmon Wireless, this is Paige. How can I help you?"

"*Salmon*?"

"Sorry. I mean Landon."

Maybe Eric was right. Maybe I am too wrapped up in my mother's life.

Maybe?

Okay, I am.

Just before lunch, Joe emailed me to say that he and his ex got back together and were going to try and work things out.

And then to add insult to injury, my supervisor called me into her office and fired me.

"I'm sorry, Paige," my supervisor, Sheila, said, "but we have to start making some cutbacks companywide, and when we went over the stats for each department, yours were the lowest. Nothing personal." Then she called security to come stand by my desk as I packed up my things. "Nothing personal," Sheila said again. "Company policy."

What? I'm going to steal call center secrets and sell them to China? India? Bill Gates?

As the guard escorted me from the building, I could feel everyone's eyes burning a hole into the back of my shirt. Before I was even out the door I knew the gossip mill would go into hyper drive. "Ooh, I wonder what she did to get canned? I heard that some people have been sending inappropriate emails. Do you think she was one of them? Well I heard she was seeing someone from work—you know how they frown on that." Blah, blah, blah. I shifted my box into my right arm and used my left to reach around and pluck my scorched shirt away from my skin.

We passed by Arthur's desk, but I couldn't even say goodbye because he was caught up in a customer escalation. I gave him a feeble wave. His eyebrows shot up when he saw the security guard and the box in my hands, and he pantomimed for me to call him later.

When the glass front doors to the building slammed behind me, I stood there, dazed, holding my box which contained my Degas coffee mug from the Musee d'Orsay, my Eiffel Tower paperweight, pictures—including copies of our late, great Napa balloon ride—my Impressionists desk calendar, and crayon drawings my Sunday school toddlers had scribbled for me.

Two girls I didn't know walked by and gave me a curious look, startling me out of my stupor.

I put one foot in front of the other and began the long, slow trek to my car at the far end of the parking lot. My feet were heavy and sluggish, my throat felt thick and my eyes burned, but I refused to cry. Not on company property at least. I trudged past a never-ending sea of Kias, Hondas, and dinged-up pickup trucks until at last I arrived at my dusty Ford.

Fumbling for my keys, I inserted them in the lock. Or tried to. By now my hand was shaking and I couldn't see straight for the pool of tears that had gathered against my stern orders not to. I dropped the keys on the tarmac and they fell under the car. Letting out a word I never want to hear my Sunday schoolers say, I set down the box of possessions that represented my two years at Landon, shoved my purse inside, and squatted down to retrieve my keys. Thrusting my hand under the car, I patted the ground, getting bits of dirt and gravel stuck to my palm, until my fingers closed around the keys.

This time when I put the key in the lock, it worked. I pulled out my purse from the box and slung it over my shoulder, shoving the box into the backseat. But as I did, a crumpled piece of paper fell out of my purse onto the ground. Picking it up, I realized it was one of the delivery forms from Golden Daffodils that I'd somehow neglected to turn in Saturday.

You can't do any job right, can you?

Loser.

Clutching the glaring white sign of my inability to accomplish even the simplest of tasks, I slammed the back door shut and stalked to the driver's seat. Once inside, I rested my head on the steering wheel and let the tears run unchecked down my face.

I'd never been fired before in my entire life. What was I supposed to do now? Who would hire me? The tears ran in earnest and then my nose began to run. I hadn't had a good cry in ages, though, so I decided to just let myself go. I felt like little Emily.

Only there wasn't anyone around to tell me a story to make me feel better.

At last I lifted my hot sticky face from the rubber-coated steering wheel and swiped my hand beneath my nose, coming away with a sticky mixture of snot and tears.

Thirty-five, divorced without any romantic prospects in sight, childless, living with my mother, and as of a few minutes ago, unemployed.

Quite the red-letter day.

I fumbled in my purse for my tissue packet, yanked out two, and blew. Then I grabbed two more and blew again, crumpling up the tissue and tossing it on the floor of the passenger side. I pulled down my visor and inspected the damage. My eyes were puffy and red-rimmed, my face all red and blotchy, and I had a pounding headache from crying.

Good thing I didn't wear mascara or it would have been all over my face like a cheap suit.

When I looked out my car window I saw that people were streaming toward the parking lot heading to lunch. I recognized Brooke's distinctive height and curly head above the crowd. Quickly I flipped my visor back up and started my car, reversing in a hurry and getting the heck out of Dodge before anyone spotted me.

But where was I going to go? I couldn't go home and face Mom. Not yet. I wasn't quite ready for that soap opera. So I just drove around aimlessly for a while thinking about my life and what a royal mess it was. What was I going to do now? What kind of job could I get?

I had to get a job. If I stayed home with Mom all day long I knew I'd go crazy. I decided to put off going home by stopping in at Golden Daffodils instead. I had to turn in the delivery receipt anyway.

As I pushed open the door of the flower shop, I pasted on a fake smile. At the sound of the chimes, Annie looked up from a stack of papers she'd been scowling over at the counter. Her scowl turned to a welcoming smile. "Hey Paige, how's it goin'? Did you come back for some more?"

"More?" My head was still stopped up from my crying jag earlier and I couldn't think straight.

"You know. Deliveries."

"Oh. No, but I do have a delivery receipt I forgot to give you Saturday." As I approached the counter I saw that today's T-shirt read *She who must be obeyed.*

Wonder what Marc thinks of that?

"How's Toby doing?" I set my purse on the counter.

"Much better, but still not quite a hundred percent. And of course he's milking it for everything he can. You know how guys are when they're sick. Bunch of big babies."

"Yeah, my ex was like that."

"Ex?" Her pierced eyebrow lifted. "As in boyfriend or husband?"

Now you've done it. Here come all the questions. I clutched the counter.

"Hey, you okay? You don't look so great."

"I'm fine." I reached in my purse, pulled out the delivery sheet signed by the pregnant daffs lady, and handed it to her. "That's simply the look of someone who just lost her job."

"What? What happened?"

At least we're off the subject of exes.

"Life. Life happened." I flipped my hand dismissively. "*C'est la vie.*" All at once a wave of nausea rolled over me. I fought it down and reached for the nearby bistro chair. "Mind if I sit down?"

Annie's face filled with concern. "No. Sit right there and I'll go get you some water."

She returned a moment later with a cold bottle of water and solicitous Marc on her heels.

"Paige? Are you okay?"

No. I'm definitely not okay. Who knew getting fired from a job I didn't even like all that much would affect me this way?

"Not having a very good day," I said thickly, my eyes gritty and my throat like sandpaper.

For the next five days I was down for the count with the flu. At least I didn't have to worry about using up all my sick leave.

I dosed myself with Theraflu and decided being home sick in bed was a good time to catch up on all my classics reading. Unfortunately, *The Woman in White* and *Jude the Obscure* proved to be a little too obscure for my fevered brain to comprehend, and *War and Peace* was too heavy.

Pushing the thick Russian tome aside, I opted for something lighter. I pulled out all my old musicals and burrowed beneath my quilt to enjoy a little MGM magic. I made it as far as the gorgeous Curley extolling to Laurie the virtues of a surrey with the fringe on top before falling asleep.

It wasn't an easy sleep. Nightmares of being trapped atop a burning Oklahoma haystack intruded. Only it wasn't the evil, jealous Jud who set the fire, but rather my old supervisor. As the flames licked higher, she cackled, "I'll get you for those bad stats, my pretty—you'll never work in this town again!"

Some people mix metaphors, I mix musicals.

I woke up from the nightmare sweating in my flannel pj's, stomach churning. Kicking off the covers, I raced to the bathroom and upchucked into the pink toilet I hadn't had a chance to replace yet.

My legs wobbled as I made my way to the sink where

I splashed water on my hot and decidedly green face, then scooped up handfuls to drink. I stripped off my sweat-soaked pajamas, dumped them in the hamper, and slipped on a cool cotton nightgown instead.

If this is what hot flashes are like, I'm skipping menopause.

Still wobbly, I made my way to the kitchen for some warm 7-Up and saltines. There I found my mother entrenched in her favorite soap opera.

Mom's never been good with sick people.

I was the one who always took care of my family when they were sick—bringing them tea with honey or heating up cans of chicken noodle soup that Dad got at a discount since he worked for Campbell's.

As I munched on a cracker, Mom's soap cut to a commercial and she shot me a solicitous glance. "How are you feeling, honey? You want me to have Frieda bring you over some KFC? Or maybe an Egg McMuffin?"

I gagged again and barely made it to the bathroom in time.

A few hours later she knocked on my bedroom door. "Honey, is that medication working yet? I'm really getting hungry."

Time to call in reinforcements.

"Tess," I croaked into the phone as I shivered beneath my blankets, "I'm really sick and can't take care of Mom right now. Can you help me?"

She did and more. Tess rallied all the Getaway Girls who stepped up to the plate. Even Becca. They took turns bringing food that Mom could have, along with Annette's amazing homemade chicken soup.

When I wasn't sleeping, downing my flu meds, or ralphing into the pink toilet—I seriously needed to swap it out for basic white—I slipped beneath my crisp sheets, thoughtfully changed by Annette, turned on my iPod, and let *La Bohème* take me away.

And in my weakened state, I imagined myself as the tragic Mimi dying of consumption. Except I didn't have a dashing Rodolfo's arms to die in.

Story of my life.

"Your mom *loved* my stir-fry," Jenna said as she brought over her favorite P. D. James for me to read on the third day when I was propped up against my pillows and finally starting to feel human again. "She didn't blink at the tofu and even asked for seconds. By the way," she whispered, "are those *ashes* on her nightstand?"

"Yep. That would be my dad."

Marc and Annie dropped by later that day too. Thankfully, I'd taken a shower and washed my hair (the first time in three days) and no longer looked like the crazy meat-pie lady from *Sweeney Todd*. They both felt bad—especially Annie—for exposing me to Toby's flu. She brought me some lemon sorbet to soothe my aching throat and a teddy bear clutching a vase of pink, yellow, and peach Gerbera daisies. But it was Marc's gorgeous arrangement of yellow and white roses, gardenias, lilies of the valley, and orchids that took my breath away.

"Is that a cymbidium orchid?" I asked.

He nodded. "You said you thought they were really beautiful."

"They are. I love them. Thank you." I leaned in to get a closer look. "Is that what's giving off that wonderful scent?"

"That's the gardenias. They're tricky to use in arrangements because they have no stems and tend to bruise easily, but I think their beauty and wonderful fragrance makes them worth the trouble."

I inhaled the heady scent. "I think so too. And what do they mean?"

He hesitated. "I can't remember right now. But lily of the valley stands for sweetness and humility."

He thinks I'm sweet and humble? Hah. Shows how well he knows me.

"You should get some rest now," Marc said. "Remember to take care of yourself too—you're not Wonder Woman."

"I'm not? Then what am I supposed to do with the red boots, bullet-deflecting bracelets, and golden lasso?"

16

> She had been forced into prudence in her youth, she learned romance as she grew older—the natural sequence of an unnatural beginning.
>
> *Persuasion*

I picked up the quarter sheet cake from the bakery and set it gently in the backseat next to the platter of sandwiches and stuffed mushrooms. Usually I made my stuffed shrooms with crab or sausage, but in deference to Jenna, this time I kept it vegetarian with two kinds of cheese instead.

The Getaway Girls and I were throwing Tess a wedding shower. And since our classy friend loved the elegance and ritual of an afternoon tea, we were giving her a luncheon tea over at Annette's. Sergeant Etiquette, which the girls had dubbed Annette due to her Southern, middle-aged Air Force background and penchant for wanting everything just so, was the only one of us besides Tess who had fine bone china and crystal. I had a few pieces, but they were packed away in storage.

We put our heads together to decide on a menu and how best to divvy up the food selections.

"I could bring McNuggets," Becca offered.

"Yeah, and I could bring tacos or pizza," Kailyn said.

"Tacos? Pizza? *McNuggets*?" Annette's eyebrows rose to her hairline. "Did y'all see any of those at the Ritz when we had tea there last year?"

Becca frowned, as if trying to remember. "Nah, but this isn't the Ritz and you don't want to be as stuffy as them, do you?"

"Yeah, Tess is anything but stuffy," Jenna said. "Want me to bring nachos?"

I could see Sergeant Etiquette struggling to frame a diplomatic answer, so I jumped in.

"Jenna, think you could bring some nice fresh strawberries from the farmer's market?"

"Sure." She gave me an innocent look. "Is that in addition to the nachos, or in place of?"

Kailyn started giggling and Annette finally got it. "Very funny."

"I still think we should have McNuggets."

"Tell you what," our Southern hostess with the mostest said. "When we do your bridal shower, we'll have McNuggets. French fries and Big Macs too, if you want."

Becca snorted. "No worries there 'cause I'm not getting married. Ever. So *not* going to happen."

After a lengthy discussion, at last we decided upon a selection of tea sandwiches, fruit and scones, cake for dessert, and some raw veggies to munch on when everyone first arrived.

"Becca and I can bring the veggies," Kailyn offered, "since neither of us can cook."

"Sandwiches aren't cooking."

"If you want PB&J, I'm your girl," Becca said. "Anything more foo-foo than that, I'd mess it up."

"Me too. Unless it's grilled cheese," Kailyn said.

Annette and I decided we'd take care of the sandwiches and scones while the others brought fresh veggies and fruit. And we'd all chip in on the cake.

"Do you really think we need cake too since we're already having scones?" Jenna asked.

"It's not a shower without a cake."

"Then why don't we scratch the scones?"

"You can't have tea without scones!"

The scones were my department. I had a great recipe from an English cookbook that I knew everyone would love.

Unfortunately those scones burned when Mom called me to break up a fight Mr. Spitz was having in the backyard with another neighborhood cat. By the time I shooed the other tom away with a broom and coaxed a bristling and bedraggled Mr. Spitz back into the house, the smoke alarm was blaring, the kitchen reeked of smoke, and my scones were burnt to a crisp.

I dumped the sheet of blackened disks in the sink, opened all the windows, and stacked the rest of my offerings on the counter, ready to load into the car. I'd decided last night that it would be nice to have something hot to eat in addition to all the cold sandwiches, so I'd rustled up some of my stuffed mushrooms that Tess loved.

"Mom, are you all set now?" I poked my head in the living room where she was intent on John Wayne in *Rio Bravo*. "I left you a couple of the stuffed mushrooms for lunch to have with your crab salad."

"Thanks, honey. I'm fine." She never lifted her eyes from the tube. "Have fun."

"Okay, I'll see you later." I hurried to the back door with

my stack of food. Mr. Spitz rubbed up against my legs, hoping for some of the crab salad, but I shooed him away.

On my way to Annette's, I zipped over to A Cup of Tea, my favorite tea room, and picked up a box of their signature scones to replace the ones I'd burned. Then I ran to the bakery to get the cake.

Sacramento was having one of its hot, July, pushing 100-degree days, so by the time I stopped by Golden Daffodils to pick up the arrangement I'd ordered, my face felt all flushed and warm.

Marc clutched his chest when I hurried in and said, "Be still my heart. Don't you look all rosy and pretty today?"

"Pretty hot." I lifted my hair off my sticky neck and blew up a puff of wind that fluttered my bangs.

"That too." He gave me an appreciative look that made me realize he wasn't talking about the weather. "A little color in your cheeks suits you. Especially with that dress."

I could feel my cheeks grow even pinker. "Thanks." I was wearing a V-necked magenta sundress that flared at the hips and swirled around my legs when I moved. Kailyn and Annette had insisted I buy it the last time we went shopping—before I lost my job. No more dresses like this for a while.

"Hey, Paige." Annie entered from the back carrying Tess's shower arrangement of roses and Stargazer lilies which she set on the counter for my inspection. She gave a low whistle. "Great dress. You really look hot."

"That's what I told her too." Marc sent me another appreciative look.

"Thanks." Flustered, I focused on Annie's green tee that said *Never judge a book by its movie.* "Now that's a shirt I need to get. And speaking of get, I'd better get going or I'm going to be late." I paid her and started to reach for the flowers.

Marc whisked the arrangement out of my reach. "I'll carry

it out for you. It would be a sin to get a pod stain on that gorgeous dress."

He loaded the flowers into my car and waved as I pulled away. And when I glanced in the rearview mirror, I saw that he was still standing there, staring at the back of my car. I hoped my exhaust wasn't belching black smoke again. I really needed a tune-up.

I mentally added that to my financial to-do list once I got a new job. Monday, I would start pounding the pavement. This time, though, I was going to try and find something a little more flexible where they wouldn't mind me ferrying Mom to all her appointments and errands.

Once I arrived at Annette's, I carefully removed the flowers from the front seat, mindful of Marc's instructions to hold them away from me. What a thoughtful guy. I think he still felt bad that my T-shirt got stained that day I did deliveries.

"Oh, those are gorgeous," Annette said as I carried them in and set them on the table. "These are from your friend Marc's shop, right? He really does great work."

"Yep. He's a talented guy."

Cute too. I've never been that big on beards before, but on Marc, it works.

Well. Really well.

Don't go down that road. He's a friend, remember?

"I'm going to have to go check out his shop one of these days." Annette sent me a knowing smirk. "Then I can check him out too."

"No need. He's just a friend. Don't put on your matchmaking hat."

"You must admit, it worked pretty well for Tess."

"True." Annette and I arranged the tea sandwiches on a crystal platter, alternating her pineapple-cream cheese and cucumber-and-dill with my crab salad and goat cheese-and-watercress.

As we were setting the dining room table with Annette's Old Country Roses china atop pretty Battenberg lace placemats, we heard the back door open and Becca's voice ring out, "Never fear, the cavalry's here." She sauntered into the dining room and plopped down a plastic shrink-wrapped container of carrot sticks, celery, and cherry tomatoes on one end of the table.

Annette blanched and caught Kailyn's eye, who'd followed Becca in. "Uh, baby girl, would you take this into the kitchen and arrange it on that china platter I have sitting out on the counter? There's some parsley in the sink too that you can use for decoration."

"Sure, Mom." Kailyn mouthed "Told you" to her roommate, plucked the plastic offender off the table, and headed back to the kitchen.

"What's so wrong with plastic?" Becca asked.

"Nothing if you're having a barbecue or a Super Bowl party." Annette continued setting out scalloped-edged place cards on each plate with each Getaway Girl's name calligraphied on the front. "But it doesn't go with a ladies tea. Presentation is everything." She glanced down at Becca's feet.

I did too, expecting to see her ubiquitous, well-worn Birkenstocks.

Instead, I was surprised to see a pair of pretty white sandals, flat-heeled and feminine, that matched her white tank top above pleated navy shorts.

"Gotcha," Becca said. "I can clean up when I want to."

"I never had any doubt." Annette gave her an approving smile. "You look very nice." She nodded to the end of the table where a group of crystal water goblets stood. "Now would you be an angel and set a glass next to each plate for me, please? Upper left-hand corner of the plate."

"But won't they tip over if I balance them on the edge of the plate?" Becca flashed her a devilish grin.

Jenna arrived then with strawberries, her gift, and two bottles. "I knew we'd want to toast the bride, so I brought champagne and sparkling cider. Hope that's okay?"

"Perfect. I have punch and tea, but that will be a nice complement," Annette said. "Now let's all go out to the kitchen and finish up. Tess should be here pretty soon. And I don't know about y'all, but I'm dying to take a peek at the cake."

"Me too. Lead the way."

I carefully opened the lid of the bakery box for their inspection.

Kailyn clapped her hands. "Oh, that's perfect!"

"It's great!"

"Tess is going to love it."

The doorbell rang.

"Ooh, she's here. Quick, close the lid."

We scurried into the living room behind Annette, who nodded to Kailyn to cue the music. As Annette opened the front door, "Going to the Chapel" blared from the stereo and we all sang along. Loudly and lustily.

Tess grinned. "Well that's the noisiest welcome I think I've ever received."

"Well don't just stand there, guest of honor. Come on in."

"Am I allowed to bring my own gift?"

A familiar head peeked around the doorway.

"Chloe!"

"Bonjour, mon amies."

Tess got shoved aside in the melee as we group-hugged our long-absent friend. But I could tell Tess didn't mind. She was smiling from ear to ear as we peppered her niece with questions.

"What are you doing here?"

"When did you get back from Paris?"

"What are you wearing? You look fabulous!"

"Have you lost weight?"

"I thought you weren't coming home until next week."

"I came home a few days early. I couldn't miss my favorite aunt's bridal shower, could I?" She hugged Tess's neck.

Chloe was wearing a sleeveless black linen sheath, with gold bangles on her wrist, a thin gold anklet, and glossy, jeweled black sandals.

"Look at you, all cosmopolitan and sophisticated." Becca munched on a carrot stick. "Could this be my same roommate who last year at this time was living in jeans and T-shirts?"

"I still live in jeans and T-shirts, but I wanted to dress up for Tess," Chloe said. "Plus, I thought it would be fun to make you all think I'd gone Parisian."

"Well haven't you?"

"Maybe a little. At heart though, I'm still a California girl."

"A California girl who knows how to accessorize," Kailyn said, grabbing Chloe's wrist. "Love the bangles. Did you get them in the bowels boutique in the Metro?"

"Okay, everyone, let's go sit down now," Annette said. "We can continue with the Chloe grilling at lunch."

While the girls took their place-marked seats, oohing and aahing at how pretty everything looked, Annette and I returned to the kitchen where we loaded up two tea trays with teapots, scones, jam, lemon curd, and clotted cream which we then carried out to the dining room.

"Yummy."

"Looks delish."

"Pass the clotted cream, please."

We nibbled on crustless tea sandwiches and listened as Chloe regaled us with her adventures from Paris, telling us about her visits to Giverny, frequenting the bouquinistes—bookstalls—along the Seine, daily walks to her beloved Eiffel Tower, dining in sidewalk cafes, but mainly, haunting her favorite art museums, and painting.

Always painting.

A pang of envy pierced me. Not that I wanted to be a painter—I couldn't even draw stick figures—but I could tell that in Paris, Chloe had found her purpose. What she was supposed to do with her life. And her next statement confirmed that.

"I've decided to go back to school and get my Master's in Fine Art," she said. "I'd really like to teach art so I'm going to see if I can work just three-quarter time while I take classes."

I listened with only half an ear to the babble of Getaway Girls voices around me. I was nearly a decade older than Chloe and I still had no idea what I wanted to do with my life. What I was *supposed* to do with my life.

Besides take care of my mother.

"But enough about me," I heard Chloe say. "This is our day to celebrate Tess and her upcoming union with James." She sent her aunt a look filled with love. "I'm so glad that God has brought James into your life, and I'm sure Uncle Ted is too." She raised her glass. "To the bride."

"To the bride," we all said.

"Thank you." Tess looked around the table. "And thank you all for doing this. It's wonderful. I couldn't have asked for a better shower."

"And we haven't even gotten to the presents yet."

Annette laughed and stood up. "I'd say that's our cue." She tugged on Kailyn's hair as she passed her chair. "Leave it to my baby girl to bring up the presents." She and I herded everyone into the living room where we made our engaged club member sit in the largest chair next to a stack of gaily wrapped packages.

"Tess, since you already have your own home, we knew you didn't need the normal household gifts," Annette said. "So we did something a little different that we think—we hope—you're going to like." She nodded to me and I handed Tess her first flat-wrapped package.

"That one's from me," Becca said. "Sorry, I forgot the card."

"That's okay." Tess unwrapped her gift and burst out laughing. She turned the cover of the book toward us: *Dave Barry's Guide to Marriage and/or Sex.*

"I figured since it's been awhile you might need a little help," Becca said slyly.

Tess's cheeks pinked beneath her red glasses. "Thanks. I'll take all the help I can get."

The next gift was from Jenna: *Men Are from Mars, Women Are from Venus.* Then Paul Reiser's *Couplehood* from Kailyn, and *The Five Love Languages* from me.

"I think I'm sensing a theme here."

"It's a book shower!" Kailyn beamed at Tess. "We've never done one before, but Paige came up with the idea and we all thought it was pretty appropriate."

"Certainly is. Thanks, Paige." She looked at us over her red-rectangled glasses. "Although I hope you all don't mind if I don't invite you along as I start to live out the adventures in these books."

"Really?"

"Bummer."

"We won't even make you give us a book report," Annette winked as she handed Tess her final book gift.

The bride-to-be burst out laughing again when she saw the title. *A Marriage Made in Heaven or Too Tired for an Affair.* "I've always loved Erma Bombeck. That woman can make me laugh like nobody else. Thanks, Annette. Thanks, all of you. I'm looking forward to reading all of these and sharing them with James."

"Maybe you can start on the honeymoon."

"I think they'll be too busy to read on the honeymoon," Becca said.

Tess's face pinked again.

"Hey, where are you guys going on your honeymoon anyway?"

"Yes, inquiring minds want to know."

"I don't know. It's a surprise. James said that's the groom's prerogative."

"That's not fair. Don't you even get a say in it?" I could see Jenna's feminist hackles rising.

"Oh, I had a say in it, not to worry. I told him I was fine with wherever we went as long as it didn't involve countries with civil unrest, communal shower facilities, or camping."

"Camping?" Chloe stared at her aunt. "But you love camping. You always took the boys camping and backpacking growing up."

"Yeah, and who's the one who was all gung-ho about our Getaway Girls camping adventure last year?"

"And insisted it would be good for us to step out of our comfort zones?" Annette reminded her.

"That's different. And it *was* good for you, you must admit," Tess said. "But for my honeymoon, and at this age, I'm all about comfort. I've waited this long, so I want a nice comfy bed to snuggle up next to my husband in and our own bathroom."

"Go Tess!"

"Next thing, you'll say you want a Jacuzzi tub too." Becca, our no-frills nature girl, frowned.

"I wouldn't turn it down."

"Wait, there's still one more present," I said, handing Tess a large gift bag.

She rustled through the paper and pulled out an oversized hardcover book. "*The Song of Solomon*?"

"In large print," Annette giggled. "At our age, our eyes aren't what they used to be."

"You can say that again." Tess examined the Old Testament book closely. "Wait a minute." She turned it over and scrutinized the back cover. "Is this really even a book?"

"Why don't you open it?" Kailyn said innocently.

"Is this one of those gag gifts? Are fake snakes going to jump out at me or something when I open the cover?"

"Would we do that to you?" Becca asked.

"Yes, you would. Especially you."

Becca shrugged. "Guess you'll never know until you open it."

"Paige?" Tess sent me a beseeching look.

"Don't look at me."

"Annette?"

"My lips are sealed." Annette slid her compressed thumb and forefinger across her lips in a sealing motion.

"Just open it already."

Hesitantly, Tess lifted the front cover. "Aha! Thought so. It's *not* a book."

"Be afraid. Be very afraid," Jenna intoned in her best creepy monster voice.

"Don't listen to them." Kailyn's eyes danced with anticipation. "It's nothing scary. Really."

Slowly Tess removed the folded tissue paper inside the top of the fake book. "Oh my," she said, lifting out a silky white negligee edged in lace and tied with a discreet satin bow at the bodice.

"That's from all of us," I said.

"Ooh, it's so pretty." Chloe was the only one besides Tess who hadn't seen it yet.

"Like I said," Becca grinned. "I don't think they'll be reading on the honeymoon."

"We thought it was only fair that James get a gift from the shower too."

Everyone giggled.

"I'll thank you for him," Tess said. "It's absolutely lovely. Thank you. And thank you too for not getting me some skimpy black teddy or bright red thong."

"Becca wanted to, but we held her back."

"For which I'll be eternally grateful." She blew us a kiss.

"I have a gift for you too," Chloe said shyly, pulling a large flat package out of her oversized bag and handing it to Tess. "It's not a book, but I hope you'll like it."

"I'm sure I will, sweetie. I always like everything you give me. You have great taste." Tess undid the silvery wrapping paper, revealing a piece of what looked like cardboard over a flat board. She removed the protective cardboard cover and gasped. Her hand flew to her mouth and her eyes glistened. "Did you do this?"

Chloe nodded.

"It's beautiful." Tess stared at her gift, transfixed. "Just beautiful."

"Well, share with the rest of the class, why don't you?"

She turned the flat board around and then we could all see that it was a painting. Oil on canvas. An Impressionistic rendering of the Eiffel Tower lit up at night.

We let out a collective gasp.

"Chloe, you painted this?" I asked, moving forward to get a closer look. "It's gorgeous! Reminds me of van Gogh."

"You think so?" A pleased smile stole over her face. "That's what I was going for with the brushstrokes, but of course I can't come near van Gogh. Who can?"

"True," Tess said. "But who needs a van Gogh when they have a Chloe original? I absolutely love it."

"I got a Chloe halter dress from a designer outlet for a hundred bucks," Kailyn interjected.

"I think I prefer this Chloe," Becca said.

"I couldn't decide whether to give you one of the pictures I did of the gardens at Giverny or this, but since this was the view we saw from our hotel window, this seemed like a better choice."

"It's perfect," Tess said.

"Now you'll always have Paris." I hummed a snatch of "As Time Goes By."

"I also brought all of you a little something." Chloe reached into her oversized bag again and removed a rectangular lavender box with a distinctive oval on the cover.

"Macaroons from Ladurée!"

"Ooh, tell me you brought some of the chocolate ones."

"Chocolate, dark chocolate, vanilla, raspberry, pistachio, and cherry amaretto."

"Ooh la la."

"*C'est* bliss."

We munched contentedly on the round crunchy cookies with buttercream filling.

"Don't forget to save room for cake too."

"Cake?" Tess patted her stomach. "I don't think I could eat another bite."

"Well you're going to have to force yourself." I carried the shower cake over to Tess which was in the shape of an open book with writing on the top that read, "And they lived happily ever after ..."

As we noshed on cake, we continued to ask Chloe about her three-month sojourn in the City of Light.

"Did you stay in the city the whole time, or did you take trips to other parts of France too?"

"I went to Provence once—gorgeous countryside—and Normandy to visit the D-day landing beaches and the American Cemetery." Chloe got a far-off look in her eye. "All those white crosses on a cliff. Something I'll never forget."

"I know," Annette said. "It's terrible and somehow beautiful at the same time, isn't it?"

Chloe nodded.

Kailyn made a face. "Did you go anywhere fun? Someplace not as depressing as a cemetery, maybe?"

"Hey, the Père Lachaise Cemetery was really cool." Becca frowned at her roommate. "Don't be dissin' cemeteries."

"Yeah," Jenna said. "I love my souvenir photo of Jim Morrison's grave."

"That's because you're dark and twisted." Kailyn returned her attention to Chloe. "So where else did you go?"

"Well, one weekend I took the Eurostar to London—"

"Wait." Becca stared at her. "Isn't that the express train that goes underwater across the English Channel?"

Chloe nodded. "Through the Chunnel."

We all stared. "You went *under*water. In a train. And lived to tell about it?"

"Sometimes you have to face your fears head on," Chloe said.

17

The fact that I was a girl never damaged my ambitions to be a pope or an emperor.

Willa Cather

All your fears? Even those deep-seated dysfunctional family ones? Somehow I think it'd be easier riding a hurtling train through the ocean depths than upending the status quo family dynamics. At least in my family.

Although … we didn't really have much of a family left.

Dad was gone, Patrick might as well be for all that we heard from him, and Isabel … well Isabel had made it pretty obvious that she wanted very little to do with our family. Her family was now her husband.

That left me and Mom.

It was always me and Mom. Had been throughout most of my life. Definitely my marriage. Maybe if I'd focused more on Eric and less on Mom, we'd still be together. I know that's what he probably thought.

Yeah right. Like he even thinks of you at all. The man has moved on. He has the family he always wanted. The family he said he wanted with you. Only you were too busy with Mom to pay attention to his needs. Your needs, as a couple. A couple who desperately wanted a baby. How many times did he ask you to go away for a romantic weekend—just the two of you—that last year of your marriage?

I couldn't. Mom needed me. How could I turn my back on my mother after her husband had just died?

She didn't have anyone else.

Sometimes I wished I could be more like Isabel. It would be nice to move away from all my duties and responsibilities and start a whole new life somewhere fresh. Maybe even meet someone and fall in love again.

Get married.

Have a baby …

I thought back to something Iz had said the last time we'd talked. "You need to stop letting Mom run your life and manipulate you into taking care of her. She's a grown woman, not a child. And you've got your own life to lead."

"But she needs me. She doesn't have anyone else."

"Don't be such a martyr, Paige."

"Paige?"

"Huh?" I blinked and realized that the girls were all looking at me expectantly.

"We asked if you wanted to join us for Mexican food," Tess said.

"What? *Now?*" I looked around at the half-finished plates of cake dotting the surface of the table. "How can you still be hungry?"

"Not now," Annette said. "Tonight for dinner. We thought we'd continue the celebration, only this one will be celebrating Chloe's return. *Bienvenue* instead of *Bon Voyage!*"

"*Merci,*" Chloe said. "I've been craving good Mexican forever.

That's the one thing I missed in Paris. There are a few Mexican restaurants, but none that I'd want to write home about. Unlike most of the restaurants there, which I simply loved. The French just don't know how to do burritos. Or tacos. And I am so longing for enchiladas. And chips and salsa." She licked her lips. "And nachos ..."

"Nachos?" Jenna sent a victorious look to Annette.

"So Paige, you gonna come or not?" Becca asked.

"No. Sorry. I can't. I've got to go home and make Mom dinner."

The girls exchanged looks.

"Can't she just nuke something in the microwave?"

Becca scowled. "You're always missing stuff because of your mom. Like our Yosemite trip."

Last month I'd had to call and cancel at the last minute for our *Into Thin Air* climbing adventure when there had been a mix-up at the pharmacy over one of Mom's prescriptions.

I spent the weekend watching John Wayne with my mother. At least the Westerns had mountains in them that resembled Yosemite.

"And don't forget the Mendocino beach house swap we did with Jenna's granola friends for our *Tara Road* adventure," Kailyn said.

"Yeah, that rocked. You really missed out."

"It's always something."

"I think it's time to stage a mom intervention," Jenna teased.

At least I think she was teasing.

"You guys stop ragging on Paige," Tess said.

"But don't you think she needs to stop letting her mom rule her life and set some boundaries?"

There was an uncomfortable silence.

Tess gave me a gentle look. "Yes, actually I do. But that's

not our call. It's Paige's and she'll know when she needs to make it."

If it was any group of women other than these women, these dear friends, saying such things to me, I'd have gotten up and walked out. But these women had earned the right over time and our shared Getaway Girls adventures.

As I drove home, I kept thinking about what the girls had said. Jenna's Mom-intervention crack had really hit home. And others agreed with her. Like Marc. And Isabel. And they were all right. Things couldn't continue as they were.

I couldn't continue this way.

But how was I going to tell Mom that? Dad was gone, she hadn't seen Patrick in years, Isabel only came home for a duty visit once every couple years. I was all she had.

She has God.

I was thinking more of someone with skin on.

You've been God with skin on to your mother for years. Serving others doesn't mean being a doormat.

But we're supposed to serve and give with no thought of anything in return.

Yeah, if you're Mother Teresa. If you can do it wholeheartedly and unreservedly, fine. But have you? Are you? Haven't you been resenting your mother for a while?

I shifted uncomfortably in my seat.

As if this inner lecture wasn't enough, I was suddenly hit with words of down-home wisdom from TV shrink Dr. Phil.

"How's that workin' for you?"

It wasn't.

When I got home, I was too tired to unload all my food containers, so I decided to leave them in the car and take care of them later. I did carry in a bite-sized dark chocolate macaroon from Ladurée, however, for Mom.

Yes, she's usually not supposed to have sweets, unless

they're sugar-free. And since I'd moved in, I'd earned my Food Police badge by making sure that the fridge and cupboards were all stocked with low-carb, diabetic-healthy foods—like her luncheon crab salad. But once in a blue moon, a smidge of sugar was okay.

Only once in a blue moon.

And since Mom was never going to go to Paris, I wanted to treat her to a little taste of heaven from the City of Light. Quietly, I let myself into the kitchen, anticipating her delighted reaction when she awoke from her afternoon nap to this unexpected treat. Then I heard muffled voices coming from the living room and realized she must have gotten up early and was watching TV. I smiled as I approached the door to the living room, macaroon in hand on a napkin.

Then I heard Mom's voice.

"Paige is the middle child, so she's always struggled to find her place. I had high hopes when she married Eric—such a handsome man—but she wasn't able to hold onto him." I could hear her loud sigh even through the door. "I'm not sure exactly why," Mom continued. "I tend to wonder if there might have been problems behind closed doors, if you know what I'm saying."

I barreled through the door. "There were no problems behind closed doors, Mom. The problems were within *these* doors."

"Paige." Frieda looked up guiltily from her seat on the couch. "We didn't hear you come in."

"Obviously." My hands clenched and without looking, I knew my knuckles were tight and white.

"Well, I'd better go now, Catherine. I'll talk to you tomorrow. Good night. Good night Paige."

"Night." I never moved my eyes from my mother's face as I heard Frieda scuttle out.

"Now don't get upset, honey. Frieda and I were just talking about our daughters—"

"No, you were also talking about my marriage. And speculating about the intimate details." All the pent-up frustration and anger that I'd been stuffing down for years bubbled over. "You want to know why my marriage didn't work out? Why Eric left? Look in the mirror. *You're* the one who ruined my marriage!"

I saw the shock and hurt in her eyes, but I couldn't stop. "I've given up my whole life for you! And still it's not enough. It's never enough."

All at once, everything everyone had been saying to me—Isabel, Marc, Arthur, the Getaway Girls—all fell into place. And I saw that they were right.

"I can't do it anymore, Mom. I won't!"

She gaped at me.

"I need to get out of here."

"Wh-where are you going?"

"I don't know. Just out."

Her lips trembled. "You're leaving me. Just like your brother and sister. Your father, too. Everyone always leaves." Tears trickled down her cheeks.

My heart clenched. I started towards her, intending to wipe away her tears and soothe her fears. But then I stopped.

I realized I needed a time out.

And I wasn't the only one.

"I'll be back, Mom. I just need some time alone to think. You can reach me on my cell if you need me for something urgent—not to pick up pudding from the store—but for anything critical. I just need to go.

"Now."

I gave her shoulder a quick pat and left before I lost my resolve.

Ever the responsible daughter, I punched in Frieda's number on my cell as I pulled out of the driveway. I told her Mom and I had had a fight and I needed to get away for a while to clear my head, and asked if she could check on her to make sure she was okay or to see if she needed anything.

"Don't you worry, honey," Frieda said. "Nikki and I have had some real doozies in our day, but we've always made up. I'll go offer a shoulder to Catherine if she needs it, and bring her some of my lemon chicken for dinner. You take as much time as you need."

Little Frieda was all chipper and in control. And she seemed really anxious to get back to Mom. I knew that my mother had bragged to her over the years that she and I never fought. Was Frieda eager to go gloat? Or wanting to hear more, since she and Mom were just getting to the good part when I interrupted?

Whatever. I simply couldn't deal with that now.

As I drove aimlessly through the neighborhood, I cried. And prayed. And cried some more. But the closeness of the neighborhood began to suffocate me and I couldn't breathe. I had to escape.

The ocean was too far away, so I headed east toward the foothills instead. Ten miles out of Sacramento, the strip malls and their beckoning signage grew sparse and soon I was cruising on a highway cut through pine and oak-studded hills saved from developers because of the steep terrain. Here, houses had views and people had elbow room. As I looked in the rearview mirror, I could see the smog of Sacramento behind me.

I could also see myself. And take a long, hard look at my relationship with my mother and my resentment towards her—how I'd been blaming her these past few years for the breakup of my marriage. And I realized it wasn't my mother who destroyed my marriage; it was my response to my mother.

My always giving in to her, being at her constant beck and call and not putting my husband first. My marriage first.

The Scripture from Genesis that had even been a part of our marriage ceremony resounded in my head. *For this cause, a man shall leave his father and his mother and shall cleave to his wife, and they shall become one flesh.*

I'm sorry, Eric. For never cleaving to you.

I took the next exit, pulled over to the side of the road, turned off the engine, and laid my head on my arms and wept. Scenes from my marriage—both good and bad—brought a fresh onslaught of tears, and I wept anew. And when the weeping was done, I closed the coffin on my dead marriage. No more tears. I'd mourned enough.

Then I tentatively opened myself to new doors, new possibilities.

18

> Edmund was already feeling uncomfortable from having eaten too many sweets ... but he still wanted to taste that Turkish Delight more than he wanted anything else.
>
> *The Lion, the Witch and the Wardrobe*

When I returned from my drive, I apologized to my mother for losing it. "But Mom," I said firmly, "we do need to make a few changes if our living together is going to work."

"My former marriage is off-limits. It's over, and I'm over it. End of that chapter. Eric has a new life, a new wife and baby." I fixed her with a steady gaze. "That's the past and we need to focus on the present and the future." I took a deep breath. "And part of that means I won't be able to cook dinner for you every night."

"What? Why not?"

"Because I won't be here every night. On Wednesdays, I'll be helping out with child care at church and in the fall I want to start taking night classes on Mondays. Meanwhile, at least one Saturday a month will be designated as my night out with the girls."

Or guys. If anyone should ever ask me out.

However, I didn't feel the need to share that with my mother. I simply let her know that a couple Saturday nights a month would be reserved as my time to cut loose and have some fun. Sometimes that fun would be with the Getaway Girls, sometimes with friends from work, and sometimes just for me to steal away to browse the bookstore shelves and curl up with a good book in one of Dunkeld's comfy chairs for a couple hours.

I decided not to mention the latter, however. She'd just be hurt, look around at my myriad bookcases, and ask why I couldn't curl up with a good book at home.

Some things are better left unsaid.

"But what am I going to do for dinner?" she asked.

"Well, on the weekends I'll cook extra and freeze the left-overs in individual plastic containers that you can easily pop into the microwave when I'm not here. And I thought we could talk to Frieda and see if she'd like to come over and have dinner with you one night a week maybe?"

Mom's eyes brightened. "Maybe we could do that on Wednesdays when you're at church?"

"That's a good idea. And then the two of you could watch your favorite reality show together afterwards."

I called Frieda and she loved the idea. "I'll even cook and bring dinner over," she offered.

"You don't have to do that—I'll keep the freezer stocked with plenty of meals."

"I know I don't have to. I want to."

"Thanks, Frieda. I'll pay you, of course."

"Nah. I have to cook anyway and there's always enough for

two. Besides," she said, "I'll enjoying watching your mother's TV. It's much bigger than mine."

We agreed, however, that she would let me give her gas money and a little extra, to ferry Mom to the store or doctor's appointments if need be.

Another item checked off my setting boundaries to-do list.

I searched online and found a senior center nearby where Mom could go a couple afternoons a week for a modest fee to have lunch and do activities with other seniors. The center would even pick her up and bring her home.

"What kind of activities can I do with my bad eyes?" Mom asked when I took her to visit the center.

"We have several seniors with poor vision who work on large-piece jigsaw puzzles together or participate in chair exercises to help strengthen their leg muscles," said Jill, the center coordinator, who was giving us a tour. "They also enjoy afternoon concerts, talks, and demonstrations from various speakers and compete in oral trivia contests."

Mom went to the center grudgingly at first, but she soon made new friends her own age. And now, going to the center was one of the highlights of her week.

The highlight of mine was my new job—working part-time at the flower shop. I'd pounded the pavement every day for two solid weeks searching for work, but to no avail. People just weren't hiring. Or they weren't hiring me. Maybe it had something to do with the big letter *F* on my forehead.

Failure.

Flop.

Fired.

"You weren't fired; you were laid off," Marc said. "There's a huge difference."

"I guess."

After my latest rejection from an insurance company, I'd stopped by the flower shop on my way home to whine to Annie and Marc. Annie's T-shirt was black with white lettering that read *English major—You do the math.*

"Maybe that's my problem," I said.

"What?"

"That I'm lousy at math. I couldn't find my way around a financial spreadsheet if you paid me. Which is why no one wants to pay me to be a secretary or an administrative assistant."

"Is that what you want to do?" Marc asked.

"Not particularly. But that's what I know. Well, thought I knew. Things have changed since I last worked as a secretary." And no way was I going back to work in a call center again.

"Do you have to work full-time?" Marc asked.

"Not necessarily. Well, not right away."

"Why don't you work here?"

"That's a great idea!" Annie said. "We need a back-up delivery driver for Toby—he'll be at summer school in the mornings and Mom's not available."

"It doesn't pay a lot," Marc said, "but you did a great job for us that one day and for now at least it would get you out of the house and still give you some income."

"Really?"

"Plus, you'd be saving on gas money since you could walk to work," Annie said.

"I don't know ... I'd need to get a full-time job eventually."

"So work here while you're looking," Marc said. "It's easier to find a job when you already have one."

"Are you sure? Even though I'm directionally impaired?"

"No problem. We just got a portable GPS system."

"Well in that case, you've got yourself a new driver."

"Yes!" Annie said.

Marc offered me a huge smile. "Welcome to Golden Daffodils."

"Thanks." I gave him a hopeful look. "And maybe sometime one of you could teach me how to do flower arrangements?"

"I think something can be arranged."

The next morning to show my gratitude and celebrate my first day at my new job, I brought in homemade banana-nut bread fresh from the oven.

"Mmm. This is so good," Annie said as she scarfed down a piece.

"And it's still *warm.*" Marc closed his eyes as a look of bliss stole over his face. "Forget delivering flowers. I'll pay you just to cook every morning."

"No way. A deal's a deal. I can't wait to try out that GPS system, plus I want to learn the art of flower arranging."

He inhaled another piece of bread. "If I teach you how to make beautiful bouquets, will you bring in more goodies?"

"I think something can be arranged."

He wasn't the only one lusting after my baked goods.

"Honey, do you think maybe you could make some of your zucchini muffins for me to take to the center on Thursday?" Mom asked. "Jerry and Frank really loved your banana bread. Alice, too. And I told them, 'You think that's good, just wait until you taste my daughter's wonderful zucchini muffins!'"

Jerry and Frank were Mom's new trivia contest cronies. Apparently, Jerry was the center's reigning trivia champ—until Mom came along. Her first day there, they had a contest on the films of John Wayne. And Mom knocked it out of the park. Or rather, knocked him off his horse. She and Jerry had been friendly rivals ever since.

Frank was Jerry's straight man and a fount of World War II knowledge, and Alice was Mom's exercise chair buddy who cheered her on.

I was so grateful to Mom's new friends for taking some of the pressure off me and giving her some new interests at this time, I'd have baked them muffins, cupcakes, and a decadent triple-fudge chocolate layer cake. But that would have sent Mom's sugar levels off the charts.

"How'd you like zucchini muffins *and* my blueberry-peach ones? And for dinner, your favorite baked chicken Parmesan?"

I made enough chicken to take to work the next day for lunch with Annie and Marc. And after Annie swallowed her first bite, she sighed. "Paige, would you marry me?"

"Hey, no fair." Marc frowned at her. "You beat me to it."

"You guys. You act like you never get home-cooked food."

"I don't," Marc said. "Unless you count my pathetic attempts at pasta, which now that I've tasted yours, are even more pathetic."

"I'll say." Annie smirked.

"Says the woman who burned basic macaroni and cheese."

"What can I say? I was at the end of *Persuasion.* You wanted me to leave Captain Wentworth and Anne for boring mac 'n' cheese?"

"*Persuasion* the movie, or the book?"

"Book, of course. Always better than the movie."

"Annie's a book snob," Marc said.

"You should think about joining my book club. Although I'm not sure if all our choices would appeal to you. We like to mix it up between classics and contemporary fiction, with a few children's books thrown in now and then for good measure."

"Like what for instance?"

"*Heidi, Little Women, Anne of Green Gables, Huck Finn* ..."

"I'm all over it."

"Can I join too?" Marc asked. "I like *Huck Finn*."

I laughed. "Sorry. Girls only."

"That's sexist. Reverse discrimination."

"Somehow I don't think you'd want to be part of a group called the Getaway Girls."

"Can't you change it to the Getaway Girls and Boys?"

"Are you serious?"

"Why not? Why does a book club have to be limited to girls? Men read too. Or do you have some secret girls-only ritual you do that men can't be a part of—like the Ya-Ya Sisterhood or something?"

"Yes we do. It's called slumber parties. Somehow I can't see you in footie jammies or bunny slippers with a mud mask on your face." I gave him a sweet smile. And as I looked at Marc's cute bearded face, a sudden image of him hairy-chested in plaid flannel bottoms smiling at me over the breakfast table flashed before me.

Down girl.

I averted my eyes, praying the telltale flush I felt creeping up my neck would go unnoticed.

"Give it up, Marc," Annie said. "You guys have had your men's only clubs for centuries. Now it's our turn."

"Fine. Be that way. Guess I'll just have to start my own book club then. I'll see if I can find a bunch of guys who want to read Tom Clancy or Raymond Chandler and we can get together and smoke cigars and belch and scratch." He finished off the rest of his chicken and washed his hands. "Paige, come on over and I'll show you how to strip."

My eyes flew to his face and I blushed again. Had he read my thoughts?

"Sorry. Roses. Strip roses, I mean."

Marc explained that all the thorns had to be removed from roses before they were ever put into bouquets or arrangements.

For smaller, domestic roses, he used a small metal stripper which he just clamped onto the stem and pulled down, stripping off the thorns. For larger, imported Ecuadorian or Brazilian roses, the stems were too thick for the stripper, so he used a knife instead, holding the rose at the bottom and cutting off the thorns in an upward motion. "Just be careful when you do it so you don't cut yourself," he said. "I'd hate to see blood on those pretty hands."

As Marc put together a birthday bouquet of red and yellow roses, he showed me how to remove the "guard petals," the outer layers of petals that protect the rose from the elements while it's growing outside. Once I removed the outer, slightly bruised and battered petals, the inner rose revealed herself in all her untouched, natural beauty.

"Ooh, so pretty."

"Sure is," Marc said with feeling.

I've never known a man who appreciated flowers so much.

"So, how are things going with your mom these days?" he asked. "You still ready to join a Mom-Anon chapter?"

"Nah. At least not right now. Ask me next month though, and I may give you a different answer. She can still make me crazy, especially when she blows off her doctors and thinks she knows more than them. But thanks to the senior center, I think it's given her a new lease on life of sorts. She's not as housebound or reliant on me anymore, which is good."

"For both of you," he said. "So … I'm guessing this gives you a little more freedom to go out?"

"Yep. Especially with Frieda making her dinner on Wednesday nights now."

"Wednesday?" His brow furrowed for a moment. "That's today." He looked over at me. "So would you be free tonight for dinner and a movie?"

"Sounds like fun. Annie told me how you guys have employee nights out sometimes. I can only have dinner though. I have to be at church by seven to do child care."

A strange look flickered over Marc's face. Was it disappointment that I couldn't go to the movies too? Before I could ask, Annie joined us in the back with a new order.

"So, where are we going to dinner?" I asked. "Do you guys have a favorite place? I'm game for just about anything. Except Indian." I scrunched up my nose. "I'm not a big curry fan."

Annie looked over at Marc, raising her ringed eyebrow.

"What?" I asked. "You both love curry?"

19

> All you need for happiness is a good gun, a good horse, and a good wife.
>
> *Daniel Boone*

Tess made a beautiful bride.

She wore a sleeveless pale-blue column dress, elegant in its simplicity, a delicate bouquet of white roses, lilies, freesia, and heather, and happiness like a gossamer cloak. Joy shimmered off her. She'd considered wearing a suit, but discarded that idea when they chose a July wedding date.

Outdoors. In Sacramento. The valley of the scorching sun.

James, her silver-haired groom, didn't let that scorching sun stop him from wearing a wool kilt in his colorful MacDonald clan tartan of blue and green plaid criss-crossed with lines of black and vivid red.

"Don't you look handsome?" I said as I pinned on white rosebud and heather boutonnieres to the blue collars of Tess's twins, Tommy and Timmy, and James's sons, Duncan and James Jr., which I'd helped Marc make late yesterday.

He'd shown me how to wire and tape the boutonnieres, which was harder than I'd realized, and he also taught me the florist's trick of putting a wet cotton ball in the boutonniere stem before taping it to keep it fresh.

I was still too green to work on wedding bouquets, so I just watched in fascination as Marc and Annie worked their floral magic on Tess and Chloe's hand-tied bouquets. I was able to help with the centerpieces though—removing white roses from their stems and floating the flower heads in low square-cut bowls of water on the backyard tables.

As Tess appeared on the patio, flanked on either side by her two sons, a bagpiper clad in a kilt and full Scottish regalia piped her down the flower-lined walkway to the sound of an ancient Scottish song that made me think of mountains and the windswept Highlands. A Highland cathedral.

I caught my breath. And so did all the Getaway Girls gathered near me. "Beautiful," Annette breathed.

I've always loved listening to the bagpipers at the Highland Games, but I'd never heard a piper play at a wedding before. There was something primordial and almost otherworldly about it that stirred my long-neglected Scottish roots. Right then I decided that if I ever got married again, I'd have bagpipes at my wedding too.

The piper finished his stirring song and Tess's pastor asked us all to pray as he began the ceremony.

When Tess and James said their vows, my eyes grew wet. You could *see* the love shining between them. However, it was when the couple took Communion as their first act of marriage to the piper's haunting rendition of "Amazing Grace" that I really lost it.

The tears streamed down my cheeks. Annette's and Kailyn's too. I noticed Chloe's cheeks were also wet.

We were all blubbering.

Everyone except Becca, who wasn't big on weddings.

When the pastor said, "You may now kiss your bride," James grinned and dipped Tess backwards in a major lip lock.

"Yeah!" Timmy and Tommy cheered.

"Whoa. It's nice to know that even at their age there's still passion," Kailyn said.

"You'd better believe it." Her dad, Randall, squeezed Annette's shoulder and sent her a look that made her blush.

"Oh, get a room," I told them with a smile.

We all stood as Tess and James made their way down the aisle to the piper's stirring recessional of "Scotland the Brave." As Chloe followed on her cousin Timmy's arm, I saw Ryan send her a slow smile full of promise, and I wondered how long it would be before we'd be attending another wedding.

Annette dabbed at her eyes. "Wasn't that just beautiful? I've never seen Tess so happy."

"Me either," Jenna said. "It must be love."

"Either that or honeymoon anticipation," Becca snarked.

Kailyn shook her head at her roommate. "You're so cynical. I don't think you have a romantic bone in your body."

"Probably not. Hopefully not. Someone's got to keep those footloose and fancy-free fires burning."

We ignored her.

"Have we heard yet where they're going on their honeymoon?"

"Uh-huh. To the coast for the weekend—Monterey or Carmel. Tess wouldn't say exactly where. Then James has to return and wrap up some things at work, but next Friday they're leaving on a," Annette paused for effect, "three-week honeymoon to *England, Scotland, and Wales.*"

"You're kidding."

"Three weeks?"

"That's great."

"James said he wants to show Tess his family's homeland."

"I'm jealous."

"Me too."

"That's not fair." Becca pouted. "We're supposed to do a Getaway Girls trip to Great Britain. Remember, Paige?"

"That wasn't set in stone. Besides, it probably wouldn't even be until next fall when rates are lower. *If* it even happens. It's not going to be cheap."

"Yeah. We'd better start saving now."

"And besides, we can still all go to Britain as a group. I'm sure Tess won't mind going again." Annette fixed Becca with a penetrating stare. "You wouldn't begrudge our Tess her honeymoon, would you?"

"I guess not."

"Hey, let's go congratulate the happy couple and then get something to eat," Kailyn said. "I don't know about anybody else, but I'm starving."

"Me too."

"I hope there's something vegetarian."

Before we could approach the table, however, the piper began to play another Scottish tune with great fanfare, leading a small procession in his wake. James followed the piper, proudly holding a large sword upright, his son Duncan close behind bearing a silver tray with some weird-looking mass on it that looked like a giant gray slug. And James Jr. brought up the rear carrying another tray with a bottle of Scotch whiskey on it.

"Ooh, it's the haggis ceremony," Annette said. "I saw this once when I was stationed in England."

"What's haggis?"

"You don't want to know." She grimaced. "Trust me. Winston Churchill once said that haggis is traditionally served with a large glass of Scotch whiskey to take your mind off what you're eating."

After Duncan set the tray down on the table, James Jr. poured a thimbleful of whiskey into a small glass and set it off to one side. The piper finished his song and asked for our attention.

"Traditionally at this point in the haggis ceremony, I'd recite the famous *Ode to the Haggis* by Scotland's greatest poet, Robert Burns," he said. "But as it's a wee bit long and a mite too descriptive for some with sensitive stomachs, in deference to the bride I'll just be sayin' the first three lines. And when I'm finished, I'll ask ye all to join me in a toast." He cleared his throat and recited in a rich Scottish brogue:

Fair fa' your honest, sonsie face,
Great chieftan o the puddin'-race!
Aboon them a' ye tak your place.

Then he stabbed a knife into the haggis, lifted his whiskey glass, and toasted the haggis and the bride and groom.

We all raised our glasses and joined in the toast.

"Aw come on, Mom, give us the haggis scoop," Kailyn said. "It can't be that bad."

"Want to bet? Jenna, you'd better cover your ears. You're not going to want to hear this."

"I think I'll just go get some more punch." She strolled away.

Once Jenna was out of earshot, Annette told the rest of us that haggis was usually made up of assorted organs from a sheep mixed with oats and then boiled in a sheep's stomach which held it all together.

Kailyn blanched. "I'm not all that hungry after all."

"I am," Becca said. "I'll just skip the sheep guts."

Chloe and Ryan walked up then, holding hands. "Hi everyone."

Becca sent a pointed look to their clasped hands. "Is this the same guy who thought things moved too fast with Chris and Chloe?"

"Yep. And I was right." Ryan squeezed Chloe's hand. "The difference is I've known Chloe for ages."

"And we're not engaged," Chloe added. "Just dating."

"Uh huh. We'll see."

Annette jumped in. "Speaking of dating," she looked around. "Where's your latest fella du jour, Becca?"

"I never bring a date to a wedding. Don't want to give them any goofy ideas."

Ryan grinned. "Yeah, that could prove fatal, Ms.-Never-Going-to-Get-Married."

Chloe changed the subject. "Paige, all the flowers are just gorgeous." She nodded to the baskets of roses and heather perched in strategic spots around the yard. "That Marc's really talented, isn't he?"

Annette gave me a knowing look.

The back of my neck grew warm. Sacramento in July is really a scorcher. "Both he and Annie are. I'm learning a lot from them. I never had any idea of all the work involved with being a florist."

I'd come early to the wedding to help Marc set up the flowers and when we arrived, Annette, Kailyn, and Chloe were already there putting tablecloths on the tables. Annette scurried over the minute she saw us. "Paige, honey, is this that wonderful florist Marc that Tess has been ravin' about?"

Before I could even answer, she thrust out her hand. "Hi Marc, I'm Annette. I've just been dyin' to meet you. Tess and Paige have said such nice things about you. Although they didn't say how good-lookin' you are. Aren't you a cutie-pie?"

"Well thank you." Marc set down the box of flowers he was carrying and took her proffered hand with a wide smile. "It's nice to meet you, Annette. I take it you're one of the Getaway Girls?"

"That's right, darlin'. One of the oldest ones, I'm afraid. Tess and I are the senior members."

"So what does a poor guy have to do to become a member of this book club?" He gave her a big wink. "Shave my beard and legs and say I like Jane Austen?"

Annette giggled. "Not only cute and artistic, but funny too." She wagged her finger at him. "It's a good thing I'm happily married or I'd snatch you right up."

She slipped easily and naturally into automatic flirt mode — something I've never been good at. Probably because I'm not from the South. Flirting is a second language to Southern women. While the rest of us are learning how to conjugate verbs in French or Spanish in high school, I'm convinced Southern women are taking Flirting 101.

Annette continued. "And don't you dare shave that nice beard. Makes you look handsome and distinguished." She stole a glance at me. "Isn't that right, Paige?"

After I flushed and stammered out an embarrassed response, I said to Marc, "Hadn't we better get these flowers set out?"

"See what a slave driver she is? Hasn't even been with me for two weeks yet and already she's ordering me around." Marc grinned to show he was teasing. "I'm just putty in a pretty woman's hands." Then he gave me a slow smile that made me flush again.

After Marc left to return to Golden Daffodils, Annette sought me out. "What a doll. No wonder you've been keeping him under wraps. If my baby girl caught sight of him she'd be all over him like a cheap suit."

"I haven't been keeping him under wraps," I sputtered. "You're being ridiculous."

"I'm ridiculous? Have you not seen the way that man looks at you?"

"You're crazy. Marc doesn't think of me that way. We're just good friends."

"I hope he doesn't look that way at all his friends."

Chloe's mom Karen—Tess's sister—walked up to me then, carrying her granddaughter Sophie. "Hi Paige. Nice to see you. How's your mom these days?"

"Doing well, thanks. She's gotten quite involved with the senior center and is really enjoying being around people her own age. I think she's more comfortable there."

"That's good to hear. I felt bad when she stopped coming to quilting, but I also understand. I could tell she felt a little out of place as the oldest one there even though we tried to make her feel welcome. But she was a little embarrassed by her vision problems and felt she was taking too much time and holding the others up."

"Well, she's in her element now. She's duking it out with one of guys at the senior center for the title of trivia champ, and I think she just might win."

My baby radar kicked into overdrive as I peered at little Sophie. "She's so adorable. And she's gotten so big! How old is she now?"

"Seven months. Would you like to hold her?"

"Can I?"

Karen handed her to me and I bounced her gently in my arms. Sophie gurgled with delight.

"Who's a pretty baby?" I cooed. I nuzzled my face into her soft baby neck, inhaling that wonderful baby smell of talcum and shampoo and something indefinable that is more intoxicating than Kailyn's latest designer fragrance.

Somebody really should figure out a way to bottle it.

"Hey Paige, have you gotten anything to eat yet?" Kailyn asked. "Better hurry before everything's gone."

"Oh thanks. I told Mom I'd bring her a plate too." Regretfully, I handed Sophie back to Karen.

We avoided the end of the table that held the haggis and grazed the buffet of smoked salmon, platters of roast beef and several kinds of cheese, rolls, fresh fruit and veggies, and a plate piled high with Scottish shortbread.

Tess and James opted against the whole bouquet and garter-toss tradition, much to the collective relief of all the single Getaway Girls.

Except Kailyn. "Aw, I was hoping to add it to my collection. I've caught seven bouquets in the past two years."

"And you're still not married?" Becca lifted an eyebrow. "Gee. Guess that archaic ritual doesn't work after all."

"Maybe it only works if that's your goal. I, of course, have a higher calling." Kailyn gazed heavenward, apparently listening for that call from on high.

"Better hope a pigeon doesn't decide to lower his calling on you," Jenna said.

Kailyn quickly dropped her gaze and we all laughed.

My purse, sitting next to hers on the table, vibrated.

"Is that you or me?" she asked.

"I think it's mine." I pulled out my cell, which I'd turned off during the ceremony and set to vibrate during the reception. Oops. Three missed calls from my mother, who was probably dying to know how the wedding went.

I flipped my phone open. "Sorry, Mom. I had my phone

on vibrate and didn't hear your other calls. The wedding was beautiful."

It wasn't Mom.

"Paige?" a quavery voice said.

The bagpipes started up again.

"Frieda? Is that you?" I pressed my hand against my other ear to block out the music. "I can't hear you. Can you speak up?"

"Honey, I'm so sorry."

Frieda was crying and it was hard to understand her with all the background noise. "I don't know how to tell you … your mother's gone … She passed away."

The phone slid from my hand.

20

> "It's all very well to read about sorrows and imagine yourself living through them heroically, but it's not so nice when you really come to have them, is it?"
>
> *Anne of Green Gables*

I didn't understand.

After Frieda's phone call, everything happened in a blur.

The girls shepherded me to Annette's car. "Tell Tess I'm sorry," I said numbly to Becca.

"Don't even worry about it." She gave my arm a squeeze.

Annette and her husband drove me home and Kailyn followed in my car. The paramedics were just pulling away as we arrived. Was Mom with them? Maybe Frieda was wrong and it was all a mistake.

It was no mistake.

Inside, we found Frieda and a man I didn't know who turned out to be the coroner.

The coroner.

As in the official person who confirms that a person is dead.

No longer breathing.

Gone.

It was a blood clot, the coroner said. Happened suddenly while she was napping. She didn't suffer.

"Just think. She went to sleep and woke up with Jesus," one of the ladies from church said when she called to offer her condolences. "Hold onto that. It will give you comfort."

It does give me comfort. I'm happy that my mother's with Jesus, but what about me? I'm still here. And I can't imagine a world without my mom in it.

I take the trash out to the curb and shield my eyes against the sun.

How can the sun still be shining?

Neighborhood kids pedal past on their bikes, while others whiz by, laughing, on scooters.

How can kids be playing?

I notice the realtor across the way scurry out to his car and stick Open House signs in his trunk.

And how can people be going off to work every day as if nothing happened?

Don't they know the world has changed and will never be the same again? It's as if the earth has shifted on its axis and everything is a little off.

Crooked.

Tilted.

I couldn't wrap my head around it. When I left for the wedding that morning, she was fine. And then three hours later she was gone. How could that be?

Apparently Frieda had stopped by to take Mom shopping for some new diabetic socks, and when she arrived to pick her up at the agreed-upon time, Mom was napping.

Or at least, that's what Frieda thought.

"Catherine, are you ready?" she told me she'd called as she let herself in when Mom didn't answer the door. "Come on lazy girl, up and at 'em."

Only Mom couldn't get up. Would never get up again.

I didn't understand. When I'd left that morning, she was fine. She was eating cereal and drinking her coffee.

"Bring me back a piece of wedding cake," she teased.

"Sure. You want a middle piece or an end piece with gobs of frosting?"

"An end piece of course. Let's see if I can get my sugar levels off the chart."

"Right. Dr. Pond will really love me for that."

"Oh, what does he know? He's just an old worrywart." Mom kissed me on the cheek. "Have fun. And try and catch the bouquet. Don't let that young Kailyn get in your way. She's strong, but you can take her."

Those were the last words my mother ever said to me.

Isabel caught the next flight out.

I'd had to call and tell her the news. Annette offered to make the call for me, but I knew it was something I had to do.

"Iz?"

"Hey little sister, how's it going?"

I couldn't form the words. I couldn't say the *D* word.

"Paige? Are you okay?"

"No ... It's Mom ... She's gone." Then I handed the phone to Annette to give her the details. I just couldn't.

I sank down on the couch. The hideous brown-and-orange velvet couch that I had hated and Mom had loved.

The couch she would never sit on again.

All at once, Marc was there. Standing in front of me. In my living room.

Frieda or one of the Getaway Girls must have called him.

I looked up at him dumbly. "It's my mom."

"I'm so sorry." He dropped down next to me and gathered me in his arms as I sobbed.

Isabel took charge when she came out, which made sense. She couldn't handle Mom when she was alive, but now that she was gone my MBA sister was a machine of brisk efficiency, handling all the myriad, necessary details that have to be coped with when someone dies.

Good thing because I went through the days in a fog. I couldn't bring myself to do anything other than the basics.

Get up.

Shower.

Brush my teeth.

Shovel tasteless food into my mouth.

Accompany my sister to the mortuary.

Surprisingly, for all Mom's clutter and disorganization, she had left us clear instructions as to her last wishes in an envelope in her nightstand marked "To my children in the event of my death."

The first thing she wrote in her letter—typed in 16-point bold font on her computer—was that she didn't want to be buried in the ground. *I don't know that they make a casket big enough for me anyway. LOL. Besides, they're way too expensive. Just cremate me like Dad. Maybe you can put me in a matching urn?*

She also requested a memorial service at church and wanted Jennie Jameson, who usually sang solos at Easter and Christmas and had "such a beautiful voice," to sing "You'll Never Walk Alone" from *Carousel*, another one of her favorite musicals.

Of course she wanted Marc to do the flowers. *All pink please. No gladiolas or white lilies. They have too much of a funeral air to them.*

As for the food at the reception afterwards, she'd set aside money for a caterer and asked that I throw out my Food Police badge for the day and stop counting carbs and worrying about sweets. And ... if it wouldn't be too much trouble, could I make my delicious stuffed mushrooms for everyone? She'd have liked for me to make all the food but thought that might be asking too much.

Patrick didn't come home for Mom's memorial service.

But then, he didn't know about it. We sent an email to the last address we had for him, but it came back as undeliverable. Isabel placed a call to the ashram in India, but they said he'd left over a year ago with no forwarding address. Her web-savvy husband, David, spent hours on the Internet, googling Patrick's name and leaving messages on various message boards all over the world in hopes of finding him. Still no luck.

Finally, we had to face the fact that Patrick was lost to us. Had been for years.

The service was beautiful. Everyone said so.

Vases brimming with pink roses, carnations, daisies, stock, and hydrangeas flanked an elegant, silver-framed photo of my mother on her fortieth wedding anniversary. Isabel created a slideshow presentation with the most flattering photos of Mom throughout the years set to songs by Josh Groban. And I wrote the eulogy which I had the pastor deliver, ending with a quote from C. S. Lewis: *Has this world been so kind to you that you should leave with regret? There are better things ahead than any we leave behind.*

It was gratifying to see all the people who came to pay their respects to my mother: Dr. Pond, Dad's old boss from Campbell's, several neighbors including Frieda and her daughter, Nikki, Arthur and Addie ... even my old supervisor from Landon. Karen and some of the ladies from quilting came too, as did Mom's new friends from the senior center, Frank, Jerry, and Alice. Jerry gave me a tinfoil crown he'd made that had "Trivia Champ" written on it with a Sharpie.

Even Eric came.

He sat alone at the back, and there was genuine sorrow in his eyes when he clasped my hand after the service. "I'm so sorry, Paige," he said.

"Thanks." I squeezed his hand and locked my gaze with his. "So am I." Then I released his hand and nodded toward the reception hall. "Be sure and get some food. There's plenty."

"Thanks, but I really have to get going. You take care."

"You too." I watched him leave for the last time without regret. Then I returned to my guests.

All the Getaway Girls came to the service, of course, including Tess, who would be leaving on her three-week honeymoon the next day. Ever since that awful phone call, all the girls had rallied around me, offering love and support and stepping in to help and do whatever was needed.

Annette and Kailyn brought casseroles and insisted on doing my laundry.

Chloe brought Chinese and vacuumed and dusted.

Jenna brought strawberry protein shakes and mowed the lawn.

Becca brought mochas from Dunkeld's and washed my car.

Tess came back early from her weekend in Monterey with her brand-new husband. When she showed up at the front door, she took one look at my face and knew.

"Paige, don't feel guilty. That's the last thing you need to feel. You were a wonderful daughter to your mom. Don't ever think any different."

"But I hate that I wasn't there when she died."

"She died in her sleep, honey. There was nothing you could do. Actually, as a mother, I'm glad you weren't there. I'm sure your mother would be too. That would have been so terrible for you to have gone in and found her. I don't think you could have handled it."

Frieda had said the same thing—that she was glad she was the one who found Mom, and not me. It would have been too hard for me to handle.

Her leaving was too hard for me to handle.

The grief rolled over me in waves.

I'd grieved when my father died too, and it wasn't any less because we'd known he was dying and had time to get used to the idea. Grief is grief—no matter how prepared you think you are for the person's dying. The difference there was, I was able to say good-bye.

I never got to say good-bye to Mom.

Marc understood.

Actually, Marc was amazing. You really find out who your friends are when something like this happens. He was there for me whatever I needed.

To lend a quiet, listening ear and a shoulder to cry on.

To run interference between Isabel and me when he saw how her cold efficiency nearly made me lose it one day, and I wanted to chick slap her size-six butt back to the Windy City.

And to talk me down when people said thoughtless things. Like the neighbor who said, "Time heals all wounds. Weeping may last for the night, but a shout of joy comes in the morning."

I'll give you a shout in the morning, and it sure won't be of joy.

"I heard the same sort of comments when my mother died," Marc said. "I know they were trying to be kind, to say something that would help. But it would have been kinder to be silent. People who haven't lost someone they love don't have a clue."

"You wonder how things can go on as normal when it's

not normal that the person you loved is no longer here," he said. "You want to share something with them, but then you remember that you can't. Or you go to call and tell them something funny, but then you realize they're not there to answer the phone anymore."

When I had a normal moment, I'd find myself heading toward Mom's room to see if she wanted biscuits with my crockpot stew. It wasn't until I knocked on her door that I remembered she'd never answer again. I'd grown tired of always cooking dinner for her, but when she left, it was the only thing I wanted to do.

Mom had left one other final instruction in her 16-point, bolded font letter—a startling request that took us by surprise.

> *Paige honey, remember that old song, "You take the high road and I'll take the low road, and I'll be in Scotland afore ye"? And remember when you asked me that one time where I'd like to go if I could go anywhere in this whole wide world?*
>
> *Do you think maybe you could scatter your dad and me on "the bonny, bonny banks of Loch Lomond"? Or somewhere in the Highlands where there's some heather on the hill? I always loved that scene in* Brigadoon. *And then we'd be back home with our ancestors.*

I looked up through blurred eyes at Isabel when I finished reading.

"This is crazy," she said. "Mom never talked about Scotland. Or was ever big on the whole ancestor thing. It doesn't make sense. And I don't know if it's even legal to take ashes across the ocean."

"I don't care if it's legal or not. I'm taking my mother and father to Scotland. I wasn't here when she died. The least I can do is honor her final wish."

Isabel puffed out a sigh. "Okay. Well I'm going with you."

"What?"

"I'm going with you. You shouldn't have to do this alone."

"Why not? I did everything else for Mom alone. Why should this be any different?"

That was mean, I know. But I couldn't help it.

"She was my mother too."

"You sure didn't show it when she was alive."

Isabel bent her head. "I know. So let me show it now."

"A little late, don't you think? Besides, what would David say?"

"David will understand." She gave me a sideways glance. "And he could come with us."

"No. This has nothing to do with him. He never liked Mom."

"That's not true." She sighed. "But I'm not going to argue with you. So, do you want to make the travel arrangements, or should I?"

21

From the end spring new beginnings.

Pliny the Elder

Scotland. We were on our way to Scotland. Home of the Brave.

Heart, that is.

For years, I'd dreamed of going to Great Britain. As an armchair traveler, I'd devoured tale after tale of epic sagas set in that historic, ancient land of rolling green hills, rugged moors, and ruined castles. I'd dreamt of soaring stone cathedrals and thatched-roof cottages. Of haunting Celtic music and rousing Highland dancers. Of tea and shortbread and men in kilts who sounded—and hopefully looked—like Ewan McGregor. I'd also dreamt of hiking through the Highlands, exploring misty lochs, and hearing the sounds of a lone piper on a distant hill as the sun set over the mountains. I'd even hoped that someday, somehow, I'd be able to talk Mom into going with me.

This wasn't exactly how I'd planned it.

I glanced down at the carry-on package beneath the seat

in front of me. Then I looked over at the matching package beneath the seat in front of my sister.

After the memorial service, I'd wanted to get on the next plane to Scotland to honor my mother's wishes for her and my father's final resting place, but it wasn't that easy. It took awhile to research and get the necessary permits and myriad other details. And the fact that we wanted to scatter ashes overseas complicated things.

Isabel emailed and said she found an international company that offered to do the scattering for us. She sent me a link to their site which I checked out and then emailed her my thoughts. *There's no way I'm going to send my mother through the mail, Iz. Not even FedEx. I've seen* Castaway *with Tom Hanks.*

That same company also offered an additional service. If we wanted, we could order a handcrafted piece of jewelry—maybe a locket or a cross—that would "retain a portion of our loved one's remains" as a keepsake.

"I'm not going to wear Mom around my neck," I said. "That's creepy and morbid and wrong on so many levels."

"I agree."

Well that's a first. Isabel and I never agreed on anything, which was never more evident than in those first emotion-filled days after Mom passed.

David, Isabel's husband, flew back to Chicago the day after the memorial service, but she stayed behind, offering to help me go through Mom's things and start packing them up. "We can finally get rid of this nasty old couch and those cheesy figurines in the curio cabinets," she said.

"It's only been a week and you're already trying to remove every trace of her?" I clutched one of the worn throw pillows from the fake velvet couch to my chest.

"I'm not trying to remove every trace of her. I'm just trying to help."

"Why don't you help yourself back to Chicago where you belong? This is still Mom's house and I'm not changing a thing in it."

"Okay," she said in a placating voice as if I were a recalcitrant child. "But at least let me strip her bed and wash the sheets."

"No. I'll do that later." There was still a Mom-shaped indentation on my mother's bed that I didn't want to disturb. Sometimes at night when I couldn't sleep, I'd slip down to her room and curl up in that indentation. And once the sheets were washed, it would remove the scent of her White Shoulders perfume, a smell that would surely disappear soon enough—too soon—from the house.

I couldn't concentrate on my travel guide on the flight from San Francisco to Chicago, where I'd meet Isabel for the next leg of the journey to London and then on to Scotland. It didn't seem possible that Mom had been gone for over two months already and that it was now the last week of September. We'd missed the Edinburgh Fringe Festival, considered the world's biggest single arts festival, and the famous military tattoo, both in August. I was disappointed not to get the chance to see the massed bands and bagpipers at Edinburgh Castle, which I'd heard were goosebump-inducing, but I was happy to bypass the crowded streets filled with frenzied Festival partygoers.

I wasn't really in a party mood.

I wasn't in an Isabel mood either and decided to take a sleep aid for the long flight across the pond. But once we met at O'Hare and boarded our next flight, I forgot about sleeping, especially since Isabel got the window seat first—with promises that we'd switch halfway through the flight. And then my sister laid out her detailed plans for our trip.

Before leaving, we'd decided to make the most of Scotland.

As long as we were traveling all that distance, Isabel said, we might as well see some of the country's natural beauty and historic sites.

It made sense. And I had always wanted to see Scotland. My eyes would be the eyes for my mother, father, and grandfather who'd never been able to make the trip.

We had already decided on our stopping points and I'd booked our B&B's, but when Isabel handed me her trip portfolio, I knew we had two very different Scotland trips planned.

"Where are the historical sites?" I asked, pulling out my portable travel guide with dog-eared pages and highlighted text. "Staying at the best hotels isn't really my idea of experiencing Scotland. I want to see a castle."

Isabel sighed the my-sister-is-so-embarrassingly-quaint sigh. "I looked at the places you booked and decided we needed to make a few changes. If you'll look at point 4, it's a hotel in a completely restored sixteenth-century castle—with central heating, I might add."

"That's not what I mean, sister," I said with the my-sister-is-high-maintenance voice.

The drink cart came rumbling down the aisle just in time to break the building tension. I ordered a cranberry spritzer and Isabel ordered a 7-Up, which surprised me. I thought she always liked to have a glass of wine when she flew.

"What's with the 7-Up?" I asked. "I thought you were a wine girl."

"Usually. But it dehydrates me when I'm flying." She glanced at the sheet of paper I was holding. "What's that?"

"Tess gave us some great recommendations of places to go and must-see sights she and James visited on their honeymoon," I said. Thinking of Tess reminded me of how much I wished I was traveling overseas with the Getaway Girls rather than Isabel.

Isabel inclined her head to the dog-eared travel guide in my lap. "Did she give you that too?"

"No, this is from Marc. Check it out—he went through and highlighted several towns and areas in the Highlands that he thought might be good final resting places for Mom and Dad."

Marc and I had become much closer since Mom's passing. He really lived out that Scripture in Ecclesiastes, "If one falls down, his friend can help him up. But pity the man who falls and has no one to help him up." Marc was the only other person close to me who had lost their mother, so he understood things no one else did.

"So, are things serious between you two?" Isabel asked.

"Me and Marc? We're not dating. He's my friend. Come to think of it, I guess you could say he's become my best friend. He's a sweetheart."

Isabel leaned in. "When I first met him, I thought he was gay."

"Stereotype much?" No way was I going to tell my know-it-all sister that I'd jumped to that same conclusion when I first met Marc. But I'd learned a lot since then. "Just because a man is creative and sensitive doesn't automatically make him gay. I hate the way people label other people. God made each of us unique." Marc was especially unique—and funny, and kind, and generous—which was why I liked him so much.

"Relax," Isabel said. "I was just sayin'. So, are you still working for him at the flower shop?"

"Uh-huh. Part-time." I didn't have the energy or desire to look for a full-time job right now, and Marc and Annie did a good job of keeping me busy and distracted. We'd usually hang out a few times a week. We'd either go out to dinner somewhere after work, or I'd have them over and cook, which they especially liked.

I liked it too. It was nice to have someone to cook for and it made the house less lonely.

Annie was a kick. She'd joined the Getaway Girls and fit in perfectly. Although Marc still pouted that he couldn't become a member. I'd raised the prospect of opening up our book club to men, and although Annette and Tess were open to it—hoping they could get their husbands to come—the others were adamant that we keep it girls only. So I simply told Marc which books we were reading so he could read them at the same time. Then he and I could discuss them together. Currently, we were reading *The Prime of Miss Jean Brodie* in honor of my Scotland trip.

We changed planes at Heathrow. Confusing would be an understatement. So many people! They didn't look quite as bright and shiny as they had in the opening scenes of *Love Actually*, and hard as I looked, I couldn't see Hugh Grant anywhere.

Too bad. Love the thick, rumpled hair and the accent.

Accents were the order of the day at Heathrow. And most of them I couldn't understand. This must have been what it was like at the Tower of Babel.

A crush of humanity flooded the security check lanes—only two were open—and I gripped the handle of my rollaway bag tightly and held Mom close to my chest. Isabel had found a company who would let us hand carry our parents' ashes on the plane, using special containers that met airport security guidelines.

I'd taken Mom, she'd taken Dad. My father was now perched precariously on the top of one of my sister's many suitcases. You'd think, seasoned traveler that she is, that she'd pack light.

Not my sister. She invented the term "clotheshorse."

And that clotheshorse was now rearing back on her

stiletto-shod hind legs and neighing and flailing for balance after being jostled from behind. As Iz fell, her feet flew out from under her and kicked one of her suitcases, causing the rest to go down like dominoes and our father to fly up in the air.

We both lunged for him at the same time and missed.

Thankfully, a stocky young guy in a striped rugby shirt leapt up and caught Dad neatly, to our relief and the cheers of his teammates.

After that, I took possession of both Mom and Dad.

After we finally made it through the interminable security line, we found our gate and sat down to wait for boarding. Exhaustion mixed with adrenaline. It was so exciting to be in *London*, but disappointing that we were this close to Big Ben and Westminster Abbey and couldn't see them.

So close and yet so far.

With thirty minutes until boarding, I decided to review the Edinburgh section of my guidebook. The castle—a castle! We were actually going to see a castle!—was at the top of the hill with the Royal Mile, a one-mile-long road, leading to the Palace of Holyrood where Mary, Queen of Scots, once lived.

I felt a curious mixture of excitement and sadness. It was exciting to finally be in Great Britain and know that soon we'd set foot on the soil of our ancestors. Who knew? Maybe we'd find some long-lost cousins. We didn't have much to go on, however, other than Mom's family name, Gallie.

"I wish Mom could have done this," I said more to myself than to Iz.

"Mom would never have done this. We would have missed our flight if Mom were here. And with her weight—"

"Welcome to British Air," a cheery voice said over the intercom, saving my sister from the flood of words I was about to unleash on her. "We are now boarding at Gate 5—"

I knew it was a commuter plane, but I wasn't prepared for

it to be quite so small. Only three seats across, no more than twenty rows long. Good thing we're only going to be here for an hour or so.

The flight attendant handed us menus.

Menus? On a plane?

Actual menus with lots of choices. Like a café. An airborne café. And the attendants all had wonderful English accents. I asked questions just so I could hear them talk.

Isabel decided on the roasted vegetable hot pizza slice, but since we were in England after all, I opted for the full afternoon tea that was more like a lunch—two small sandwiches, plus a scone, jam, and cream. Clotted, of course.

Not as fabulous as our tea at the Ritz, or even Tess's bridal shower—it was still airplane food after all—but all in all, fairly good.

Everything would have been great if it hadn't been for the baby opera singer behind us. As much as I love kids and am still longing for a baby of my own, after traveling all night and it now being lunch time, I was just too tired for crying babies.

Maybe they don't have pacifiers in Great Britain?

Looking out the window, I saw something I'd never seen before—layers of clouds. There was a layer of wispy clouds—if I remember correctly from junior high science class, they were called nimbus—through which we could see the cauliflower-like clouds. (Cumulus, I think?) Great effect.

As we took off and left London behind—too far away to see Big Ben or anything famous I'd recognize—I looked down upon the English countryside and a gorgeous crazy quilt with all the greens of fields and forests and farmland in irregular parcels with trees lining them all.

Sitting in my café-in-the-clouds, it all became real.

We're here. We're not in the States anymore. I reached

under the seat in front of me and patted the special travel box. Not much longer, Mom, and we'll be in your homeland.

Edinburgh Airport was so much easier than Heathrow and we were quickly in our taxi and on the way through the city to our B&B. Although it was a bit pricey, taking the taxi was well worth it so we didn't have to mess with public transportation, luggage, and jetlag all at the same time.

That had been Isabel's suggestion—due to all her bags. But my weary body was grateful for it.

"Will we be driving by Edinburgh Castle?" I asked our cab driver, rhyming Edinburgh with Pittsburgh.

"Not from around these parts, are ye?" He smiled at us in his rearview mirror. "Sure, I can take you that way. The scenic route."

He went on to teach us the locals' pronunciation of the city—Ed-din-bruh—and suggest we try the double-decker bus tour to orient ourselves and learn a little bit more about his native city at the same time.

We'd done this in Paris, at Tess's suggestion, and it had proven invaluable.

True to his word, our cabdriver drove us past the castle which sat high on a hill overlooking the city. We couldn't see a lot because the entire castle is surrounded by a high stone wall, but I was surprised to see how spread out it was. And it wasn't just one building, but several.

I couldn't wait to explore it tomorrow.

Our bed and breakfast was just a couple miles past the city center on a quiet, residential looking street. At least if you consider three-story-tall buildings residential. It reminded me of San Francisco the way the buildings were tall and right up next to each other. Unlike the Painted Lady Victorians of San Francisco though, these buildings were mostly made of stone. Very old, tan stone with gabled roofs and bay windows.

"How old world," I blurted out.

"Pretty amazing, huh?" Isabel snarked. "Since it *is* several hundred years old."

Sabrina, our innkeeper, showed us to our room. "Is this your first trip to Edinburgh?"

Our cabdriver was right about the pronunciation.

"Yes. First time in Scotland."

"Well then, let me be one of the first to welcome you to this wonderful city. Your rooms are on the second story. Let me help you with your bags."

Second story. A flash of memory from Paris. That will mean the third story, as we think of it. Our first story is their ground floor. They call the next flight up the first story.

Judging from the area and the outside of the building, I was expecting our room to be old-world charming with antiques and tartan plaid. I was surprised, albeit pleased, to see a large, contemporary room with two beds done up in dark greens, with a green leather couch under the window and a pristine bathroom in a rich green marble tile.

Sabrina was explaining things, and I have to admit I was having so much fun listening to her accent that I wasn't paying all that much attention to what she was saying. Something about the shower and a string and hot water. Oh well, we'll figure it out. Meanwhile, we're in Edinburgh.

Time to sightsee.

"Let's wait a while," Isabel said, looking longingly at her bed. "I need to take a short little nap."

"We can't stop now," I said. "We need to push through the day. The open air bus will do us good. Sunlight's the fastest way to reset our internal clocks."

Isabel had wanted to start our exploration of the city on foot, but I put my foot down. In Paris, the double-decker bus tour gave us a great overall introduction to the city, so I insisted we do the same in Edinburgh.

"Well look at you," Isabel said. "My little sister's gotten all cosmopolitan."

With Sabrina's instructions, we caught the city bus to the Tourist Information Center and picked up a couple different guidebooks, then walked over a block to where the open air tour buses started.

We sat on the top of the bus listening to the local guide tell us about the different buildings and the history of the city. The old town has layer upon layer of buildings built on top of each other, he said, and in some places, you can go several stories underground to see how people lived centuries ago.

"Why are so many of the buildings so dark—almost black?" Isabel asked.

"That's years and years of accumulated soot, my darlin'. It's too dear to have them cleaned."

I'd always heard the Scots were thrifty. This proved it.

He pointed out The Scott Monument, named after Sir Walter Scott, Scotland's most famous writer, as we passed—a towering Victorian Gothic spire whose stonework was also stained black with soot. "In Victorian times, Edinburgh was nicknamed 'Auld Reekie'," our guide said, "which means 'old smoky.'"

Although the old stone buildings in Edinburgh weren't as pristine and creamy as the architecture I'd seen and fallen in love with in Paris, these ancient stone buildings had a gritty, lived-in charm of their own.

And so much history.

Looming above everything else in the city is the castle. Built atop a volcanic hill, it's been destroyed and rebuilt "with horrible regularity" in all the battles between the English and the Scots. Our guide explained that Edinburgh has been at peace since the mid-1700s, when Bonnie Prince Charlie unsuccessfully tried to regain the throne. Since then, the city has thrived with the addition of New Town, and has been the birthplace of many of the world's greatest scientists and writers.

Most of the rest of the tour was a blur. Jet lag finally kicking in.

We saw the new Parliament building, a funky dome-looking thing with spikes sticking through it—definitely not from the days of Old Town. The Palace of Holyroodhouse looks interesting. Arthur's Seat …

"I didn't know King Arthur went this far north. Is there a Guinevere's throne or Lancelot's couch?"

The tour guide smiled at me. "No, love, Arthur's seat is an extinct volcano and has been called by this name since the fifteenth century. Some say the extinct volcano is probably named after a local hero that had nothing to do with King Arthur, but it's also thought to be a derivative of the Gaelic phrase *Ard-na-Said*, meaning Height of Arrows."

Definitely jet lag. Time to head home. Back to our B&B.

Exiting the city bus at our B&B street, we stopped in a market for a few provisions—some bread and cheese, chocolate, and bottled water. Way too tired, we opted for a picnic in our room and an early sleep.

So much for Edinburgh's night life.

22

"Isn't it splendid to think of all the things there are to find out about? It just makes me feel glad to be alive—it's such an interesting world. It wouldn't be half so interesting if we know all about everything, would it? There'd be no scope for imagination then, would there?"

Anne of Green Gables

We both felt better in the morning, although I guess we woke up too late to get the hot water. I washed and rinsed as best I could in the cold water. At least it wasn't too cold out.

Shivering, I stepped out of the bathroom. "Brrr. I wish I had my bathrobe."

"You just finished showering," Isabel said. "The room's not that cold."

"Maybe not, but the water was freezing."

"Is the water heater broken?"

"That, or it's just empty."

She stared at me. "What *are* you talking about?"

"The water heater's empty."

"It can't be. It's instant heat."

The blank look on my face must have spoken volumes. "The cord in the shower is the instant water heater," she explained. "Sabrina showed it to us yesterday."

"Oh, I thought that was the shower vent."

Ten minutes later, Isabel was blow-drying her hair after her nice hot shower.

Brat.

When we entered the dining room, we were greeted by Sabrina's husband, Tony, who had a great smile and prematurely gray hair. He offered us several breakfast choices and we went for the when-in-Rome scenario, opting for the traditional Scottish breakfast.

As we were enjoying our morning coffee, a middle-aged couple entered the room. It was obvious that this wasn't their first morning here. They went straight to "their" table. Tony reappeared and the couple already knew their breakfast order: coffee and porridge for him, tea and toast for her.

When our breakfasts arrived, we realized why.

Our plates were filled to the rim with eggs, bacon and sausage, fried tomatoes, sautéed mushrooms, fried toast, the dreaded haggis, and a dark black thing that resembled a hockey puck.

The middle-aged couple smiled at the looks on our faces.

"Your first Scottish breakfast?" he asked in an American accent.

"How could you tell?" I leaned over and whispered, "What's this black thing?"

"Black pudding. Blood sausage."

I lost my appetite. But not wanting to be rude, I pushed the hockey puck to one side with the haggis and just ate the bacon, eggs, and mushrooms.

After breakfast and a short bus ride, we were back on the

Royal Mile. According to Isabel's map, we were near the midway point. So much for starting at the castle and walking the mile downhill. Oh well. Best-laid plans. As we passed a pub on the right, I noticed the name: Deacon Brodie's Tavern.

"Deacon Brodie!" I said. "He was the inspiration for *Dr. Jekyll and Mr. Hyde.* By day, Brodie was a well-respected cabinetmaker and a member of the Town Council, and by night he led a band of thieves. Eventually, he was caught and hanged—supposedly on a gibbet he'd helped design."

"How'd you know that? And just when did you start reading more classics than me?" my sister with the master's degree asked.

"Research for our book club discussion on *Jekyll and Hyde.*"

"I've been meaning to read at least one classic a year, but with my job, I just don't have the time."

Of course you don't, Ms. High-Powered Executive. What you need to do is just downscale to part-time like your humble little sister and then you can read all the classics you want.

We continued walking, passing tons of great-looking shops that Iz wanted to check out, but I was on a mission. I had to see my first castle. Up close and personal.

As we got closer, I could see that this was no Disney castle, all blue and pink and shiny with Tinkerbell flying around it spreading her fairy dust. Instead, it was old, majestic, and reeking with history. Walking up to the castle gate, I overheard another visitor say this was the esplanade where the military tattoo had been held last month.

"I wonder if you have to have a tattoo to get in." Isabel waggled her eyebrows.

Hmm. My sister made a funny. A lame one, but still. Who knew?

We entered the castle through the Gatehouse with bronze

statues on either side of the arched entrance of Robert the Bruce and William Wallace—who didn't look much like Mel Gibson—guarding the castle gate. Inside the castle grounds, a tour guide took us up the hill and gave us lots of history as we wound our way between all the buildings.

So many wars, so much violence in the struggle for power. So much destruction and lives lost.

All this was brought home when we visited the Scottish National War Memorial with all its bronze friezes and stained glass windows showing images of "the great war to end all wars," World War I, and the figure of Michael the Archangel soaring overhead.

Heartbreaking.

We sought solace by going into St. Margaret's Chapel, the oldest building in the castle—and in all of Edinburgh—which was nearly a thousand years old. Apparently there had been many other buildings built before this little chapel, but they'd all been destroyed and rebuilt. It seemed ironic that the only structure to survive was a church.

Or not so ironic.

The tour guide told us the chapel was still used for weddings and christenings. "Fathers of the bride love it because the chapel only holds twenty people—makes for a very inexpensive ceremony," he said with a roguish grin.

I'd always thought that the Scottish being frugal was a stereotype, but there's a lot of truth to it. When he showed us the one o'clock gun, he said that the gun has been fired from the northern defenses of the castle every day except Sunday and a couple holidays for more than 150 years to let the ships at sea reset their clocks. Traditionally, other countries fired off twelve rounds at noon to signal their ships, but the thrifty Scots realized they could save a lot of ammunition—eleven rounds a day—by waiting an hour.

Next he showed us the huge, medieval siege gun, Mons Meg, which weighs six tons and used to be trundled around the countryside in action at battle sites against the English. However, the massive gun soon became too cumbersome to travel, and by the mid–1500s was taken out of military service. Iz and I took turns posing next to the behemoth cannon and then took tons more pictures from the castle walls looking down over the city.

Walking back down the Royal Mile, we decided to pop into the Edinburgh Woolen Mill. I mean, how often can you buy woolens from the very mill right there in Edinburgh? The shop had a clan room full of both women's and men's kilts, tartan cloth, Highland jackets, and masses of clan-crested accessories, but we looked and didn't find anything saying there was a Clan Gallie. I picked up an Edinburgh T-shirt and a red plaid scarf.

Then I saw the cashmere. Stack after stack of cashmere sweaters.

I fell in love with a red, button-down cardigan and tried it on—although wool sweaters are usually too scratchy for me. Not this one. It was like a soft caress against my skin. I looked in the mirror, admiring the fit.

Then I looked at the price tag. I took it off, folded it neatly, and set it back on the pile.

Isabel bought a pair of hunter green cashmere gloves and a matching scarf as well as a black cashmere scarf and gloves for David. "Our hands freeze in the winter," she said. "That's one thing I miss about Sacramento—no nasty Midwest winters."

After we finished our shopping, we noticed St. Giles Cathedral and decided to take a peek inside. There was a bronze statue of John Knox, leader of the Scottish Protestant Reformation who lived during the time of Martin Luther and Henry VIII. But the most remarkable thing was the stained glass.

Window after window.

Panel after panel.

Each gorgeous scene followed by another equally spectacular one.

Any thoughts of a quick peek of the cathedral were washed away by bits of colored glass. We sat and absorbed the magnificence, then moved to a different spot to look at different scenes.

Now I understood what Chloe was talking about when she tried to describe Ste. Chapelle in Paris. We'd all gone together to visit Notre Dame, but Chloe, Tess, and Annette made a side trip to a smaller nearby church the day I was taking an extra cooking lesson from Jacqueline. She'd been unable to describe the experience adequately, except to say that it was transcendent.

Here now, I knew what she was trying to explain.

Thoughts of the Scottish Reformation made me think of the beginning of the German Reformation and of Martin Luther. I kept myself from singing aloud his words, but they rang loud and strong in my soul—"A mighty fortress is our God. A bulwark never failing."

The words reminded me that he would never fail me. No matter what.

Walking around the cathedral, the hymn's melody still playing in my mind, I noticed a plaque on the wall. Anticipating some deep, spiritual insight, I walked up and read: "Thank God for James Young Simpson's discovery of chloroform anesthesia in 1847."

Okay.

Hungry now, we decided to find somewhere to eat dinner. Deacon Brodie's seemed a little too loud and touristy, so we kept looking, hoping for something quieter. As we wandered through the city streets, we found a small pub down the steps of a small side street called the Halfway House.

Small seemed to be the norm for most of the places we frequented.

Once inside the pub with only four tables and a bar, we saw a plaque that said it had won the Scottish Pub of the Year for 2005. We also learned from our friendly server that it was the smallest pub in Edinburgh. He was from London but had been living in Edinburgh for twenty-three years. "I think I'll stay a bit longer," he said, with a wink.

The menu was posted on a blackboard and I opted for the border lamb with rosemary while Isabel tried a traditional Scottish dish called a stovie—potatoes cooked with corned beef and other vegetables and served with oatcakes.

Starving, I took a bite of my lamb and nearly swooned.

And I thought the food in Paris was good. Wonder if they'd give me the recipe?

Isabel was equally happy with her stovie. "It's like beef stew, only with corned beef," she said. For dessert, we shared a bread pudding that was indescribable.

Our server told us about a fascinating house in the city he thought we should visit called Mary King's Close. It was sealed up during a cholera epidemic, and then new buildings were built over the top. He said it's now three and a half stories below street level and the best preserved three-hundred-year-old house in Europe. Although other buildings are older, they've been altered over the centuries. Mary King's Close was a time capsule.

Sounded fascinating, except we were both way too tired to climb up and down that many stairs. We decided to just head back to our inviting B&B. And when we returned, I got the chance to talk to our innkeeper, Tony. I noticed that his accent sounded different than what I'd heard all day.

"I'm not a native," he explained. "I was born in Portugal, but my heart is Scottish."

I was beginning to know how he felt.

Although I'd loved Paris and had found it beautiful with a graceful, feminine feel to it, Edinburgh was more strong and masculine. I could actually feel the strength of that ancient city seeping from the stones.

Maybe it was from all the haggis they eat.

"So, Tony, what's the deal with haggis anyway?"

"It's everything left over from the cow or sheep, mixed with oats."

"Waste not, want not?"

"Exactly. Comes from a poorer time."

"But do you actually eat it?" I grimaced.

"Not really. I don't know anyone who really does anymore. It's now mostly a tourist thing."

"Remind me to just have toast and porridge for breakfast, okay?"

The next day, our last in Edinburgh, I did have the toast and porridge.

Big city girl that she is, Iz wanted to stay a little longer in Edinburgh, but I was anxious to move on to the Scottish countryside and see the Highlands, so we decided to cram as much as we could into our last day.

We walked all over the city, stopping to see the statue of Greyfriars Bobby, the Skye Terrier who wouldn't leave his master's grave and kept guard over it for fourteen years until he died. Iz, who had her own devoted Bichon Frise waiting for her at home, sniffed as she recounted the story to me.

Following Tess's recommendations we visited the tiny Writer's Museum, a former residence that now honored three of Scotland's most famous writers: Sir Walter Scott, Robert Louis Stevenson, and Robert Burns, who is considered the national poet of Scotland and who wrote, among other things, "Ode to the Haggis" which the piper had quoted at Tess's wedding.

Isabel and I wound our way up and down narrow stairs to explore rooms crammed with pictures, manuscripts, and exhibits that included Burns' writing desk, Scott's chessboard, and the printing press on which his Waverley novels were produced.

"I've never heard of the Waverley novels, much less read them," Isabel whispered to me. "Have you?"

"Nope. The only Scott I've ever read was *Ivanhoe* back in high school."

"Good. Then I don't feel so stupid. Have you read *any* of these guys?"

"Just Stevenson."

"What did he write?"

"Um, *Treasure Island. Kidnapped. Dr. Jekyll and Mr. Hyde.*"

"I take back my stupid comment. And as soon as I get home I'm starting a book club."

"I can give you a list of titles to choose from if you like."

"I like."

At the small counter near the exit, I picked up leather bookmarks with the Writer's Museum embossed in gold for each one of the Getaway Girls.

Afterwards we visited the National Gallery, which houses the national collection of fine art from the early Renaissance to the end of the nineteenth century.

Small, but mighty.

We wandered past Rembrandts, Rubens, Gainsboroughs, and amazingly lifelike portraits by John Singer Sargent. Then I came upon a van Gogh I'd never seen or even heard of—*Olive Trees.* I stopped, mesmerized by the intensity of the writhing brushstrokes and colors. I know Chloe had fallen in love with Monet in Paris, as did I.

But there was just something about van Gogh.

I read that this painting was one of at least fourteen canvases of olive trees that van Gogh painted while confined to the asylum at Saint-Remy.

That explained it. The agitation. The frenzy. The torment.

"Ready to check out the basement wing?" Iz asked.

Downstairs, where Scottish art was highlighted, we saw several serious portraits of famous Scots including Sir Walter Scott done by an artist I'd never heard of, Henry Raeburn.

And then we came upon something completely different. A whimsical painting of what looked like a red-cheeked minister clad in a black frock coat and hat, skating on the ice. I peered at the title, and sure enough: *Revd Dr Robert Walker Skating on Duddingston Loch.* Done by the same artist, Raeburn, and commonly known as "The Skating Minister."

I could feel myself smiling. And when we stopped to buy postcards to send home, I picked up a key chain of the skating minister for myself.

For lunch, we had leek and onion soup at the gallery café followed by cups of tea and Victoria sponge cake. And then we were off. A couple more shopping stops and then good-bye Edinburgh, hello countryside.

We took a taxi to the airport where we picked up our rental car, a tiny thing that reminded me of a Mini Cooper. I didn't plan on driving, however. Not with my directional impairment. Also, the steering wheel was on the right side, the driving was on the left, and it was a stick shift. That's what you call a recipe for disaster.

I willingly ceded the driving responsibility to my older

sister. Which meant I had to be the navigator. Which involved reading maps.

Would we even make it out of the Highlands alive? Our entire family might wind up scattered in the hills, not just our parents. Oh well. We'd be just the latest in a long line of ancestors going back *thousands* of years as it turns out.

In another one of the Edinburgh shops offering clan tartans and accessories, we asked a clerk whose specialty was genealogy if he'd ever heard of the name Gallie.

According to him, Gallie is a sub-branch of the Gunn clan.

We have a clan! Woo-hoo.

Between the two of us, we almost bought out the entire stock of green plaid Gunn merchandise: two kilts, three scarves, two hats, three pins, and two key chains. We had to honor our heritage, didn't we?

We also learned that our new clan motto was *Aut Pax Aut Bellum,* which means "Either Peace or War."

The next few days would bear that out.

23

> A journey is a person in itself; no two are alike. And all plans, safeguards, policing
> and coercion are fruitless. We find that after years of struggle that we do not take a trip;
> a trip takes us.
>
> *John Steinbeck*

I wonder if there's such a thing as genetic memory?

As we drove through the lush, open countryside on our way to the Highlands, it felt somehow familiar, as if I'd been there before. Probably from all the movies I'd seen.

An hour and a half later we pulled into the southern Highlands picturesque village of Dunkeld on the banks of the River Tay. Dunkeld, we read, translates to "Fort of the Celts." The area became a religious center over 1400 years ago when Celtic monks chose the location as the base for their missionary work in East Scotland.

We were here, however, in honor of the Getaway Girls and Dunkeld's Bookstore. I wondered if Becca's boss even knew there was a Dunkeld in Scotland. I took a picture of the village sign for show and tell. We sauntered down the narrow streets and saw signs to Dunkeld Cathedral. Since we were there, we decided we might as well check it out.

I sucked in my breath, and even Isabel let out a gasp at the idyllic picture postcard scene spread out before us. The ancient stone cathedral stood amidst wide green lawns that swept down to the river on one side and forested hills on the other. Tall trees swayed in the breeze as we approached the ruined cathedral with tall gray stone walls open to the sky and a grassy carpet for a floor.

As I looked up through the roofless edifice, I thought of *Brother Sun, Sister Moon,* the Zeffirelli movie from the seventies of Saint Francis of Assisi, and I remembered how Saint Francis had said the church was outside. Here, in this sacred place, the clouds were the ceiling and there was a sense of timelessness and tranquility in the air. A cool breeze drifted through the ruined nave and fluttered my hair as I knelt among the ancient tombstones, some dating back to the fifteenth century.

Outside the stone walls, four-foot-high Celtic crosses dotted the ancient cemetery. As we walked among them reading the names and dates on the tombstones, I realized they'd lasted for centuries. My fingers trailed over the names that made me wish that we could erect some kind of enduring marker in my parents' memory.

We entered the parish church part of the cathedral where weekly services were still held, and there we learned that Dunkeld was once the ecclesiastical capital of Scotland. While Iz wandered around quietly checking out the surroundings, I slipped into a pew and bowed my head, wondering as I did how many others had prayed in this very spot before me hundreds of years before.

We decided to spend the night in Dunkeld and found a

B&B right in town, just a few minutes from the cathedral. For dinner, Isabel encouraged me to spread my wings a little, so we ate at an Indian restaurant where she had chicken tikka masala, which is apparently Queen Elizabeth's favorite dish and the most popular dish in Britain. Since I still didn't like curry, I opted for the mustard chicken instead.

The next morning we hurried through breakfast since we needed to drive a ways to the designated spot where the representative from the ashes scattering company had instructed us to meet him.

We didn't talk as Isabel made her way through narrow winding roads to our destination—the whole reason we were in Scotland. She was intent on the road and I was intent on the sad packages in my lap.

I gripped Mom tightly, knowing the time had come to say good-bye but not sure I was ready. I tried to take solace in the fact that I was fulfilling her final wish, but that didn't stop my throat from tightening or my eyes from blurring.

An hour later, a lone piper stood on a nearby hill that was covered in heather and piped "Amazing Grace," while we released my parents' remains into a rushing waterfall that would eventually carry them into Loch Lomond.

And my tears flowed with the water as I said my last farewell.

After this difficult good-bye, the next item on our Scotland itinerary was to visit Culloden Battlefield—the last battle on British soil.

I trailed Isabel into the Visitor's Center where we learned that on April 16, 1746, thirty years before our own successful War of Independence, Culloden ended Bonnie Prince Charlie's hopes of regaining the throne. The battle lasted less than an hour and would affect the entire future of the Highlands.

Civilians who were not at the battle—including women

and children — were slaughtered, and the Highlands culture began to be erased. Kilts were outlawed, clans were disbanded, and all weapons had to be surrendered. Including bagpipes.

Bagpipes? Weapons?

We walked out of the Visitor's Center onto the battlefield, which looked like a lot of the Highlands, only flatter. Mostly wild grass with an occasional tree or shrub. A lone thatched roof cottage was the only building, and that wasn't even technically there at the time of the battle. Most of the farmhouse had been rebuilt, and an open moorland with flag markers showed where the armies had gathered.

We passed the Well of the Dead with its stone plaque marking the place where one of the clan leaders was killed. Two hundred and fifty-odd years later there is still water in the well. Refusing to dry up, like the stories of these brave people.

Lining both sides of the walkway were the gravestones marked simply with the names of the clans. Too many bodies for individual graves? Or simple disregard on the part of the victors? The Highlanders were confined to mass burials.

I could almost hear the voices of the dead crying out and see the ground running red with blood.

Stupid to come to a battlefield on this, of all days. I fought to keep my emotions in check. The grief and loss. For these people, but even more so, the loss of my parents, my heritage.

Gone.

Scattered in a field.

We got to the twenty-foot-high stone memorial with its simple inscription: The Battle of Culloden was fought on this moor 16 April 1746. The graves of the gallant Highlanders who fought for Scotland and Prince Charlie are marked by the names of their clans.

"Is that it?" Isabel blurted. "I don't get it. It's just an empty field with a flag."

I whirled on my sister. "You're so thick." What my voice lacked in volume, it made up for in tone. "Don't you care about anything? Sometimes you have to not think. Sometimes you have to feel."

And the tears started to flow. Tears into sobs that wouldn't stop.

"Paige?" was the only thing that Isabel said before she walked away.

Deserting the family once again. Embarrassed to be seen with a crazy woman falling apart in a battlefield.

I became aware of other tourists giving me a wide berth. They probably thought I'd become caught up in the emotion of this place.

Not knowing that even at age thirty-five, a woman still needs her mother. However imperfect their relationship.

I knew the emotional explosion would happen in Scotland. I'd figured it would be when we were spreading Mom's ashes. I never dreamed it would be in public. But once set free, the breach could not be contained. So I walked. Through the battlefield, away from the people. Away from the woman birthed by my mother yet somehow not really family.

Later, when the tears stopped flowing, I walked back to find Isabel sitting on a bench. Though she saw me coming, she waited until I got to her before she stood up.

"I'm sorry. I don't know what—"

"It's okay," she said, giving me an awkward hug. "I understand."

Our drive to our B&B was mostly in silence, which was fine by me. We had agreed to skip the nearby prehistoric Clava Cairns. Even though it was considered one of the best-preserved Bronze Age burial sites in Scotland, it was still a burial ground.

And we'd been to enough burial grounds that day.

Inverness must have been beautiful, but I hardly noticed anything until we got into our room. And that was only because Isabel started complaining.

"Three diamonds," she muttered. "I should have insisted on four."

"What are you talking about?"

"This guest house was supposed to be rated three diamonds."

"And?"

"Hello? Didn't you hear the toilet running when we came in? I had to jiggle the handle to get it to stop."

"Okay?"

"Can't you smell the mildew?" She paced around the room.

I sniffed. "Now that you mention it, yes."

"It's growing in the shower. You can actually see the mold. Disgusting."

I crossed the creaky floor into the bathroom and shuddered. "You missed the best part." I grabbed a tissue and wiped up a small pile off the counter top. "Someone's toenails."

"That does it. We're outta here. The bathroom probably hasn't even been cleaned since it was originally installed in the fifties." Isabel looked at the sink and toilet and shuddered. "Fifties pink, just like at home."

"You always did hate that color."

"Not nearly as much as I hate it in this place right now." She began to roll her suitcases to the door.

"Come on, Iz, you can't run from everything unpleasant."

The words were out of my mouth before I realized what I was saying.

Isabel spun around, her eyes blazing.

"I'm ... I'm sorry. I didn't mean it like that."

"Oh yes you did. That's the second jab in as many hours," she said. "I wasn't going to say anything at the battleground—too public. I thought it best to let you have your drama on your own. Thought it would pass and you'd cool down. Obviously, I was wrong."

I realized that this room was about to become another battleground.

"Fasten your seatbelt, it's going to be a bumpy night."

"Don't quote me movie lines, big sister," I said. "That's my territory."

"You mean like Mom was?"

"Excuse me?"

"You heard me. You loved being the perfect, self-sacrificing, long-suffering daughter."

"No," I said, clenching and unclenching my fists. "I just tried to take care of her as best I could since her other kids hated her and deserted her."

"I didn't hate Mom. I loved her."

I snorted. "Sure had a funny way of showing it. You left home the minute you could and moved clear across the country."

"It was the only way I could break away from her. Her control. Her passive-aggressive manipulation."

"But you also broke away from me. You left as soon as you could and left me holding the bag." My turn to pace.

"I had to. I couldn't stay in that house any longer. Mom drove me crazy."

"You don't think she drove me crazy too?"

"Yeah, but you always knew how to handle her better than I did. You didn't argue and make waves. That's why you were her favorite."

"*I* was her favorite?"

"Oh yeah. Whenever I talked to her, all I ever heard was Paige this, Paige that. Paige cooked this amazing dinner for me. Paige made me a sugar-free birthday cake from scratch. Paige is the next Martha Stewart. Blah, blah, blah."

"Well all I ever heard was Isabel has a fabulous career. Isabel is best friends with Oprah. Isabel walks on water."

"Oprah? You're kidding, right?"

I shook my head.

"Where did she ever get that crazy idea?"

"From you."

"Are you kidding?" Isabel sat down on the only chair in the room, a smile tugging at the corners of her mouth. "Little sister, I think we've been played. I think what we have here is a failure to communicate."

I started to sit on the bed, but the faded bedspread gave me pause. I'd read all the gross stories about hotel bedspreads on the Internet. I pulled the spread down and began to laugh.

Isabel noticed and joined me.

The blanket was very loud, very bright, and very pink.

"I haven't seen that neon a color since the eighties," she said.

"Me either. What do you say we get out of here and talk over dinner?"

"Deal. But I'm telling you, I'm not staying here more than one night."

"Deal."

We found a nearby restaurant where we ordered fish and chips and swapped years of Mom-loved-you-best stories.

"Remember the time she made you your costume for the nativity pageant?" I asked. "You were the best-dressed angel in the pageant. I was so jealous of your glittery halo and all those sequins that sparkled under the lights."

"And I was jealous of your costume," Isabel said.

"My costume? I played the donkey!"

"I know. But you had really cool ears and a tail."

We giggled.

The waitress approached. "Would you like anything else?"

"Yes," I said. "A couple glasses of white wine."

"None for me, please," Isabel said.

"But I want to make a toast to Mom."

"Could I just have a Sprite or 7-Up?" she asked the waitress, who nodded and went to get our drinks.

I looked at Isabel across the table. When had my cosmopolitan sister become a teetotaler? She didn't have wine on the plane either.

And then I knew.

"You're pregnant," I said.

Isabel blushed and sent me an anxious look. "I didn't want to tell you."

"Why not?"

"Because I know how much you've always wanted a baby. I didn't want to rub your face in it," she said. "Especially on this trip."

My sister's going to have a baby. I turned the words over in my head.

My older sister.

How did that make me feel?

Jealous?

Angry?

Envious?

I tested the words again, this time aloud. "My sister's going to have a baby," I murmured.

Isabel reached for my hand across the table. Tentatively. "Are you okay?"

Was I? Six months ago this news would have cut me to the core. Even three months ago. Two.

But not now. Tears pricked my eyes and I squeezed my sister's hand. Then I sprang up and hugged her tight. "I'm going to be an aunt!" I felt a lone tear splash my cheek. "I'm just sad Mom's not here. She wanted to be a grandmother so much."

The waitress returned with Isabel's Sprite and my wine. I sat back down and lifted my glass. "To Mom, who's probably dancing for joy in heaven right now that at long last she's going to be a grandma."

Isabel clinked her glass with mine and we each took a drink. Then I raised my glass again. "And to my sister, who's going to be a mother and who's going to have an absolutely beautiful baby who will be spoiled rotten by his or her Aunt Paige."

"That would be a *his*. Iz's face split into a huge grin. We're having a boy!"

"Woo hoo! To my nephew!" We clinked glasses again and drank.

Then I raised my glass a third time. "And to yours truly, who's also going to be a mother."

Isabel's jaw dropped. "Paige! You're-you're pregnant?"

I parroted our mother. "You'll catch flies that way."

Iz closed her mouth, yet still stared at me wide-eyed.

"No, I'm not pregnant," I said. "But when we get back home, I'm going to check out my adoption options—find out what I need to do to become a single adoptive parent."

"You'll make a great mother," Isabel said softly. She grinned. "But start the process soon so my kid will have a cousin to play with when we come out to visit."

"I'll see what I can do." I remembered from my Internet surfing that most single women who adopted had established, successful careers. "I think it might also be a good idea for me to go back to school and get my B.A.," I said. "Maybe in early childhood education ..."

"That's a great idea!" Isabel said. "I'd be happy to check out schools for you and find out which ones have a good education program. I think Berkeley might."

I quirked an eyebrow at her.

"Or you could do that perfectly well on your own."

"Actually, Iz, I'd welcome the help. Especially since I'm also going to have to get a full-time job soon to start saving up for the myriad adoption costs."

We talked long into the night, discussing all the different possibilities. And when we got back to "Scotland's Armpit," as Isabel had christened our tacky B&B, she pulled a flat tissue-wrapped package out of her suitcase and handed it to me.

"What's this?"

"Open it and see."

I undid the tissue paper and there was the red cashmere sweater I'd tried on our first day in Edinburgh.

24

> One's prime is elusive. You little girls, when you grow up, must be on the alert to recognize your prime at whatever time of your life it may occur.
>
> *The Prime of Miss Jean Brodie*

The next morning it was dreary and foggy as we drove through the mountains.

I guess there were mountains. We mostly saw only clouds. And rain. Lots of rain. At one point we realized we were driving alongside the famous Loch Ness. Not that we could see the other side of the lake (loch) but we could see the edge of the water. According to the map, this was Loch Ness.

The rain stopped shortly before we arrived at the castle. From the car park we had a great view of the ruins silhouetted against the backdrop of white mist. It was like something out of the King Arthur stories, only instead of Camelot, this was Urquhart.

I had to stop along the pathway to take it all in.

This was so different from Edinburgh Castle or anything I

saw in Paris. The tower, half crumbled and roofless—a grand remnant of the past. Struggling to find the right word, all I could come up with was ethereal. That always seemed kind of a woo-woo word, but here and now, that's exactly what it was.

Ethereal.

Otherworldly.

We decided to watch the short informational video before going to the castle. Isabel and I entered the theater and took our seats. Six hundred AD, the 1200s, 1400s ... I tried to fit all this in with the limited Scottish history I knew.

And I wondered how it all related to *Braveheart*.

Invaded by the English, the castle was no longer needed or wanted, so the soldiers blew it up so no one else could use it. Chunks of wall still lying where they are today. That was over three hundred years ago. Way before George Washington and our American Revolution.

I was thinking about the colonies—people ruled by another country, finding the common ground between my American heritage and Scottish ancestry—when the movie ended. The screen rolled up and I noticed the curved backdrop curtain began to open.

There directly in front of us and across the field was the ruined tower.

Oh my. Talk about bringing history to life.

The castle sat on a little peninsula-like thing, surrounded on three sides by the lake. The crumbled walls of the many buildings were at staggered heights, meandering like the hilltops. Where there were once floors, grass grew in its lush greenery. While I appreciated the green, I was glad the rain had stopped.

Amazing that there were any walls still standing. And people were walking in there. Even up in the tower.

I stood in an arched stone doorway and looked back toward

the Visitor's Center. The modern wooden ramp and hand rail leading to the ancient cobblestone floor. Knee-high stone wall in front of another waist-high wall. Green hill sloping in one way meeting the zigzag of a partial building and the misty tree-covered hill and the white sky.

Feeling adventurous, I decided to climb to the top of the tower. It looked like five or six stories tall, and although the stairs were open-air and wet, other people were up there so it couldn't be too dangerous.

Could it?

The stone stairs were weathered and rough, so not all slippery—the different levels in the tower allowed for various views. And the best view, of course, was from the top. The clouds were patchy now so I could see bits of the other side of the lake. The tower was built on the edge of the lake with a sheer drop down to the water.

A tour boat passed slowly by, although I couldn't make out the individual people.

I felt at peace.

Maybe it was the fog. Enveloped in the coziness. The plush green of the trees and grass. Maybe it was coming to terms with my life. Thoughts of my family, my old job, of Paris, of Culloden, and the sheer history of these ancient stones.

I'd come home.

The realization was startling. Sure, my ancestors came from Scotland, but that was generations ago. My home was in Sacramento.

No, that was my house, the place I grew up, the church I attended, the restaurants I went to. Yes, that's my home. But this was something deeper—ancient even.

So this is what it means to be home.

A noise behind me made me turn back towards the water. A line rippled its way through the water. A wake. Something was moving in the water. I remembered the tour boat, but strangely, could no longer hear the motor. Must be the fog clouds muffling the sound.

I laughed out loud.

This had to explain at least some of the Loch Ness Monster sightings. I shared my theory with Isabel.

"Grandpa used to tell us fun stories about Nessie when we were little," she said.

"I don't remember those stories."

"That's because you were only two. I was four, almost five ... that's when Great-Grandpa Gallie died ... He said he'd seen Nessie when he was a wee lad and thought maybe the monster was hungry so he threw her/him/it the rest of the candy bar he'd been eating."

Just then we saw a couple tour buses pull in and the children piled out yelling, "Nessie! Nessie!"

We read in our guidebook that the first recorded Nessie story came from the sixth century. Supposedly Saint Columba was on his way to see the king and he discovered a man being attacked by a water beast in the loch. Apparently Columba drew the sign of the cross and ordered the monster to leave.

The beast turned and fled.

In the gift shop, I found some more Gunn clan items, including one very special one—the smallest kilt I'd ever seen. But I made sure Isabel didn't see me buy it because it was going to be a Christmas present for her son. My nephew. So adorable. I couldn't wait to see his tiny little legs peeking out from his Gunn kilt!

At the gift shop we also bought box after box of Scottish shortbread, which was nothing like the kind we got in the States. This shortbread melted in our mouths the moment it touched our tongues. And it was especially good with a hot cup of tea.

With milk and sugar of course.

That night we stayed in one of our favorite B&B's of the trip—a far cry from "Scotland's Armpit," although we had a hard time finding it initially. Isabel had called ahead to an accommodations agent in town and told them that we wanted to stay in a clean, quaint, charming country inn or bed and breakfast with two beds, en suite (bathroom in the room).

And it had to be at least four stars.

No more three stars for my sister.

Me either.

I didn't think I could handle another person's toenail clippings ever again. That seriously turned my stomach. And I wasn't even the pregnant one.

The booking clerk told us she had just the place. A small country inn with just six rooms en suite that had recently opened, but had already received a four-star rating. They served dinner and one of the owners was a gourmet chef renowned for his steaks.

Would we be interested?

Does Mr. Spitz like to catch mice?

The only downside was that the inn was down a desolate country road out in the middle of nowhere and the directions to get there were a bit tricky.

Were we good with directions?

I started to shake my head no but Isabel held up four fingers, mouthed the words *gourmet chef* and *steak* and patted her tummy that was showing just the slightest hint of a pooch. Then she stuck out her lower lip.

I gave in. And then proceeded to get us hopelessly lost for the next forty-five minutes.

In the dark.

And the rain.

In a foreign country.

Next to a really big lake.

"You know I'm no good with directions, Iz."

"I did know that. Years ago. But I thought by now you might have gotten better."

"That's like saying you thought by now I might have gotten taller. Sorry. It's a genetic abnormality."

"Genetic-schmetic. I'm getting you a universal GPS system when we get home."

"Okay." I began to sing, "On the soggy, soggy banks of Loch Lomond."

Iz giggled. Then she snorted.

Yes, my MBA sister from Chicago who's best friends with Oprah.

Pretty soon we were both snorting. And laughing so hard we almost missed the turnoff to our country inn. An inn that was every bit as charming as the booking agent told us. And then some.

Huge, inglenook fireplace in the sitting room, old-world antiques, white down comforters, 800-thread-count sheets, and deep claw foot tubs with hot running water that you didn't have to remember to pull a string to heat.

In the dining room when we came down to dinner, there were white linen tablecloths and napkins, Staffordshire blue-and-white plates, and crystal water goblets.

We both ordered steak—the thing to do in Scotland, apparently—from Hamish, our kilt-clad host with a great Scotch brogue. I had pepper steak with pepper sauce, Iz had a petite filet.

Both melted in our mouths.

After dinner, I took a book into the sitting room and curled up in front of the huge fireplace while Iz paged through a magazine.

"Well hello there," I heard my sister say in a syrupy, totally un-Isabel voice. "Who are you? Aren't you just adorable?"

I set my book down in time to see a white flash of fur scamper up to my sister.

"Fergus (only he pronounced it Fairr-gus), are ye behavin' yourself or are ye bothering the lovely ladies?"

Isabel scooped the white Scottie into her lap. "He's not bothering me at all. He reminds me of my dog whom I'm missing like crazy." She made sweet cooing noises to the fluffy lapdog.

Hamish asked us how long we'd been in Scotland and what we'd seen so far.

I told him of our adventures, highlighting our latest stops.

Turns out he was a direct descendant of one of the clans buried at Culloden by the well.

"We saw that yesterday," I told him.

What I hadn't seen at Culloden because I was too busy having a breakdown were the engraved stones on the pathway to the visitor center that were called the Culloden Walk. A fundraiser from the National Trust, the Culloden stones are available for anyone to purchase as a memorial to their loved ones with a message of their choosing, Isabel informed me.

"Really? A stone? How long do they say it will last?"

"Indefinitely. And you can also get a replica of the stone for yourself. To put in a backyard or a garden or whatever," Isabel said.

"Let's do it!"

She smiled and flashed the paperwork at me. "Way ahead of you, little sister."

Isabel was tired and went to bed a little later, but I stayed up in the sitting room staring into the fire and thinking over the past several days and all that had happened.

I'd said good-bye to my mother, hello to my sister, and found a new heritage and a second home in the process. Yes, I'd fallen in love with Paris when I visited there, but the rugged Scottish countryside with its ruined castles and cathedrals stirred something primeval in my soul and I knew I had to come back again.

And again.

On our way home, when we changed planes in London, they told us our flight back was overbooked so they were asking for volunteers to stay overnight and catch another flight in the morning. They'd put us up in an airport hotel and give us vouchers for meals. Were there any volunteers?

Isabel and I thrust our hands up at the same time.

Then we scurried to the Underground stop, caught the tube into the heart of London, and raced to see Big Ben and Westminster Abbey. Seeing the names of all the famous English writers I knew and loved immortalized in Poet's Corner of the Abbey made my heart go pitty-pat.

I couldn't wait to tell the Getaway Girls.

We also snagged tickets to see a musical in the West End.

A revival of *Brigadoon.*

25

> A man travels the world over in search of what he needs and returns home to find it.
>
> *George Moore*

I opened the front door, rolled in my suitcase, and collapsed on the couch.

Boy it felt good to be home.

But as I shifted on the sagging couch, I realized it was definitely time to get rid of this old thing and bring mine out of storage. I glanced at Mom's curio cabinets crammed to the hilt with figurines.

Maybe it was time to retire the Precious Moments too. I'd set one aside for both my sister and me as a memento, then offer Frieda first crack and take the rest to the senior center.

I glanced around the living room, considering other changes I might make.

Definitely paint the walls. They hadn't been painted in years.

And maybe add some crown molding.

Mom had left me the house in her will. Not me and Isabel so we could sell it and split the proceeds. Just me.

"That doesn't seem fair, Iz," I said to her that night we stayed up so late in the musty B&B talking about anything and everything.

Was Mom playing us against each other again?

"It seems perfectly fair. You're the one who's been there all the years taking care of Mom and you're the one who moved in with her. Not a problem. Doesn't bother me a bit."

She grinned. "Especially since David and I are putting our condo on the market and planning to buy a house in the suburbs soon. With a dedicated guest room of course, so Auntie Paige can come out and babysit."

"You got it. Just make sure it's on spring break or around the holidays, or I'll be in school."

The great thing about Mom leaving me the house was that it was paid off and mortgage-free, so I didn't have to worry about a rent payment anymore. Sure, there would be taxes and utilities and maintenance costs, but no house payment.

That would give me more flexibility.

And next year when the Getaway Girls went to Great Britain, I'd be the travel guide. At least to Scotland.

I decided to flip on the local news to see what I'd missed while I was gone.

A pudgy thirteen-year-old girl with mousy-brown hair badly in need of a trim and glasses held together with duct tape was speaking to the camera. "Everyone always wants to adopt or foster babies or cute toddlers," she said. "I don't blame them. I would too. Babies are cool. But there are also kids like me, in between, who need a home and family too."

She stared at me from the TV screen, naked pleading in her eyes. "If not more."

My heart clenched.

Okay God, could you be a little more subtle? I thought you didn't do the thunderbolt between the eyes stuff anymore.

I glanced back at the screen. But a teenager?

The airbrushed anchor was smiling a plastic smile at the awkward adolescent and pretending to bond with her for the cameras. "Thank you, Syd. That's short for Sydney, right? As in Sydney Bristow from *Alias*?"

"As in Cyd Charisse."

"Cyd Charisse?"

"The dancer. MGM musicals. You know, *Singin' in the Rain, The Band Wagon, Brigadoon*? My mom liked all that retro stuff."

"Okay. Well thank you again, Cyd." The camera cut to a closeup of the anchor's face. "If you'd like to find out more information about becoming a foster parent to children like Cyd who need your help, please dial the number on your screen or go to our website at www.blah, blah, blah."

I scribbled down the phone number, then flipped off the TV and sank back into the couch. I felt like I'd been sucker-punched.

Looking at that lonely girl on the screen was like looking into a mirror. I never had the taped glasses, but I definitely had the pudge factor. And the in-between factor. And I also had two parents who loved me. Sure, with a little manipulation and some dysfunction, but who's perfect?

She didn't have anybody.

I glanced at the number in my hand. Should I call right away?

Wait a minute, wait a minute. Aren't you being, oh maybe, just a little bit impulsive? I mean, think about it. You with a teenager? You don't know the first thing about raising a teen. You're best with babies and cute toddlers, remember? That's the route you're planning to take.

God's plans are not our plans.

So what are you waiting for? Are you going to call or not? Do you want someone else to get to her first? What if it's some creep or something? That's all the poor kid needs.

I punched in the number.

And after the voice on the other end told me she'd send me the necessary information to start the foster parent screening process, I punched in another number. Who better to share my momentous news with than my best friend, Marc?

Only it went right to voicemail, which meant his phone was off.

He was probably out delivering flowers.

I looked at the clock. Not this late.

So maybe he was at the movies or something. Leave him a message.

As I finished leaving him a voicemail, the doorbell rang. I opened it to find Marc himself beaming and holding a large basket of white gardenias.

"I just left you a voicemail," I said.

"Welcome home." He handed me the flowers.

"Thank you. They're gorgeous! What a wonderful surprise. Come on in." I set the flowers down on the coffee table and turned back around to face him.

He grabbed me by the shoulders, pulled me into his arms, and kissed me.

Definitely not the kiss of just a friend.

Oh.

My.

It had been years since I'd been kissed like that.

Marc pulled away slowly and caressed my cheek.

"By the way," he said, "gardenias mean secret love."

"Not so secret anymore." I pulled him to me for another kiss.

Some people go through life trying to find out what the world holds for them only to find out too late that it's what they bring to the world that really counts.

Anne of Green Gables

BOOK SELECTIONS IN *TURNING THE PAIGE*

Kidnapped, Robert Louis Stevenson, 2002 (originally published in 1887).

Into Thin Air, Jon Krakauer, 1997.

Around the World in 80 Days, Jules Verne, 2001 (originally published in 1873).

Tara Road, Maeve Binchy, 1998.

The Prime of Miss Jean Brodie, Muriel Spark, 1961.

ACKNOWLEDGMENTS

Some books are harder to write than others—for myriad reasons. This was one of those. So it's with gratitude that I thank the following for their help and support:

Jean Baumann for her memories of Scotland.

Jan Coleman for early brainstorming and for the foothills drive description.

Lisa Cook, Annette Smith, and Karen Grant for answers to medical questions—with a special shout-out to Karen for going above and beyond.

Jennie Damron for the "booty-head" scene inspiration.

Cathy Elliott for her willingness to be a first reader and for her fast replies and sweet, generous, and encouraging spirit.

Karissa Lucas and Josh Cook for answering all my call center questions.

Cindy Martinusen Coloma for helping to brainstorm new scenes and letting me know when something didn't work. (Also, for the great short stack line!)

Dave and Dale Meurer for their gracious hospitality and for Dave's insight.

Debbie Thomas for the pop-ups on the Internet line.

A big bouquet of thanks to Sarah and Char Ireland for all the behind-the-florist-scenes help.

My wonderful and patient editor, Andy Meisenheimer, who even when he doesn't get some of my "girl" stuff, always challenges me to be better. Also to Becky Philpott and the rest of the Zondervan team, including the talented designers who came up with the great castle cover even before I'd written the Urquhart Castle scene!

To my beloved Michael for sharing his travel journal and

reminding me of so many of the details from our Scotland visit, but most of all for his continued sacrifical love and support. You're my rock and I thank God that he brought us together.

And as always, to God, who makes all things possible and always provides.

> Think only of the past as its remembrance gives you pleasure.
>
> *Elizabeth Bennett*, Pride and Prejudice

A GETAWAY GIRLS NOVEL

Laura Jensen Walker

AWARD-WINNING AUTHOR

Read an excerpt from Laura Jensen Walker's next book in the Getaway Girls series, *Becca by the Book*. Coming soon!

1

Look! Up in the sky. It's a bird. It's a plane. No, it's me, Becca Daniels. Skydiving. Which totally rocks. Lynyrd Skynyrd's "Freebird" fills my head as the wind whips my face and I plummet towards the ground. Wow. Who knew this would be such a rush?

Jenna.

And she told the rest of our Getaway Girls group about it, so here we are. Sharing airspace with eagles. How cool is that?

Cool. And cold. My skin tingles and my cheeks flatten into my skull from the force of the wind and the tight goofy glasses they make us wear. But who cares? I'm free falling. Tom Petty's free-spirited anthem replaces "Freebird" in my head.

I feel a tap on my shoulder and Zach, my instructor who's strapped against my back for our tandem jump, lets me know it's time to pull my chute. I reach down by my hip and pull the cord. The harness jerks my body and we come to an abrupt halt. Only it's not really a halt. Just an immediate slowing down—a huge change from when we were hurtling towards the ground mere seconds ago. Now instead of speeding downward, we're gently floating. Zach gives me the handles which control our descent and I lead us into a spin. And then another.

Definitely the best adventure ever.

I glance above and behind me and spot Annie's flame red T-shirt off in the distance. Annie's cool. She always wears these great slogan T-shirts. Today's red one said Out of my mind—will be back shortly.

"Y'all sure are out of your mind," Annette had said when we met up at the airfield. "Jumping out of a perfectly good airplane."

Pushing fifty-two, Annette is the oldest member of our book club and the only one who's ever served in the Air Force. And as such, she'd tried to talk us out of our skydiving adventure. "The pilots I worked with said the only way you'd ever catch them jumping out of a perfectly good airplane was if the plane was going down. Doesn't that say something to you?"

"Yeah," I said. "It says they were a bunch of wusses."

"Ya got that right." Jenna flexed her toned biceps. "No wusses allowed."

Our wusses, Annette, Paige, and Kailyn, stayed on the ground. Chloe and Tess were busy with their guys, but Jenna, Annie, and I headed up into the wild blue yonder, eager to spread our wings.

And spread them we did. Wide. As we soared through the air, I felt like Kate whatshername in Titanic with my arms outstretched and hottie Zach behind me as Leonardo DiCaprio.

Only so much better.

"What'd you think?" Zach asked after we landed and he unbuckled the harness that strapped us together.

"Loved it! Can we do it again?"

"A woman after my own heart." He favored me with a sexy, gap-toothed smile.

I never did like guys who were too perfect. Zach's slight space—the width of a thin stick of gum—between his front teeth just made him all the more appealing. "Another hundred and fifty bucks and we're back up there," he said.

That wasn't as appealing. I'd hoped Zach might offer to take me up again. For free.

In my dreams.

I heard a squeal behind me. As I turned, the squeal turned into a roar as Jenna, my adventure buddy in crime, rushed towards me. With a giant bear hug, she tackled me, knocking me to the ground.

"So, was that sweet or what?" Jenna was usually a high-five girl, but your basic high five was totally inadequate for the moment.

"Oh, wow." I untangled my arms and legs, the adrenaline still pumping. "It rocked! I want to go again."

"Y'all are seriously crazy," Annette said as she and the others joined us.

"Seriously," Kailyn echoed. "I can't believe you really did it."

"And I can't believe you didn't. Oh wait. Yes I can. You wouldn't want to break a nail."

Kailyn, with her designer flip-flops and Niagara Falls blonde hair, is the girliest roomie I've ever had. And I've had plenty of roomies over the years. Of them all though, Chloe was the best. Even though she was a church chick.

Too bad she had to dump me to go find herself in Paris.

Not that I blame her. I'd dump my grandmother for the

chance to live in Paris for three months. Or Rome. Sydney. Singapore. Beijing … anywhere overseas. The more exotic, the better.

My roommate thinks I'm crazy for wanting to live in China. Or anywhere exotic, for that matter. "Don't they eat cats and dogs in those places?" She's another church chick. One of those perky ones. Do Christian girls take lessons in perkiness or what? Maybe it's one of the Ten Commandments: Thou shalt always be perky.

Whatever.

Sometimes though, it's like fingernails on a chalkboard. Especially in the morning. Kailyn's one of those disgusting morning people. She bounds out of bed at seven a.m.—even on weekends—all bright-eyed and squirrel tailed, humming and dancing around like some Disney princess with a halo of happy bluebirds twittering around her head.

Good thing I'm a pacifist. Otherwise, I'd blast those stinkin' bluebirds to kingdom come.

Our first Sunday as roommates, she sang in the shower while she shampooed her perky blonde hair, rummaged through her closet for her perkiest outfit to wear to church, nuked two perky cinnamon rolls, and then rapped on my door, singing out in her perky blonde voice, "Rise and shine, sleepy-head, breakfast is ready. Want to go to church with me?"

I lifted my Seven Dwarves Grumpy head from beneath my pillow and yelled something I know she's never heard in Sunday school.

But we're good now.

Kailyn knows not to wake me before nine o'clock on the weekends, not to even attempt to make conversation before I've had my first cup of coffee, and that I'm more a fruit and granola girl in the morning. (How she can eat all the junk she does and still have the best body in book club is beyond me.)

She also knows better than to ask me to go to church. Not my thing. Too many rules and regs. And glitz. Some of those churches, especially those big ones, really creep me out. Too much Splenda razzle-dazzle.

Like Mister Rogers on crack.

Dancing girls, bright, shiny choirs with Marie Osmond smiles, and men with Italian leather on their feet and more product in their hair than I've used my entire life. And don't even get me started on the Stepford women in their ice-cream-colored suits, matching pumps, and perfect makeup.

My ratty Birkenstocks would definitely be out of place.

And what's up with all the committees, meetings, and campaigns? Is it a church or a corporation? Then there are all those holier-than-thou types putting on a show on Sunday like they're all that, and then turning around on Monday and hitting on their secretaries or gossiping.

Don't get me wrong. I don't have anything against Jesus.

Jesus was cool. He took care of the poor, hung out with the lepers, and treated women well—unlike most of the men of his time. Really, if you think about it, Jesus was a feminist. But to some people, that F-word is a dirty word. And applying it to Jesus? Heresy.

Another reason I'm not into church. Everyone gets so uptight if you take Jesus out of their churchy box.

And that whole women and submission thing? Not in this universe.

Later, after I got home, I logged onto my laptop to scope out my Visa statement. Last I checked, I was close to maxing out my card. It didn't help that my last job turned out to be a bust. Marketing, my foot. I didn't get a degree in English to be a sign waver.

Like Teddy Roosevelt said, "A man who has never gone to

school may steal from a freight car, but if he has a university education, he may steal the whole railroad."

I didn't want the whole railroad, but I did want a job with a little more meaning.

The girls all told me I should never have quit Dunkeld's, but I'd been there over three years and gotten bored of the same-old, same-old. Yeah, it was great to be surrounded by books all day long, but at the end of the day, it was still retail.

Unfortunately, in the two months since I'd quit the bookstore, all I'd been able to find was a telemarketing job—where I got tired of people yelling and hanging up on me—a part-time barista job where I spent most of my paycheck on lattes, and this last marketing job where I spent an entire day waving a 30% OFF ALL FURNITURE! sign on a street corner.

Really meaningful, that.

I needed something exciting to get me out of my unemployed funk. And as I checked my credit card statement, I found it.

The next day, I was up in the air again with Zach. Free falling in that wild blue yonder on a clear, crisp April morning. And it was just as cool as the first time.

Until the landing.

Daring Chloe

Laura Jensen Walker, Award-Winning Author of Reconstructing Natalie

When Chloe Adams' fiancé dumps her—the night before their wedding—two girlfriends from her book group decide a little adventure is in order for the three of them. After all, why let a perfectly good honeymoon cruise go to waste?

Adventure? Chloe Adams? No way! Chloe's lived in one town her whole life. The closest she's ever gotten to actual adventures is reading about them. But her girlfriends won't take no for an answer.

One good adventure calls for another as Chloe's friends try to coax her out of her post-dumping funk, and soon she finds herself living out the adventures in her book club's latest selections. Hiking. Sailing. River rafting. Traveling to new places and eating exotic food. The play-it-safe Chloe begins to blossom into a new, daring Chloe. A Chloe who just might be ready to take on her biggest adventure of all ...

Laura Jensen Walker has a knack for quirky heroines and real-life humor. In Chloe, she's created another memorable character who will live on in readers' hearts.

Softcover 978-0-310-27696-8

Share Your Thoughts

With the Author: Your comments will be forwarded to the author when you send them to *zauthor@zondervan.com.*

With Zondervan: Submit your review of this book by writing to *zreview@zondervan.com.*

Free Online Resources at

www.zondervan.com/hello

Zondervan AuthorTracker: Be notified whenever your favorite authors publish new books, go on tour, or post an update about what's happening in their lives.

Daily Bible Verses and Devotions: Enrich your life with daily Bible verses or devotions that help you start every morning focused on God.

Free Email Publications: Sign up for newsletters on fiction, Christian living, church ministry, parenting, and more.

Zondervan Bible Search: Find and compare Bible passages in a variety of translations at www.zondervanbiblesearch.com.

Other Benefits: Register yourself to receive online benefits like coupons and special offers, or to participate in research.